OPERATION: NIBIRU 2012

OPERATION: NIBIRU 2012

Arn Lou

Bogkanten

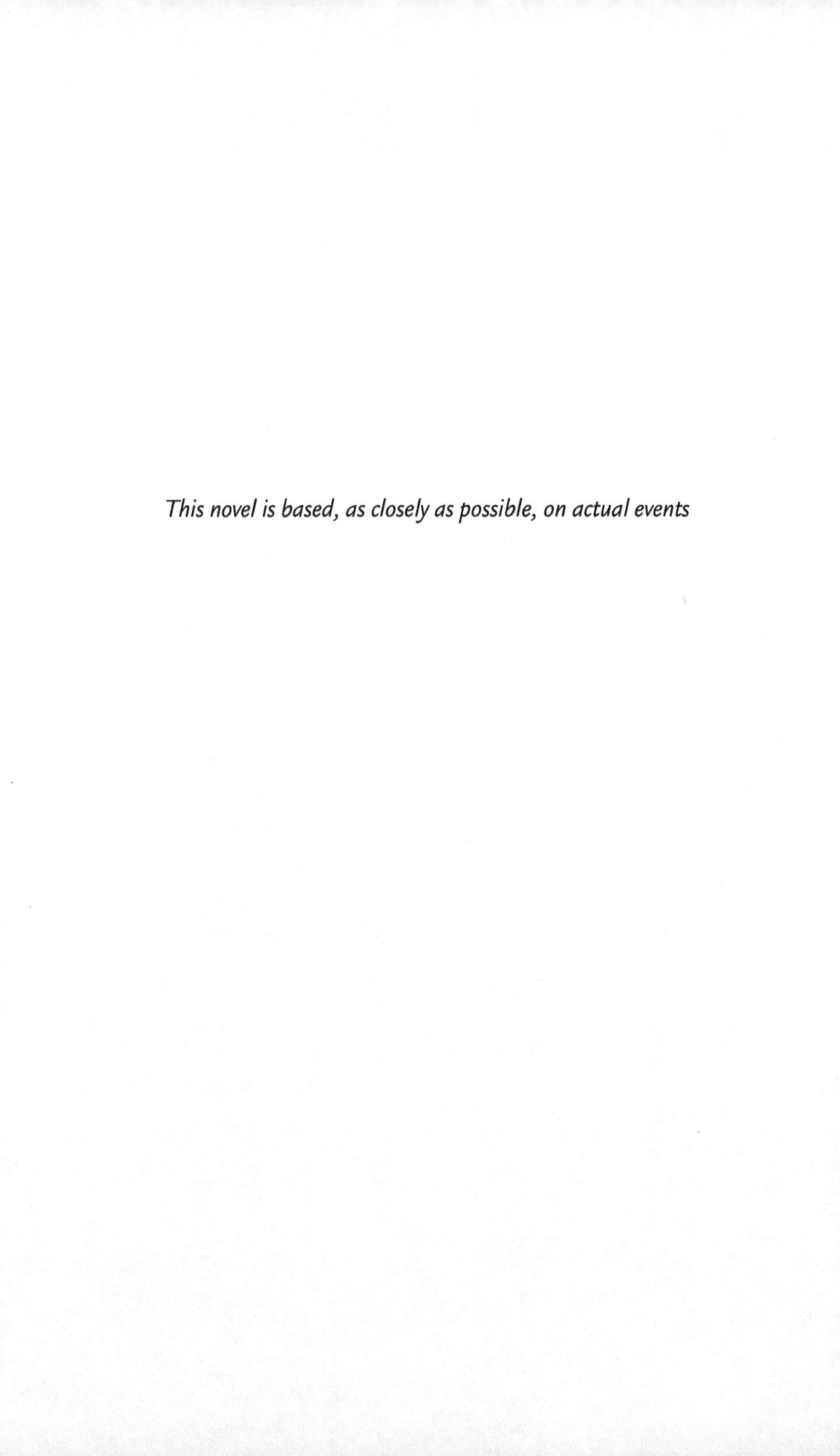

This novel is based, as closely as possible, on actual events

And there was light. Still at the edge of darkness, yet separate. Shimmering. From green to red and blue.

A light that culminated in the precise second that the little spacecraft broke through the atmosphere. So far from the space station that the craft could easily have passed unnoticed if it wasn't for the light.

Even though the International Space Station - the ISS - was home for several months for at least three astronauts at a time, it was not designed as a place for people to relax or enjoy themselves. The only thing the engineers had considered was how the space station would function as a workplace, and that meant that there were no creature comforts - none whatsoever. Whilst other progressive companies had long-since cottoned on to the benefits of designing work environments that employees were comfortable with and that could boost their efficiency, the space station was far behind.

Despite the fact that NASA had considered a number of competing designs for both the interior of the space station and the equipment that was in it, it was going to take another ten years before, for example, MIT's *Bio-Suits* would be ready for use. Everything was still heavily influenced by rational engineer-thinking, and designed to do a job. Not to look good. The astronauts could compensate though. With windows in the floor and ceiling the view was indescribable and far, far more spectacular than any man-made design. The view of the earth, the moon and the sun and the view out into the vast emptiness of space.

The expedition commander, 42-year-old Holly Burkana, was a two-mission veteran now about two thirds of the way through her third expedition. After waking from a well-deserved nap on her day off she climbed out of her sleeping bag and turned off the little alarm clock. She had never really been able to acclimatise to the numerous sunrises during a 24 hour period, so she wore a mask when sleeping. Several of the other astronauts did likewise, though there were others who could just roll up somewhere in the module and fall asleep just like that. Weightless sleep was not as romantic as you would think though, and sleeping pills were still in widespread use.

Mission specialist Alexander Leshenko came drifting towards her. Alexander, who was the Russian representative on the crew, was also the second in command.

"Who would've thought you'd just woken up. Did you sleep well?"

Alexander considered Holly and smiled charmingly.

"Fine thanks. As always. You should try it. All I have to do is put my mask on."

Alexander hesitated and it was clear that he wasn't keen on the idea. He preferred just to strap himself in to stop his limbs from floating about rather than filling his body with sedatives.

"Hmm," said Alexander.

"With no pressure on your body you relax more. I do anyway."

"I will consider it," he answered. "But only if you would accompany me."

Holly smiled at his flirtatious joke.

"I've got a teddy you can borrow."

The ISS was almost 360 by 168 feet on completion and thereby the world's largest manned space station. A conglomerate of American, European, Japanese and Russian technology and crews had successfully replaced the Russian-made MIR space-station, which burned up as planned on its way through the atmosphere in March 2001.

The plan was for ISS to pave the way for the further exploration of space, until this space station too was scheduled for destruction around the year 2016.

Though ISS had been plagued by accidents, including the fatal *Columbia* space shuttle disaster, optimism was starting to return and the station would soon be up to its full compliment of six crew members again. Crew members who lived in the station for up to six months at a time. However, currently there were just three astronauts aboard the station. And that meant there wasn't much time to do anything except work and complete their daily hour-long exercise period. Physical training that was necessary to prevent the body's muscles from wasting away.

Holly manoeuvred herself through one of the many nodes - a sort of corridor connecting the individual modules with each other - and on to her breakfast, which, just like every other type of food in space, had had to be tested before departure. A test that consisted of a flight in one of NASA's *KC-135* zero-gravity planes - if the food survived the trip without breaking up or misbehaving in some other way, then it was allowed a place on the menu.

Holly ate a couple of Mexican fried eggs and then found herself a carton of juice whilst she began running through the day's schedule with the control centre in Houston.

Though a 15-16 hour working day was standard and many of the tasks were routine, everything was checked and double checked again and again just to be on the safe side. For that reason, Holly had to move back and forth between appliances and her laptop repeatedly.

Living and moving around in a zero-gravity environment was something you got used to very quickly, and the obligatory 'space sickness' was now a thing of the past. Space sickness occurred within the first week and consisted primarily of dizziness and disorientation. Not what you would call serious, but pretty gruelling all the same.

The light was just a faint glow when it was first spotted. So weak and nondescript that it almost passed without notice. When it really started to show it was almost over.

Alexander Leshenko, who was in one of the service modules, turned around and was on his way over to wake the third and final astronaut *Flight Engineer* James Waskiel, when the light changed character and passed to the red end of the spectrum. A change that made Alexander Leshenko redirect his focus.

He reached for one of the many hand-held microphones that were attached to the wall with a magnet and called laconically:

"Mission control. Do you see what we see?"

"Negative, Leshenko. What do you see?"

Silence.

"ISS, come in. What do you see? There aren't any unusual readings down here."

"Houston, this is not coming from the ISS."

"Come again, please."

Holly entered the module as they were speaking and took control. She took the little microphone out of Alexander Leshenko's hands and looked at him seriously.

"This stays between the two of us. All right?!"

"You know what it is?"

"Yes."

Then Holly changed frequency to the so-called *Houston Appendicitis*. The rather odd slang term for the radio channel reserved for top-secret communications.

"Can I have a couple of minutes?" she asked Alexander Leshenko.

A difficult and unusual request since the astronauts had, per definition, complete confidence in each other. They had to to work together. Mandatory when working in space. What one astronaut knew, the others knew too. But this was an exception. An unpleasant but necessary exception, which Holly knew she would have to talk through with Leshenko later. With help of course. With a little help from her superiors.

Some information was only divulged on a need-to-know basis in order to secure the classified task as well as possible. If individual operatives were only aware of their own functions - their one little brick in the big puzzle - it was next to impossible for even the smartest amongst them to deduce what the whole picture looked like. To get a total overview.

However, Holly had also decided to take Alexander's feelings into account. She knew how much was at stake, and as they had all become close friends during their stay, she would do anything to protect her fellow astronauts. Holly was furthermore certain that what she said to Alexander would not go any further. That way the third astronaut James Waskiel would be spared totally. And that was a great relief for her right now. The fewer that knew anything the better, and the more certain they were to make it through this alive.

The red light with shades of green had reached its saturation point and now shone right through the entire space station, only to disappear completely seconds later. When Holly Burkana took up the microphone again everything had returned to normal.

The two soldiers carried out their normal patrol and approached the East gate of the top-security military installation. A military base with a subterranean stockpile of nuclear missiles. An important component of allied defences, that meant that the base should have been particularly well-protected from unwanted intruders.

That is why it came as something of a shock for the soldiers when a powerful light suddenly broke out in the sky and traced across them from a low altitude. Only to descend into the nearby woodland shortly afterwards.

A couple of seconds later everything went out and both soldiers' military radios and powerful tactical flashlights were totally dead.

The two soldiers stopped abruptly as one of them pointed in the direction of the area the explosive light had ended in.

"What the f...! Did you see that?!"

The second soldier looked in the same direction and nodded eagerly.

"Yeah, yeah. What was it?"

"It must have been a plane. It can't have been anything else. It must have crashed!"

They jumped into their jeep and drove towards the crash site.

As they approached the two soldiers noticed another light. This time a multicoloured one. White, red, yellow. In a swirl that seem to culminate in the middle of a flying object hovering just about five hundred feet above their heads.

"Shit!"

The object seemed to just hang in the sky for several long seconds, before moving off toward the place where the first light had disappeared a few minutes previously.

The soldier driving the jeep put the brakes on hard and jumped out while the vehicle was still moving.

"This is too much! I'm not going any closer."

The second soldier ran round from the other side of the car to his shocked friend.

"Pull yourself together! Nothing's happened okay! It's just some lights and, and, and a chopper. Come on we're going to call HQ and get reinforcements."

The second soldier shook his head.

"If that was a chopper how come we didn't hear the propellers?"

Suddenly their equipment started working again and the sudden light from their flashlights and buzz from their radios made them jump.

"Jesus!"

"Look I wanna get out of here! This is just too weird."

The second soldier grabbed his colleague's arm and shook him heavily.

"Fucking relax OK?! You're a soldier. It's what you're paid for. You're not going to fuck up and you're not going to run away. Do you copy?!"

That seemed to help a little. At any rate the soldier stood his ground, but kept a watchful eye on the peculiar craft that had now moved further in over the nearby woodland.

"Echo Four to Alfa One. Over."

The second soldier had called their base and a few seconds later the scratchy answer came through.

"This is Alfa One."

"Illegal entry. Repeat, illegal entry! Probably a chopper with suspected landing in a westerly direction about one click from Gate East. Request immediate back-up. Over."

"Echo Four, what did you say, a chopper?!"

"I'm presuming the craft is a chopper yes sir. No markings. We request immediate back-up. Over."

For a while the only sound was the radio's crackle then came the reply.

"Stand-by! Reinforcements are on their way."

"Roger that," the soldier replied. Then he pulled out a crumpled packet of cigarettes, took one himself and tossed the packet to his still nervous friend.

"Do you really still think that was just a chopper?"

"Look shut up and smoke your fag all right?!"

They smoked in silence whilst the final glow from the lights in the sky gradually faded out in the forest in front of them.

Minutes later a small team of soldiers reached them. Soldiers they didn't know, silent soldiers. Their reinforcements. Driving the characteristic 'Supacats'. So-called All-Terrain Mobility Platforms (ATMPs). Light-weight six-wheeled vehicles that could handle both hilly terrain and shallow lakes. Surprisingly they were lead by Base Commander Lieutenant Colonel Gordon Halt, and, just as surprisingly, they were equipped with radiation detectors.

The two soldiers on patrol threw away their cigarettes in a hurry, straightened up and saluted, whilst snatching hurried glances at the new arrivals. There was something about these other soldiers that didn't fit in. Their whole attitude was noticeably different to the sort of soldiers they were familiar with.

Gordon Halt returned their salute rapidly but his focus was clearly elsewhere and his arm only completed a half-hearted movement.

"Yeah, yeah. At ease. Which direction were they moving in when you last saw them?"

The two soldiers tried to relax but it wasn't easy.

"I think it landed over there, sir. Just behind the hill," said the calmer of the two soldiers and pointed in the same direction.

"Good work, soldiers. You may return to base."

"Sir?"

"This didn't happen. Okay? And that's an order."

"But..."

One of the newly-arrived soldiers slowly raised his rifle and aimed at them. Almost casually.

"Bullets are cheap," continued Gordon Halt and stared at them with such a cold expression that they both looked away.

Then the moment passed and the Lieutenant Colonel and the little group of soldiers returned to their vehicles. They drove off quickly into the forest towards the area in which the soldiers had seen the craft disappear.

"Who were those lads then?"

"I've never seen them before. And I've never seen that sort of kit before either. That was an XM8 he was pointing at us."

"An XM8? Isn't that what the American special forces use?"

The other soldier nodded seriously.

"Yeah."

"Fuck," the first soldier all but whispered.

"We saw nothing okay?! Nothing at all."

The first soldier straightened up and tried to smile, without quite being able to hide his continued nervousness.

"What are you talking about? Saw what?"

The second soldier patted his friend's back encouragingly.

"Exactly."

They went to their jeep, started it up and drove back to the base.

It was hot. The water in the strait rippled lazily, but inaudibly, given the noise from the aerial flapping around on the roof of Christian's car. The aerial that had been loose as long as Christian had owned the car, an elderly Polo estate, but which he had never quite been able to get it together to do anything about. Even though it really irritated him. As it did now as he drove down the coast road.

He had rolled the side window down long ago - by removing the wedge that held it in place. The summer breeze cooled his tired face but could not alter his meditative dozy state. Underscored by the repeated clicking noises from the roof.

This evening Christian was tired in a healthy kind of way. Tired after a long afternoon spent wandering in and out and up and down. After an early evening spent taking atmospheric photos with his cell phone. Just to recreate a little of the scenario he had been thinking through again and again. And even though his cell phone was not able to take the best pictures in the world they were still good enough to give an impression of what it was like. So Christian was satisfied. Something of a rarity for him, as more often than not, his mood, like his clothing, was black.

Whilst others perhaps thought of him as depressive, he considered himself a realist. Cynical maybe, but a realist. Tired, long ago, of lies and pretending. Tired of acting and playing a part. Tired of pleasing others and the fear of being far-fetched. Even though everyone shouted about individualism and the here-I-come mentality. A trend that just made them the exact opposite. Made them dull and featureless - one of the herd.

Christian took a deep breath and focused on the music he was listening to.

The classical music from the car radio playing quietly in the background - what he always listened to when he needed something calming.

He took his eyes off the road a couple of times as he grasped and started the dictaphone that was lying on the passenger seat next to a pad of hand-written notes and an empty 50 cl bottle of bourbon.

Christian began talking into the microphone.

"Monday, start training regularly. Remember to buy new CDs. Remember to empty all the old food out of the fridge. Remember to check with the bank for a new loan."

Christian had just completed a research trip to Kronborg Castle. A location that was to be central to his next novel. The first two he had written had no readers at all, and even fewer reviews. That was how it went. No reviews no sales.

Books that did not get any column inches lived a shadowy existence and were only familiar to the most devoted readers. And, as if that wasn't enough, it had taken him years just to find a publisher. On the other hand the books had made it possible for him to apply for grants. Grants which he was now doing his best to live off. And it was just about possible. All he had to do was pull himself together a bit, avoid the pub and leave off the cigarettes. But that might happen all of its own accord now. Given the recent legislation. After the most recent global mass-psychosis had spread still further. A smoker was more or less a drug addict now, rehab if you were lucky, a kicking if you weren't. All in the name of conformity. Away with anything that was a bit different, that didn't quite fit in. Away with gaudy, down with colourful. Down with anything that made life just a little fun; the things that made meeting other cultures interesting. Long live conformity, thought Christian. And what about the day when everyone thinks the same?

Christian was approaching Skodsborg, when a mid-range sports coupé suddenly appeared uncomfortably close behind him. *Where the fuck did that come from?!* thought Christian, whilst he turned off the dictaphone. Recording anything would be impossible anyway, with the throbbing bass coming from the other car.

Christian was irritated, but unconcerned. *Jerks out at night*, he said to himself.

He looked up at his rear-view mirror every now and then anyway, but was distracted by his radio which started to hiss in a highly unusual fashion. As if it had been scrambled.

Christian tried searching for other stations, but without success. All he could pick up was static and noise.

He swore to himself and put a CD on instead. But the stereo refused to make any sort of sound.

Christian knew what the solution to that was and gave the dashboard a thump with his fist. That normally worked. But not this time. Christian swore again, whilst he hit the panel a couple more times.

The man in the racy coupé, a Hertz hire car, was known as Wedlock. A thin sinewy man with slicked-back hair held in place with plenty of gel. A man in his late thirties; American through and through. A representative of the 'global power', as he liked to call his country. But also charming when he felt like it. A fast-talker, quick-thinker - a man of action. Many had remarked on the similarity between him and the actor Andy Garcia. A comparison which had actually hurt Wedlock, as he thought Garcia was a bit of a smart ass, but which had inspired him to revist some of Garcia's early films such as 'The Untouchables' and 'Godfather III'. It was the 1990 film 'Internal Affairs' that was his favourite, however. And it was from here he had, more or less unconsciously, borrowed his style. Mostly his way of moving. Many of the later films such as '*Oceans Eleven*' etc., had been a disappointment and Wedlock had now totally given up following Andy Garcia.

Wedlock focused on the deep bass from the stereo and beat time on his steering wheel whilst he swore at the sight of Christian's old wreck which filled the narrow carriageway almost completely.

"C'mon, you little shit! Move your ass."

Wedlock was a big fan of hiphop. He was especially keen on the young upcoming *T.I.* from Atlanta. And *Snoop Dogg* of course and *Black Eyed Peas* - which was what he was listening to right now.

Wedlock had tried his hand as a rapper without really making a success of it. And since he had joined the army all that had gone on the back burner. He had had the opportunity to keep rapping, but not at the same level and once his training started to intensify he had had to give it up altogether. No, in the army you were a soldier first and foremost. Wedlock had no doubts about that after his first survival course.

From there Wedlock's life had changed so radically that the only remnants of his dream of becoming a musician were his ability and the way he could spot upcoming talent. Not that he could use it to any purpose whatsoever. It was just a game.

Wedlock lit yet another cigarette but the taste was too much for him and he threw it out of the window. He swore at Christian once more, opened the glove compartment and rummaged impatiently for something. He couldn't find what he was looking for, didn't notice where he was going and only just managed stop the car leaving the road.

Christian noticed Wedlock's car swerve behind him, as if to avoid an obstacle. The car then fell back again a brief second later only to speed up again and overtake recklessly.

Christian turned his head immediately but only in time to see the car's rear lights as it shot past him.

"Jerk."

He said it quietly to himself in the cabin of the car, but was relieved to see it go past him.

His relief was temporary however. Wedlock's car had pulled into the side of the road further ahead with it's engine idling.

As Christian passed, he tried, once more, to get a look at the other driver, but without slowing down too much. And as he passed the coupé's subwoofer took over the night air again.

Christian only caught a faint glimpse of a silhouette as he passed, without being able to see whether there was more than one occupant in the other car or whether the driver was a man or a woman.

Wedlock was pulling everything out of the glove compartment. He chucked its contents onto the seat and and finally found what he had been looking for: A small bag of cocaine. He smiled, poured out a line and snorted it.

Just as Christian passed slowly outside.

Wedlock straightened up and watched him with irritation.

"Asshole."

He wiped his nose again, considered himself in the mirror and lit up a cigarette, changed the CD on his stereo and put the car back into gear.

Christian continued to watch the sports car in his rear view mirror, but was distracted by a characteristic beep from his cell phone.

He pulled it clumsily from an inside pocket and stared in amazement at the little display whilst simultaneously trying to keep an eye on the road and on his rear view mirror. An almost impossible task.

The cell phone's display showed 23 received messages, which a second later became 521 followed by some fleeting and confused text that flashed across the screen, then, the phone went dead.

Christian swore in surprise and chucked the phone onto the back seat, as his reflexes took over as he stopped the car at a red light. In a deserted junction that was completely free of traffic occupied only by a gas station on the opposite corner.

Normally he'd just have crossed the junction anyway, but not today as the coupé had rolled up behind him once more.

Christian checked his rear-view mirror nervously a couple of times, and then checked his fuel gauge. One of the few fittings that still worked perfectly.

It was showing 3 quarters empty, and was thus a good enough excuse to get off the road.

At the opposite side of the junction there was a manned gas station. Christian passed the junction and pulled into the forecourt. As he did so he noticed the coupé racing past speakers booming in his rear-view mirror.

"Asshole!"

This time Christian's outburst was louder - clearer. With the accent on the second syllable.

Christian began filling up and considered whether to pay at the pump with his card, although he had already decided. He never left a gas station empty handed.

He went into the shop and made his way quickly to the fridge where the beers were kept.

The young attendant behind the counter seemed distracted. He had a lazy eye and seemed always to be looking in an unfocused way at a point somewhere behind Christian, whilst at the same time seeming as if he was almost falling asleep. A thin fragile looking guy, who looked as if a gentle shove would knock him over.

Christian tried to catch his eye but decided to give up.

"Hey. I'm standing right here you know."

Not that that got the attendant to re-focus but he did at least answer.

"Yeah... Yeah, right."

"Is there ever any trouble here? I mean..." Christian looked briefly over his shoulder, thinking about the coupé.

"Trouble? No, nothing. Nothing ever happens here."

"No jerk-offs?"

"No. None at all actually. Errr, that'll be 451 Kroner, thanks."

Christian shrugged his shoulders.

"Okay."

"Fuck."

The attendant let the word fall in a whisper.

"What?"

Christian followed his gaze, which was now directed towards the forecourt, and was suddenly wide awake.

"451. Come on, time to pay, will ya?!"

The tone in the attendant's voice had changed. To impatience or perhaps more desperation.

Christian pulled out his credit card whilst watching whatever it was that was going on on the forecourt outside: Three black-blue Fords rolled up at high speed.

He looked back at the attendant who, surprisingly, had now started moving hectically back and forth on the spot and pointing repeatedly at the card reader.

"Just swipe the card!"

The attendant seemed like he was ready to abandon everything and do a runner. Whilst at the same time giving the impression that he knew there was no point.

Almost as a reflex Christian ran his card through the machine and entered his pin, whilst watching both the panicking attendant and the dramatic scenes outside the window.

"What the fuck is going on?"

Wedlock looked at Christian's car, as he passed the gas station. Then he drove a little bit further forward, pulled in to the side of the road and began looking around for a suitable vantage point.

He found what he was looking for and squatted down between a couple of trees at a slight distance from the road. Then he put a small pair of binoculars to his eyes and observed the gas station.

"Shithead."

Wedlock's expression didn't seem to indicate irritation, so he could just as well be swearing out of habit as actual frustration.

In the next second Wedlock spotted the same motorcade as Christian and the attendant, three dark almost identical Fords came screeching to a halt in front of the store.

"Don't tell me it's the Feds... Christ!"

24

Several grim looking men with crew cuts all wearing the same dark suits jumped out of the cars whilst they were still in motion.

They were led by a mean looking man in his late forties with a powerful presence and a penetrating gaze. A gaze which Christian, even from that distance, instinctively interpreted as dangerous. It had an almost irresponsible feel. Paradoxically, at the same time, there was something feminine about the man - perhaps it was his long eyelashes.

Two of the men assumed positions outside the door in a practised manner. Both of them were looking out away from the store. A detail many semi-professionals and rank amateurs often missed. When protecting someone one should always look *away* from the subject. Out into the surroundings. There's no point, and very little protection to be had, from keeping an eye on the subject. No, the danger would come from without, if it came.

Meanwhile the leader and two other men continued directly into the store.

Christian had difficulty taking the scene in front of him seriously. It was just too violent. As if it came straight out of a B-movie.

"What's going on?"

The two other men had quickly moved to the other side of the counter whilst the leader positioned himself in front of it - standing with his legs slightly apart.

"Lars Mortensen?"

The attendant nodded in a desperate sort of way and waved his arms around.

"Time to go."

The two men took hold of the young attendant and began to pull him out of the store, whilst the leader moved forward to Christian who had remained standing at the counter throughout.

"I'm sorry, but you'll have to leave the area. The store's closed."

"Sure thing. I'm just taking my stuff with me."

"You'd better hurry then. As I said, the store's closed."

The man kept staring at Christian, until he withdrew his gaze. Then he went behind the counter and rummaged a bit on the shelves before continuing to the back room. In this man's world Christian evidently wasn't a threat.

Christian shouted at the man's back.

"You can't just come barging in here throwing your weight around. You haven't even said who you are. Even though... I mean, it's pretty obvious from the outfits you're running round in."

Christian took hold of his 6-pack and put the bill in his pocket next to his well-worn debit card.

Just inside the double electric doors the attendant seemed to be making a last desperate attempt to escape. Something that generated additional tumult but just meant that the two crew cuts took an even firmer grip.

"Right then, you'll just have to have this on."

One of the two men holding the attendant tripped him elegantly and both men managed his fall so that he didn't hit himself. One of them put a knee in his back, whilst the other took a white plastic strip from his pocket and locked it around the guy's wrist. Modern police handcuffs. They helped him to his feet again and continued out of the door.

Christian looked on dispassionately and made his own way to the exit. He wanted to go home. It was getting late and his head was killing him. He always got headaches when people started pushing their weight around. And, anyway there was nothing more to be done here. Whatever the poor guy might have done there was nothing Christian could do to help him whether he wanted to or not.

"Wait a minute."

The leader had emerged from the back room and was making his way towards Christian, who stopped and looked despairingly up at the ceiling.

The man stood in front of Christian and fished a little leather case out of his pocket. A card that showed that he came from the police, that his name was Carsten Clausen and that he obviously liked flashing his Breitling watch about. It had to be a replica. No policeman makes that much, thought Christian.

Carsten Clausen began his career while serving his national service, where he was posted to Cyprus on a UN Mission.

After a couple of years in the Royal Life Guards, he ended up applying to the police academy, where he quickly became known for his extremely brutal manner. This reputation had followed him since his posting as a UN soldier. Here he had picked up a number of reprimands as a consequence of his rough-handed way of dealing with civilians. In fact, he had got himself quite a reputation, a reputation he liked building on.

One episode in particular was still remembered and mentioned when new colleagues were introduced to the force: After an hour's self-defence training a rookie got heavily beaten and was hospitalised for several days.

But since there were no witnesses to the assault - which took place in the locker rooms - and neither Carsten Clausen nor the rookie were interested in saying anything more specific than that they'd had a bit of a disagreement, the matter was closed.

That did not stop people talking about it, however. Especially after it emerged that the rookie in question was openly gay. In fact, after that, there was no end to the speculation. Two naked men alone in the showers and one of them at least was a homosexual...

After that incident, Carsten Clausen became more motivated, thinking more about his career. He applied for a transfer to a different department and took course after course after course until he had a piece of paper saying he could do everything under the sun. He was familiar with even the most trivial legal details and used to trip up young lawyers on a regular basis. Quick thinking and totally ruthless with anyone who got in his way, he was fast-tracked and had already achieved the rank of inspector at an age of 32. A position he was well suited to.

"Carsten Clausen, police. What's your business here?"

Christian laughed abruptly and, as usual, could not keep a tone of sarcasm out of his voice. Not that he wasn't, at some level or other, fascinated by the officer in civvies facing him. Sarcasm was just a bad habit. And he had a bit of a problem with authorities altogether.

"My business? Wow. That was a tricky one... I've just filled up and bought a couple of beers as you can see. I was just on my way home when you guys came crashing in."

Carsten Clausen stared at him - just stared. Then he reached out and caught hold of one of Christian's hands, forcing back his thumb. An action that was performed quickly and elegantly and gave Christian so much pain as to be almost intolerable.

"Chapter 14, article 119 paragraph 3 of the penal code governing offences against public authorities clearly states that a person hindering a police officer under active duty can be punished by a fine or imprisonment for up to 6 months. I assume that's not something you'd be keen on?"

Carsten Clausen spoke quickly but calmly and persuasively. A circumstance that made Christian nauseous. The feeling was perhaps strengthened by the position he found himself in: with bent knees, and leaning backwards almost out of balance.

Carsten Clausen released his grip and allowed Christian time to gather himself, even though Christian wasn't actually shaken at all. It took more than a bit of harassment to put him off his stride. After all, what was pain other than just a state of mind? It was there, and then it was gone. Just like everything else. Happiness, money, sex, life; nothing lasts for ever.

"Now that you've been so kind as to remove the attendant perhaps I could just pop behind the counter and get myself a pack of cigarettes? I'm almost out."

Carsten Clausen smiled, revealing a long row of white teeth. His expression indicated heightened respect.

"Goodnight."

He reached a friendly arm out towards the door indicating that the party was over.

"I was just starting to enjoy myself," said Christian, and rotated his thumb a couple of times.

Carsten Clausen's unnecessary display of force had provided Christian with some useful information. Information about the policeman's character defect, an insight which might well prove useful. Either fictively, in one of Christian's books, or in real life. Every cloud has a silver lining, thought Christian in a satisfied way, even though his subconscious was already working on schemes for getting even. Ways of getting revenge. Christian never forgot.

"Could you give me your name again, I didn't catch it?"

They were both now out on the forecourt. Out next to the three dark cars waiting with their engines' running - ready to go.

Christian tried to get a look at the attendant through the tinted windows of the middle car but without success. He turned his attention to the leader again.

"Christian. Christian Bang."

"And you are?"

"An author. I've cluttered up the world with even more books."

"The world?"

"You know what I mean."

"I'll keep an eye on you."

"Thanks, thanks very much. I expect I'll manage without, but thanks all the same."

"That wasn't how I meant it."

"Oooh?!"

Christian tone was one of evident surprise and the energy and tension between the two men came to the fore again.

And then the moment passed, and Christian waved quietly and smiled to the other men in the cars as he meandered towards his own.

Behind him he could hear Carsten Clausen shout questions about whether anyone knew how to lock the doors and if they did whether they would be so kind as to come and show him.

Back in his car Christian smiled to himself and drove off, while opening a beer and drinking a long draught.

Suddenly the electronics started working. The radio came back on of it's own accord and started playing again, whilst Christian's phone's beep indicated that it had come back on too. Christian shook his head

- he had long ago lost any interest in trying to work out how modern technology functioned - or didn't.

Wedlock had gone back to his car where he was sitting waiting, whilst keeping an eye on the gas station via his rear-view mirror. Impatient. Irritated. He hated being rendered irrelevant. But he was still professional enough not to let it cloud his judgement.

Wedlock followed Christian with his eyes as he drove past. He shook his head.

"Jerk."

Then he forced himself to relax and leaned back into his comfortable seat. He remained there unmoving until the three Fords came up the road and passed him. Only then did Wedlock start his car and begin following on behind.

The space shuttle Atlantis had completed it's mission. *Space Transportation System* 122 - STS 122 - had come to a complete stop right at the middle of SLF's enormous landing strip. A gigantic area complete with specially-designed facilities and vehicles and all the personnel necessary to handle returning space shuttles.

SLF or *Shuttle Landing Facility* consisted of a 300-feet-wide and a 15,000-feet-long landing strip, running north west - south east. Even though SLF only had this one landing strip at its disposal it was known as runway 15 or runway 33, depending on which direction the shuttle came in from. Something that was determined primarily by the weather and the general wind direction.

When the shuttle's cabin door opened a doctor was on hand in the re-fashioned jet bridge ready to offer the passengers a first quick health check. The jet bridge was known as the CTV - *Crew Transportation Vehicle* - and was also the place where astronauts removed their clumsy protective orange suits.

From here the two crew members from the space station were sent directly to ACQ - *Astronaut Crew Quarters* - whilst crew members whose jobs related exclusively to the space shuttle itself stayed in the area around the landing strip and chatted with VIPs and specially invited members of the press. All whilst performing routine checks to the underside of the space shuttle. To the heat shield. One of the most vulnerable points on the vessel and one that was kept under very close observation.

Holly Burkana waved smiling to the assembled crowd from her seat behind the windscreen of the white bus. The bus that was to transport her and Alexander Leshenko to the main Kennedy Space Center complex, where they would be spending a single night in the company of their respective families.

Even though Holly was looking forward to seeing her family again she was even more interested in having a shower - a real shower. Just the feeling of standing under warm running water and letting it massage her body. A privilege she had had to give up for far, far too long. A quick rub down with a cloth was pretty much all there was by way of personal hygiene on the space station.

On the following day they'd all be aboard one of the many space shuttle training aircraft on their way to Johnson Space Center in Houston. The place where astronauts underwent the obligatory medical check ups performed by so-called *Flight Surgeons,* followed by repeat debriefings with their managers.

Even though these procedures were starting to become routine, five long months of weightlessness weren't without their consequences. A stay of that sort of duration made walking extremely difficult for the astronauts, and it always took them a number of days to reacquaint themselves with the earth's gravitational field. Nonetheless, astronauts were kept under close observation for the next six weeks. A medical-physiological standard supplement that supported the obligatory daily exercises they performed during the same period.

All this seemed to be a bit beside the point for Holly, whose attention was focused on altogether different and more worrying things. Things that had made the final weeks of her stay aboard the ISS all but unbearable. Not being able to share your knowledge and concerns with others. Having to watch what you said, how you said it and who you said it to, was quite simply close to being more than she could take. And, on top of everything else, Alexander's unexpected and continuous flirting.

Had he really gone and fallen in love? That was how it seemed when she looked into his eyes. When she listened to the way he talked. The pitch of his voice and the way he emphasised certain things. And, of course, the unavoidable occasions on which they had touched each other, and where Holly had just wanted to put everything else on standby and just talk. Talk things through. Properly. Not just their flirting, which as far as she was concerned was always going to be wholly innocent - but also, and especially, what had happened outside the space station.

The only thing that had kept her going had been the many daily tasks and routines. Those of them that weren't absolutely top secret that was.

Holly looked at Alexander once more. A face that under their trip back from the space shuttle had been smiling and open. Like Holly's. The only difference being, her expression had been a charade.

Holly speculated as to whether the third astronaut, James Waskiel, had noticed anything, anything at all. Waskiel who had stayed on site as he had 82 days of his stay to complete. She was sure, in any case, that he knew nothing of the confidential *Appendicitis* conversations or the event itself. And that was the most important thing. It couldn't have escaped his notice, however, that she was under stress. Under unusual stress.

Waskiel was a good man - a good colleague. Just like Alexander, she thought. *Had he really fallen in love?*

Living under the extreme conditions they did, created, naturally, special bonds between people. When you thought about it like that, perhaps it wasn't so strange that people's feelings sometimes ran away with them.

Then her thoughts returned to the task in hand. To what she knew she had to do.

Was it wrong of her not at least to have informed the others? No, the fewer that knew about it the better, she thought. On that point she'd already made up her mind to follow the non-discussable requirement for complete silence. What had happened hadn't happened. No comments whatsoever. Not to anyone, not even close family. A requirement that had been emphasized again after astronaut Catherine Coleman's misspeak back in the 1990s that was available right across the Internet almost as soon as it had left her mouth.

Holly wished, for a brief second, that it had been her turn to sleep and that everything that had happened had passed her by - but only for a second.

The evening at the Kennedy Space Center in Florida passed uneventfully, and even though she was constantly under surveillance she'd managed to remain discrete and reticent. In fact, Holly was the only person who noticed anything. She possessed a fine feeling for details. The male agent's peculiar cautious comportment. His vigilant nervous stare. His shoes. Foot-shaped and soft and easily recognisable.

A bit like now, as she recognised the golf course at Ellington Field as the plane swung over effortlessly to the correct angle for its approach.

The agent had got back up and there were now two further agents. Still discrete but they still stuck out to the extent that they were hard to miss.

It was a while since Christie, Holly's youngest daughter, had trotted over to ask them who they were and how come they were there. A question that had produced the response that they were 'just looking after your mom'. At which point one of the agents passed Christie a little badge. One of the type that people probably only wear to official events. If at all.

Christie was happy with the somewhat unusual gift and returned to Holly proud of her treasure. A badge that she had affixed to her blouse some time ago.

"Now I'm looking after you too mommy."

Eric, her husband turned in his seat and looked at the three men quizzically.

"Who are these guys? They are not normally here," he said.

"It's just some new security procedure. It's nothing," said Holly evasively.

Holly smiled to her daughter as she sent the agents a warning glance. She was going to have to pull herself together if she was to get through this circus in one piece. There was still lots to do before she finally got some time off. But for each hour that passed she was getting closer and closer to freedom.

A mantra she succeeded in sticking to under the following official duties, where she put on a smiling and professional face and only mentioned the successful course of the mission. And everything was assessed. Everything apart from the fateful light.

The first evening Holly Burkana finally made it back home to South Carolina, was one she enjoyed as never before. Being alone with her husband and their two children was a consciously repressed need that had been emphatically saved and hidden away. And it was only now that she could let go and set her feelings free. Happiness, relief and gladness.

A rare feeling of peace and inner calm had taken hold of her and all the speculations of the previous days were all but forgotten, or would have been if Eric hadn't commented on the wrinkles on her forehead. The wrinkle which always seemed to crop up when Holly was unusually worried about something or other. Not that anybody else would notice it, but for Eric it was like a lighthouse. A wrinkle which he had, of course, already spotted that first evening in Florida. He hadn't asked about it, however, and had waited as Holly had other and more pressing tasks. But now was the time as they lay naked and satisfied under the sheets after the lovemaking that they had both been waiting for.

"Do you want to talk about it?"

Eric asked quietly whilst he stroked her hair.

"Not tonight Eric. I'm so tired. I'm just so tired."

Holly repulsed his approaches in a friendly way, but cosied up to his arm in the end anyway. Tomorrow everything would be better. Tomorrow everything would be good, she thought and closed her eyes.

Next morning when the kids had left for school and Eric had left for work, Holly was finally ready to act. She wanted to speak to her sister. Jodie. Jodie Green, who was a journalist and could give her the advice she needed to help her decide what to do next. Then the telephone rang.

"Hi Holly... It is me... Alex... Alexander."

"Alex! Great to hear your voice again."

"Yes, it's good to hear you too. How are you?"

"I'm great. How about you? Is it good to be back in the Russian cold again?"

"Yes. There's nothing like home, it's snowing."

"And the children? Your wife?"

Alexander didn't answer but changed the direction of the conversation. Spoke slowly as he chose his words with difficulty and care.

"Now it's all over... can you not explain for me what it is that has happened?"

Holly closed her eyes whilst she tried to figure out a quick and plausible answer. She shook her head.

"It was the northern lights. *Red sprites* and *blue jets*," she answered easily.

"I was more thinking between us. Or was it just me?"

"Oh, Alex. We're both married. We both have kids. It just can't be."

"Not just for a visit?"

How do you reject a man without hurting his feelings?

"I'd really like to see you again, but..."

Alexander interrupted her.

"And that's enough. Enough for me. For a start."

"Alex...," she tried gently.

He interrupted again.

"And by the way... It definitely wasn't northern lights. And sprites and jets only last a couple of milliseconds. There was no lightning where we were."

Holly shook her head quietly.

"That's what is says in my report," she answered.

"A lie? Why?"

"What do you want me to say Alex? I'm giving you the answer I can give."

Holly was obviously affected by the situation but kept her feelings out of her voice.

"Would you welcome me if I came to you?"

"Of course. But not in the way you're maybe hoping…"

"Okay." Alexander sounded disappointed. "I'd better get back to the cold. I just wanted to say hi," he said with affected happiness.

"Take care Alex."

"You too."

And so, the conversation was over.

Holly put down the phone and sat still for a while. Relieved. Relieved that Alexander had enough sense to see that there was no point in pressurizing her.

Alexander Leshenko turned off his cell phone and returned to the table where his wife and the two boys were sitting waiting. All dressed in comfortable relaxed clothing. Holiday clothes.

Alexander stood still looking at his wife for one long second before he asked them all to head back to '*Londonskaya*'. The hotel on Primorskiy Boulevard where they were staying. He needed some time to himself, and he needed a drink. They must understand that there were things he couldn't get over even though they'd been away for a couple of days.

Alexander Leshenko was 48, he had trained at Kharkov's flight academy before taking a Ph.D. in geology at Moscow University. Having become a lieutenant colonel in the air force, he was transferred to the cosmonaut division in Star City where he completed his training at the famous *Yuri Gagarin Cosmonaut Training Centre* - officially abbreviated to GCTC. After completing his training he'd been on three space missions, all aboard the Soyuz spacecraft launching from Baikonur in Kazakhstan.

Whereas his role in the first two missions had been to concentrate on the transport of equipment to the space station, his third, and most recent trip, had finally given him the opportunity to focus on a prolonged stay in space. That was what had always been Alexander's greatest dream and ambition. Actually having the opportunity to live in space. He had been a bit disappointed that his trip back to earth had been aboard the American space shuttle. Because, even though there was seldom room for nostalgia, and even though he'd actually taken part himself in the development of upcoming Russian space vehicles such as *Kliper* and *Parom*, he couldn't help feeling a bit misty eyed about Soyuz. A spacecraft which the Russians had redeveloped and improved again and again since it was first used to carry a human cargo in 1967. Alexander Leshenko was thus just a bit more than ordinarily sad at the thought of having to retire without flying Soyuz one last time. But that was just the way it was, and besides he had other more serious things to think about. Things that had led him to apply for a couple of days' recreational leave.

A trip to Ukraine which had been independent since 1991 with Odessa as one of the cultural highlights. A town that had been founded by Catherine the Great in 1794 and which was full of both life and charm with its inviting boulevards and shady squares. It was probably best known for its horseshoe-shaped opera house built in 1887 and, of course, for Sergej Eisenstein's film *'Battleship Potemkin'*, which made use of another of the city's landmarks, a 466 feet stairway, for it's main scene. The stairs were originally known as 'The Boulevard Steps,' 'The Enormous Staircase' or 'Richelieu Steps'. This last because of the statue of Emmanuel Richelieu at the top of the stairs.

The town itself had a number of nicknames. 'Wonder of the south' or 'the pearl of the Black Sea' were some of those most frequently used. The town on the Black Sea which almost anyone with a bit of money in their pocket liked to visit on holiday. Especially Ukrainians, but also Russians like Alexander Leshenko.

He'd already identified a good hang out in the form of *'Mick O'Neill's Irish Pub'* on Deribasovskaya street. A place that was both a well-loved retreat for the many foreign tourists and for the better class of local prostitutes.

Alexander chose to take a detour. Consciously and carefully planned. A detour that would lead him to the statue further along and to the right of the base of Potemkin stairs. A stair that was still populated at this hour. Especially by local youth who like to hang out there. As they were doing now.

Alexander surveyed a small group of them. A group in which a bottle was on its way round. They were discreet, and yet provokingly obvious.

Alexander smiled to himself in satisfaction at the thought that things hadn't perhaps changed much since he was that age.

He then reached his first goal, the Richelieu statue, where he nodded to a well-dressed man who was standing there smoking a characteristic brown *Sobranie Black Russian*. Once they had been hand-rolled, now they were mass produced in England and the Ukraine, amongst other places.

The two men embraced warmly and kissed each other on the cheeks.

"Alex!"

"Vadim. It's been a while. Still *Spetsnaz's* demon?"

Vadim Filitsyn, a rather overweight man somewhere in his forties, laughed hoarsely and coughed hard a couple of times. It was time he cut down on the cigarettes he thought, whilst he coughed up a thick slime from his chest and spat it onto the pavement in front of him.

"The Russian special forces aren't for faggots. I thought you knew that," answered Vadim, whilst he looked around himself reflectively. Then he continued in a more serious tone:

"What's up?"

Alexander breathed deeply and sighed before answering.

"I'm afraid I don't have that much to say."

"Despite everything we've registered?"

Alexander shrugged his shoulders.

"Northern lights and thunder. That's the official line anyway."

"And the unofficial?"

"There isn't one."

Vadim crushed his cigarette with his foot.

"Listen Alex, now you're disappointing me. All our meters are going off the scale. That just can't be right."

Alexander tried briefly to consider his words. Even though the two men had known each other for a number of years, he probably should be careful. But he wasn't. He was getting tired. Tired of the game, tired of the secrets, tired of always having to watch what he said - and to whom. Alexander decided to believe in old-fashioned notions like allegiance, friendship and honour. He chose to trust Vadim.

"Have you ever been in love? I mean really in love. You know, where it just goes boom."

"Look I've no time for games. What are you trying to say exactly?"

Vadim's voice had changed register like the flick of a switch and was harsh and cold. Alexander realised that he had made a mistake. But found that actually, somewhere along the line, he didn't care. He'd made up his mind and that was that.

"I want out. Can you help me?"

Vadim took yet another cigarette out and sucked on the golden filter a couple of times before, finally wedging the cigarette in place between his full lips. Then he fished a golden lighter from his pocket and ignited it whilst he nodded thoughtfully and changed his tactics. Alexander wasn't just a rookie who could be browbeaten.

"Who is she then? She must be really special. There are loads of women, Alex. For God's sake. You know that. What about your wife?"

Alexander shook his head.

"You wouldn't understand if you'd never experienced it."

Vadim lost it.

"What the fuck are you talking about! Are you on something? What is it exactly I haven't experienced huh - what?! I tell you I've had some

43

very nice women. The ones with really big tits. And I tell you, they'd do anything. Anything. So what exactly is it I haven't tried, what?!"

Vadim calmed down slightly and lowered his voice before continuing.

"Alexander you idiot. And now of all times. Why now when we need you the most."

Alexander shook his head.

"I'm tired of all the lies. The secrets. The pressure."

That was too much for Vadim.

"The pressure?! You're a fucking cosmonaut. You should be used to pressure. You've got the world's best - and most expensive - education. What did you expect? What is the matter with you people?! The first sign of trouble and you whine like fucking kids. What the fuck did you expect?!"

"Definitely not this," answered Alexander seriously.

Vadim studied Alexander's eyes and facial expression. Then he made a decision.

"Okay. Okay. I'll see what I can do. Really!" Vadim smiled broadly again and the two men embraced and said their goodbyes.

"Really?"

"Really. Say hi to your beautiful wife! And the mistress whoever she is."

The two men parted and Vadim stayed where he was with a dark shadow across his forehead. He nodded a couple of times in the direction of the stairs and muttered to himself: "*Death solves all problems - no man, no problem.*" A quote from Stalin lifted from the series of novels by Anatolij Rybakov Дети Арбата - Arbat's Children.

What Vadim didn't know was that the quote was fictional. Had he known he would probably just have shrugged his shoulders indifferently. The most important thing is it sounds good, would've been his response.

And it did. So he didn't really give a flying fuck who said it.

About halfway down the stairs Alexander Leshenko bumped unexpectedly into a stranger. A stranger who excused his clumsiness and was off again before Alexander had time to think twice. Altogether a harmless incident that neither he nor those around him reacted to.

Not, at any rate, before he reached the point where, at some stage, the bottom steps had been removed to make way for the road. The point at which the optical illusion was at its most effective and the stairs appeared longer than they actually were. An illusion that resulted from the broadening of the lowest steps.

A cold pain was spreading from Alexander's thigh, like the sting of a large needle and he was already afraid.

"Извините - Excuse me?!"

Alexander tried to call for help from the gang of kids before sinking to the pavement in a heap.

Then the thought hit him. Absurd yet obvious. *Ricin*. A deadly protein based on the castor bean. Just like in London back in 1978, he thought and closed his eyes. Now just refined, far more effective. How many times had they used that technique since? Easy, quick, efficient.

The doctor that later discretely removed the less than two millimetre long perforated ball from which the poison had spread to Alexander's Leshenko's body, concluded that he had been subject to a sudden and particularly virulent bout of pneumonia. In fact Leshenko had been suffering from a weak respiratory system for some time. A pronouncement that was supported by a spokesman from the Russian space organisation *Roskosmos* who went on record to say that the recent mission would in fact have been Leshenko's last one in any case. Something that would have been made public at the upcoming event for aspiring cosmonauts. And, after the President had awarded him a medal of honour, the post mortem was performed and the newspapers had written the obligatory articles and obituaries the matter was forgotten.

The world kept turning and no-one asked any questions when the responsible physician rolled up to work a couple of weeks later in the car he, until recently, had only dreamed of owning.

The three identical Fords drove in convoy up the coast road, and kept a good speed. Right as far as the highway where the front and rear cars changed their route and left the middle car on its own.

The car in which the young Lars Mortensen was sitting. Squeezed in between two silent crew cutted men, an equally silent driver and Carsten Clausen.

"Bring everything directly in to us. Over."

The radio crackled briefly as the answer came in.

"Copy that."

Carsten entered a name into the little inbuilt computer screen in front of him whilst Lars said nervously from the back seat.

"Are they on their way to my mum?"

"Chapters 107 and 110 of the penal code gives us the authority to impound any items that could potentially damage national security and independence. Was that enough of an answer for you?"

Carsten Clausen looked hard at Lars, before returning his attention to the little screen in front of him.

"Can't it wait till the morning? It's the middle of the night. And the stuff won't go anywhere. Just for my mum's sake."

Carsten Clausen didn't answer. Instead he asked a question of his own.

"Can you remember your boss's home phone number?"

"Yeah, why?"

Carsten Clausen turned towards Lars, whilst he nodded quickly to one of the men on the back seat who removed the white plastic strips round Lars' wrists with a practised movement.

"Otherwise I'd have found it here."

Carsten Clausen clicked his fingers at the little screen whilst he continued:

"Call him. Call him and say that you had to go home because you felt ill."

An expression of surprise appeared on Lars' face whilst he rubbed himself where the plastic had cut into his skin. But he was also relieved.

"Is that normal procedure?"

"It is for you. When I say it is."

Even though Lars was still both worried and under pressure he was still ready to answer back. A bit anyway. Another, more and more unpleasant thought was catching up with him.

"What about my rights? I've still got my rights."

"You've got less than nothing here boy. Do you understand?"

Lars sank back into the seat and nodded weakly. He knew they'd apply to have him taken into preventive custody for at least 27 days, and that all 27 days would be spent in isolation. He also new that they'd have plenty of time to find the one thing he wanted to prevent becoming public at all costs.

Lars had to do something. Anything. His attempt to run away at the gas station had been stupid, a bad move. Now when he had the time to think things over, he'd built up his courage a bit, even though his heart was still beating far to fast and Carsten Clausen still scared him.

Lars was just praying for a chance, any chance. No matter how small and insignificant it might be. Just a chance.

One of the two crew cuts on the back seat gave Lars' phone to Carsten who entered the number in question before turning on the speakerphone function and giving it to Lars.

"Here you are... and no funny business now, right?"

Wedlock kept his distance. The sort of distance that meant that only the most watchful or paranoid person would suspect they were being followed. Something that, of course, wasn't the case here. The chances of anybody following a police car, marked or otherwise, were infinitesimally small, a fact that Wedlock was using to his advantage. An advantage that, naturally, allowed him to make use of the element of surprise.

A small accident prevented him from achieving his goal, however, thereby saving a life for the second time that summer night.

The dark Ford left the highway and continued up the slip road to a roundabout. As it turned off the roundabout it went straight into the side of a taxi that, unnoticed, had attempted to overtake it on the inside.

Even though both cars were driven by experienced drivers the Ford completed an almost 360 degree spin, whilst the taxi was pushed off to the right across oncoming traffic and came to rest in a cycle path.

The two policemen on the back seat of the Ford jumped out and made straight for the taxi where they opened the front door and stood waiting for Carsten Clausen who was walking slowly and deliberately over to the driver of the other car.

He leaned forward and put his hand on the taxi driver's shoulder and moved the man in a controlled manner out of the car.

Whereas the cab driver was clearly both shocked and shaken, Carsten Clausen was far better at hiding his own reaction. In reality it had only been a question of centimetres. As it was the taxi's left front had battered most of the Ford's right side and had left a deep dent in the wing. Right in front of the door Carsten had been sitting behind. A couple of centimetres further back and Carsten Clausen could have suffered a serious injury.

49

"Do you have any idea of how to drive at all?"

Even though the question was delivered almost in a whisper it was clear and icy cold and there could be no doubt as to its intended menace.

The driver looked nervously at the three men facing him. Not the best of odds, he was thinking. Despite this he maintained a defiant front to the last.

"For fuck's sake man. It was an accident. How was I to know you'd suddenly swing right when you were in the outside lane all the time."

Carsten Clausen looked in both directions to ensure that no-one was watching. He pushed the taxi driver to one side.

"What are you doing?! What the fuck are you doing? You can't just start pushing people around."

However, the driver was too uncertain of himself to make any real resistance.

"Do we agree that overtaking on the inside is illegal?"

The driver spluttered in contempt in a final attempt to maintain his standing in the conversation.

"Not any more illegal than taking the left hand lane if you're going to turn right."

Carsten Clausen looked out into the night once more before directing a hard and sudden blow with the tips of his fingers to the man's solar plexus. A blow which made the driver collapse and disgorge what was left of his dinner all over himself.

"Aahh, an equal. I'll say mine first then you say yours okay?"

Carsten Clausen continued sarcastically whilst the driver continued to swallow spasmodically.

"Chapter 4 paragraph 21 of the road traffic act clearly states that overtaking manoeuvres should be performed to the left of the vehicle

50

being overtaken. Overtaking to the right is only permitted in the event that a driver swings to the left or is clearly in the process of preparing to do so. Cyclists and mopeds may also overtake other categories of vehicles to the right. Now it's your turn."

A few drops had landed on Carsten Clausen's hand and he dried it on the man's shoulder with obvious distaste.

Carsten Clausen became serious again.

"Another time I'd advise you to keep a careful eye on where you're going. You never know who you might run into, if you get my drift."

The driver didn't answer at first.

Carsten slapped him hard in the face. And after glancing around him again repeated the performance.

"Is that understood?"

The driver nodded and began to cry. Tears of anger over his complete humiliation and powerlessness. He managed to force a yes out and nodded several more times. Mocked and disgraced.

Carsten Clausen pulled out his police ID and shoved it into the driver's face.

"And by the way, we'll also be charging you with violence against an officer on active duty... Take his name and number will you?"

This last remark was directed to the two officers who now looked at each other briefly. Next, one of them approached the taxi driver hesitantly and asked to see his drivers license and taxi license.

The two crew cuts' sudden exit from the back seat had given Lars the chance he'd been praying for. The chance to slip away. He had managed to ease a seat belt into the door opening - with the result that it hadn't shut properly when the policemen slammed it. And, while the driver was following their noisy argument, Lars left the car quietly and unnoticed and crawled away behind it on all fours.

Unfortunately he only made it a few hundred feet before he heard the alarm being raised. A noise that had Lars high-tailing it with the two crew cuts hard on his heels.

Carsten Clausen sighed and shook his head. He returned his attention to the cringing cab driver.

"I hope you're insured."

Lars jumped and stumbled over a barrier in the middle of the road and on down a side street - empty at this time of night. But even though he was young and in reasonable shape it would only be a matter of time before the two athletic crew cuts caught up with him.

Lars sprinted up to a street door and heaved at it desperately in his attempt to escape, but it was locked. Then he caught sight of a passageway from which a garbage collector was just emerging with a bin.

Lars sprinted over to it and disappeared round the corner.

The two policemen arrived seconds later. But too late. Lars had gone.

Even though the searched the yard the passage led on to, they had to give up and returned eventually to the roundabout. Back to Carsten Clausen who was sitting calmly waiting on the hood of the Ford, completely at ease and almost in a good mood.

"Why do they always think they can get away? They never get away."

Carsten placed extra emphasis on the 'never,' whilst sitting himself back into the car.

"Shall we?"

The two other crew cuts followed on behind, whilst the driver looked questioningly at Carsten.

"Where to?"

One of the two policemen from the back seat answered first.

"I reckon he's gone back to his room at college."

Carsten Clausen continued unperturbed.

"Like headless chickens running in all directions."

The driver tried to follow Carsten's train of thought and supplemented.

"Yeah, or sheep."

Carsten sent his colleague a bemused look.

"Sheep? What have sheep got to do with anything? I'm talking about headless chickens, so you can't just suddenly start going on about sheep."

The driver tried to explain.

"Yeah, but isn't it sheep that just do what all the others do?"

"That's not fucking sheep. That's lemmings."

It was one of the crew cuts from the back seat that answered.

Carsten Clausen shook his head.

"Let's go in and get a new car first. There's nothing less appealing than a smashed up car. That'll give our friend here time to get all the way home too."

"And there's nothing to loose?"

This time the driver had succeeded in saying something relevant.

Carsten Clausen shook his head.

"The IP-address identifies the house in Skodsborg. The mother's house. And the others should definitely have got there by now."

He looked reflectively at his exclusive watch and then clapped his hands impatiently.

"Come on boys, time to go."

The battered Ford drove on, on through the night on the empty ring road, whilst the taxi driver cursed them all bitterly and repeatedly.

Lars crept up the stairs and on to his room. One at a time. Everything was completely quiet.

He quickened his pace and headed for the room about midway down the corridor. A small sparsely furnished and exceptionally tidy room with a desk and office chair, a bed and a small armchair standing up against the window behind a similarly nondescript occasional table.

Lars made straight for the desk and took down a book from one of the shelves above it. Hidden between a couple of the book's pages he found a single anonymous looking DVD. He took a paper knife out of the drawer and began scratching the smooth surface of the DVD. When he was finally satisfied he quickly shoved the disk into his pocket and turned his attention towards the room for a brief period. He threw a couple of books off the shelf, pulled the bedspread off his bed and knocked over a chair. Stood there briefly nervous and breathless and then left the room again.

Back on the central staircase that led off to the individual floors the lift suddenly started up, and the unexpected sound made Lars flinch. Then he stood a while before continuing downwards. He'd reached the first landing before the characteristic ping noise told him that the elevator had reached its destination and that the doors had opened. A sound that made him stop and listen. To nothing. Everything was still deadly quiet. Now scarily quiet. For a brief second Lars hoped that it was just one of the other students that had returned home after a night on the town. But the lack of activity around the elevator on the floor above just made him even more nervous and strengthened his desire to escape. To get away at all costs - where he didn't know, just away.

Lars ran out to the car park behind the hall of residence with renewed hope and headed out to the main road. He was looking busily for a garbage can in which to get rid of the DVD, found one and dropped the disk directly into it. He was too occupied to notice the little sports coupé rolling up slowly a few hundred feet behind him.

Wedlock's face was expressionless and any intention he had was completely hidden when the lights from his car lit up the area in front of him around Lars. But the sight made him growl in irritation.

"Like a fuckin' rabbit."

He knew what he had to do and he didn't like it.

Wedlock drove up to the place where Lars had thrown away the DVD and fished it up again. Then he jumped back into his car and continued in pursuit of the unsuspecting gas station attendant.

Lars had travelled some distance down a thoroughfare, before he became aware of Wedlock's car following him, and he took up his desperate almost hopeless flight once more.

Wedlock had chosen direct confrontation. Now he'd dealt with the first stage of his task the next thing to do was to eliminate Lars. Quickly, efficiently and without trace. He drove the car up onto the cycle path whilst still consciously keeping his distance. He tried deliberately to induce the exact reaction he needed. And it came.

Lars redoubled his efforts running even faster. In blind panic. This time across the road and on into the park on the other side.

Confused, scared and almost exhausted Lars wandered bewildered in the darkness and never really escaped from the dense undergrowth. Not before it was too late and a well-placed blow to the back of the neck had dropped him on all fours, followed up by a sharp sting.

The blow to the neck was intended as a diversion and a way of furthering the subject's state of panic. A blow like that could never knock a man out completely. No-matter how professional you were about it. To really get someone out of the way much more brutal methods were required than those familiar from Hollywood films where blows delivered by the edge of the hand did away with people. Methods that were, as a rule, both bloody and vicious. But not here. Not now. The circumstances required a manoeuvre that was quick and effective and under such circumstances there was no better tool than chemistry.

It wasn't the sting itself, more the feeling of paralysis that dictated total surrender. Total surrender to powers that were far, far greater than Lars could ever imagine.

The substance in question, 200 mg ketamine, would soon block the NMDA neuroreceptors with the desired effect - effective anaesthesia.

Instead of carrying him and thereby increasing the risk of unwanted attention Wedlock took Lars by the shoulder and edged him back to the car. Not without worrying whether Lars would throw up - one of the most common side effects of using the drug. Fortunately he didn't. However, it looked as if Lars was already well on the way into the so-called *K-hole*. A psychedelic side-effect that often caused users to imagine fantastic things, such as conversations with divine beings or out of body experiences. And Wedlock didn't begrudge him it. In view of what lay before him a state of joy probably wasn't a bad way to end it all.

Back in the car that was parked discreetly right against the kerb Lars was shoved into the back seat and taped up. Over his mouth and round his upper body and legs.

It was starting to get really light when Wedlock backed the little sports car right up to the quay.

He exited the car slowly and studied the surroundings. An empty and deserted area on the city's wharf. Then he went back to the car and pulled out the still groggy Lars.

Next, Wedlock took out a thick black sheet which he laid out on the pavement whilst Lars just sat swaying from side to side. Completely out of it in his own fantastic universe.

Wedlock worked quickly and efficiently and when everything was ready he fished out a little plastic bag, whereafter his attention returned to Lars.

Wedlock was now taking things very seriously. It was one thing to kill someone in self defence, something quite different to liquidate a defenceless person. He found it distasteful. And in this situation neither self-defence or *Krav Maga* were any help.

Krav Maga, or literally "contact combat," was the combat technique favoured by the majority of professionals. And even though it involved both effective and particularly aggressive techniques it could never teach you what it feels like to kill someone. Killing was only something you could master after some practise, even after you'd lost your innocence once and for all and would have to live with it for the rest of your life.

Wedlock took a deep breath and went to work. He took hold of Lars, hauled him to his feet and pushed him sharply towards the sheet. Then he pulled the bag down over Lars' head, pulled his pistol from the shoulder holster under his jacket, set the muzzle to Lars' forehead and pulled the trigger.

Even though the high calibre *Glock* pistol had been modified with a silencer the sound of the shot was enough to make a couple of surprised seagulls take flight. This being, however, the only reaction from the surrounding area.

Wedlock rolled the sheet around the corpse, carried it over and laid it on the very edge of the boot. Then he fastened a lead belt round the bag at the level of the corpse's stomach and let everything fall back into the car.

Seconds later he was back on the road again and heading for one of the main bridges into Copenhagen.

The sun was almost up and Wedlock knew he'd have to work quickly if he wanted to avoid drawing attention to himself.

The bridge was pretty empty at this hour meaning he could safely wait in the hard-shoulder for a suitable opportunity to dump the body. And within a couple of minutes he was finished.

Wedlock returned to the four-room apartment to the north of the city and opened the door to the balcony for the first time. Then he sat himself at the desk and prepared a quick and exceptionally sloppy AAR - *After Action Report* - to which he attached the DVD whereafter he sent a text consisting of a single number. The number four which meant there was post available for collection by courier.

Then he sat himself down in an armchair and held his hands. Hands that had been shaking now for several hours.

He found the remote and put MTV on at full volume but nothing seemed to help. If only the kid had had a weapon and threatened him with it.

"Fuck!"

Wedlock stood up, pulled out some powder and took a line. Wiped his nose in irritation and lit a cigarette.

The next day was going to be harder - despite the fact that he would never be in doubt as to the correctness of his actions, despite the fact that he was acting on behalf of his country and his government, assassinating a boy wasn't something you just did.

Then the doorbell rang and broke Wedlock's train of thought. It was the courier already.

Though there was an obvious layer of dust on the window shelf, several of the small bonzai trees were in pretty good shape. A circumstance which indicated that they were tended. Not with the greatest care perhaps, but tended none-the-less.

In other respects the room was a mess, with several substantial piles of paper, notes, magazines and books dotted about wherever there was room for them.

No-one had made the sizeable bed and the duvet was well-hidden by a small mountain of clothes. It wasn't possible to see how clean it was.

A couple of framed but yellowing degree certificates were leaned against the wall on the opposite side of the bed. The marks of suction cup darts from a toy gun were visible on both frames, and the wall also bore the traces of wine and coffee stains and other marks of unknown origin. At one time, of course, Christian had intended to hang them on the wall as an ironic comment on the fact that he would never use his degrees for any practical purpose, but some other task had got in the way and he'd never got any further than leaving them leaning against the wall.

Christian sat himself down on the edge of the bed and fastened the lace on one of his sneakers.

Next he retrieved a small key ring from which he removed the front door key.

The idea was that the occasional jog would help compensate for some of his alcohol consumption, perhaps also for some of his excessive consumption of cigarettes. In any case it was something he enjoyed when he finally got round to it. Running was enjoyable, even though getting back into the groove was difficult after several nights spent in various bars in the company of a corresponding number of random female acquaintances. And when it came to women there were plenty to choose from. Especially if you went in for net dating. What he resorted to when his need was strongest. It was quick and easy, without any great fuss. You mailed, you exchanged phone numbers and text messages and met at a café. From there on in it was only a matter of time before they ended up coming up to his flat. That was the easiest. No acting. No fucking about, just fucking.

Of course there were women who excused themselves and left, but not many. When he first sweet talked them a bit, something that didn't take long at all, it was all plain sailing even though, unfortunately, many of them weren't actually a very good lay. But he got his end away, that was the main thing. Better crappy or average sex than no sex at all. And the more crude and crazy he was the quicker it went, as a rule. It was one of those things that women just couldn't resist. The fast-talking nonsense he spouted. His genuinely frivolous attitude and respectless comments about everything and everybody under the sun. But the chat didn't reflect cynicism on his part. It was a technique. A technique he'd refined since high school and which he could now just turn on as easy as nothing. Apart from that it was good training. Constantly playing with words and rhythm; language's artful skills.

Outside on the stairs Christian attached the key to his shoelace and tied the other shoe.

Christian jogged off at a relaxed pace and tried to enjoy the weather - neither too cold nor too hot.

On his way he passed several other runners, all of whom nodded to him in friendly recognition. *As if they knew each other!* Just because you ran round a marsh together it didn't make you bosom buddies. Where did it come from this mania indicating that you were the member of some special privileged group? Just like bikers and bus drivers. Always waving at each other. Christian simply couldn't take it seriously and never, ever nodded back.

A man fixed Christian with his gaze for longer than was normal as they approached each other from opposite directions. Far longer than was socially acceptable. Christian stared back and flattered himself that the guy was probably gay and was trying to contact him.
Christian decided to play along and raised his eyebrows a couple of times and smiled questioningly. But instead of the expected response the man just maintained his stare without the least sign of recognition or friendliness, and without a trace of a smile. He was just totally stone-faced.
Christian turned, as did the man, and they stared at each other for some time as they both continued their run in opposite directions. Christian began to wonder whether actually they knew each other, though if so he'd no idea of where they'd met or who the other man was. Then tiredness and exhaustion suddenly took over and Christian reduced his speed over the next few hundred feet before pulling up completely as his body was racked by a fit of coughs and then finally overtaken by vomiting.

As he neared his flat Christian started to run again. Just for the sake of appearance. He crossed over the road and continued to the little bakers on the corner.
The baker seemed familiar with the routine and tossed a small carton of low fat milk across the counter to Christian.

"Have you been ill?"

"No. Oh, and two croissants."

"Oh, I just thought I hadn't seen you for a while... Don't forget your tab eh?"

"And two croissants."

The baker took a couple of croissants out, put them in a bag and handed them across the counter.

"I've just finished your book, actually."

"What did you think?"

The baker smiled in a friendly manner.

"Let me put it like this. If you bake bread like you write books then it's a good thing you're not a baker."

"What is it that doesn't work?"

"Everything! The language, the style. It's just too dull. Too long, I think. And nothing happens. Give me some drama, sex, excitement, you know. That's what people want to read about. And not all that intellectual shit, where nothing happens."

"You're lucky you've caught me on a good day."

The baker laughed again.

"I believe in honesty... It's the best way."

"What if I told you your pastries taste like shit."

The baker laughed again, still friendly.

"Anyone can say that."

"I bet you've never even tried them."

"You know as well as I do that I make the best pastries in town."

"Sure... See you."

Christian took the goods under his arm and left the store whilst the baker stuck a finger into one of his pastries and tasted it meditatively. Then he shrugged his shoulders and went out back.

Christian emerged from the bath. Dressed and towel-dried his black hair. Then he started clearing the worst of the mess from his table. A couple of empty pizza boxes and several coffee cups with the dried remains of several days' old coffee at the bottom.
The TV was still on in the background spilling out daytime TV into the room.
He took everything out into his kitchen and put it in the sink and decided to clear up properly later.
Then he sat himself down in front of the little laptop computer and turned it on whilst he dug out his dictaphone and listened to the check list of messages he'd recorded.
Even though Christian had difficulty seeing the point of tidying up generally, he had a particular mania. His hand written notes were always neatly stacked in a pile to the left of the computer. In that way he could quickly see how much he'd done and how efficiently he had been working. A good thing. Especially during the periods and the days when he was in his black mood and just dropped it altogether. The days when everything was just fucked up, and where nothing got done despite his intentions. Those were the days when he ended up going out drinking and taking women home. The days when he seriously and for the twenty-fifth time decided to do something different. Something that meant something - something you could actually earn money doing. To not have to write another word - not one, was exactly the most subtle form of pleasure he could imagine. Just letting the keyboard go. Well-knowing that he would never have to return to it. But it was always just a question of time. Then he was back, with renewed energy and ideas flowing.

When the computer was ready he began re-reading a passage from the manuscript he was working on, only to hesitate half way through and finally grind to a halt. Not because he lacked discipline. That was actually all he did have. But because he was no longer certain of the basis for the entire story. And not just that. There were problems with the language. The way he put things. He hated stories about journalists. Hated reading books that were full of quotes and mindless nonsense, full of utterly irrelevant details about gadgets and other bling, even though he could see that that was exactly what he was in the process of writing. He chose to put his work aside and checked his mail instead, though he knew that there was unlikely to be anything in his in-box apart from the ever-present spam.

Christian stared out of the window with a blank expression for a couple of long minutes. Then he found the remote control, turned down the volume on his television and put a CD on. Humming he walked over to one of the many piles of papers in search of a pack of cigarettes.

There weren't any.

He went out into the hall to check his jacket pockets. Finally. A half-empty packet was retrieved from an inside pocket along with a small pile of receipts.

Receipts he was just about to bury in his pocket again when the uppermost receipt attracted his attention.

It was the one from the gas station. A receipt that had a long sequence of ones and zeros written across it. Figures that probably meant something. Why else would you write them down when you were about to be arrested, Christian reasoned.

Even without the receipt bringing the memory of the previous evening's events back to him they'd still have troubled him. Perhaps it was the thought of them that was actually hindering him from writing his own story. The entire episode had been pretty bizarre. So bizarre that there had to be a story in it somewhere. It would be worth thinking it through anyway. Having someone present you with a good story like that on a plate wasn't something that happened every day. Because it *was* a good story. He could sense it. And even though he no-longer worked as a journalist as such, he could probably sell it anyway. Preferably with a twist that cast Carsten Clausen in an unfortunate light.

Christian went back to the living room, closed the lid of his computer, put on his jacket and went out.

In the daytime, the coast road he had been travelling on that fateful evening seemed much more inviting. Especially with the rows of exclusive houses and the rippling sea that jumped and tossed in the fresh and windy weather. Even now where the clouds had come to stay and it looked as if rain couldn't be far away.

Christian drove his beat-up car onto the forecourt in front of the gas station and parked in one of the corners.

Inside there was a queue of customers waiting to be served. To pass the time Christian went over to the video dispenser and flicked through the titles on offer, whilst he waited until their were fewer people.

Most of the videos were either action films or porn. A trivial combination he thought, whilst nevertheless picking up one with a particularly interesting cover - a woman who was being penetrated by three men simultaneously, one in the mouth, one in front and one from behind.

A female customer on her way to the counter gave him a knowing look as she passed which Christian returned with a wink that made her blush like a fourteen year-old.

She was the only customer left in the queue so Christian took his place politely one step behind her.

"There's nothing like a good picture. They're so inspiring don't you think?"

The woman in front twitched and it took her some time to compose herself and a presentable answer.

"I'm more a fan of abstract art. It challenges the intellect."

"Sure, sure. But it's probably not going to make my dick hard if you get my drift."

The women smiled and nodded apologetically as she received her receipt. Then she was on her way again.

Christian smiled after her whilst calling out:

"Does that mean we have a date?"

"What can I do for you?"

The attendant behind the desk was about 50, if not more, and looked to be both bleary-eyed and irritable behind his stuck-on customer smile. His eye's weren't in it, and revealed both tiredness and bile.

"I wanted to have a word with the guy who normally works here, what's his name...?"

The attendant glared at Christian, but was quick to reply and spat the sentences out at high speed.

"Lars. Yeah... I really couldn't care less what happens to him. What the hell was he doing calling me up in the middle of the night and getting me out of a warm bed because he suddenly felt ill. But I know him... Don't you worry, he won't be getting paid for that shift. We don't put up with tricks like that you know. Are you listening to me?! Just shutting up shop without so much as waiting. Do you know how much that costs?"

"You don't know where I could get in touch with him do you?"

The attendant continued his rant.

"At home, I guess."

"Home?"

At which point a new customer entered the store.

"Yes, the Egmont hall of residence, or whatever. The campus down town. But he's probably just screwing around... What is this all about anyway?"

"My sister. I never know where to find her. And she never answers her phone. But her boyfriend... Lars... he works here I think. So..."

"Lars Mortensen, Egmont hall of residence."

The attendant scribbled down a telephone number and handed it to Christian.

"Maybe you'll have more luck with this than me. He doesn't pick it up when I call him. And if you do find him tell him to come in to work again this evening all right?!. Or I'll bloody well find someone else. You can't play games with me. Did you want to buy anything or what?"

Christian shook his head.

"No thanks, but thanks for your help."

On his way back into town Christian tried ringing Lars' number but no-one answered. He hadn't expected them to.

Christian reached his destination, leaned into the right-hand turn in front of the campus building and rolled to a halt, finally, in the parking lot, where a single parking space had just become available.

Christian made his way up to the first floor kitchen where some students were busy with some sort of group work.

"Hi, can you tell me where I can find Lars Mortensen?"

"532."

"Okay. Thanks."

Christian found room 532 and knocked on the door, just as a young woman passed by with a bag over her shoulder and the day's mail in her hand.

"He's not home."

"Do you know where I can find him?"

"If he's not in class then he's probably round at his mother's. Why?"

"Oh, it's just for an article about student work."

"Are you a journalist?"

"Yeah."

"Which paper? Do you have a press card?"

The young woman just sounded curious in an everyday kind of way and wasn't threatening.

"It's in the car. But I have got a business card."

"Can't you use me? I've got a student job. I'm Sofie, by the way. Sofie Breinholdt."

Christian studied her reflectively whilst she offered him her hand. Short, slim, fair-haired, attractive. With a peculiar mixture of intelligence and sensual appeal. She came across as quick on the uptake but with an analytical bent. And she seemed like the type to take a friendly interest in other people generally. Plus - and not least - she was good looking.

Christian returned her greeting and handed her a worn business card that was curling at the edges. It was a leftover from his time on the newspaper and the only thing on it was his name, e-mail address and phone number.

"That sounds interesting, but I've actually already got enough subjects thanks. I'd love to meet over a glass of wine though."

"I'm actually Lars' girlfriend."

"No problem. What are you doing tonight?"

Sofie shook her head in a serious fashion, though her glimpse betrayed a hint of humour.

"Anyway, you're too old."

"36, that's no age for someone like you."

Christian smiled his best smile, but on this occasion all he got in return was a cold, frosty stare.

"Gotta go."

Christian fished the receipt up from his pocket.

"Oh, hey. By the way, do you know what this is?"

Sofie glanced briefly at the receipt. And her eye's flashed as she answered seriously.

"It's a receipt from a gas station with lots of ones and zeros written on it."

Christian had anticipated the answer, but looked genuinely disappointed. He put the receipt back in his pocket.

"You know what? I think it would do you good to hang out with an adult sometime."

"But I do already. His name's *dad*."

Sofie walked off without so much as a backward glance.

Christian chuckled darkly behind her back and found his way back to the staircase.

On his way home Christian tried to weigh up the pros and cons of taking the matter further. On the one hand it could be interesting, but on the other hand Christian could well imagine that it would just end up being some frustrated student who'd been mucking around with shoplifting or something like that. Basically harmless, in other words, but, as so often, an excuse for the heavy handed police to turn up with their lights flashing.

Christian parked his car in front of his flat while deciding to try one more time. Recalling the name on the card the policeman with the psychotic streak had shoved in his face. A card which most of all recalled a garbled driver's license without any title beyond the usual insignia at the top. All and all he found that it just irritated him too much to just let it go. The guy's face just kept popping up in his head again and again. The complacent, self-important Carsten Clausen.

Christian turned on his laptop and rang a number on his cell phone. Even though he no longer used his regular phone he still had to pay for a subscription, as he could only get Internet access if he also paid for a phone line. A small extra expense but it riled.
The receptionist at the other end sounded friendly in a routine way.
"Just a moment... ... Do you know which department he works in?"
"No actually I don't."
"But he does work here at the station?"
"Yeah, I think so."
Christian surfed the net for images of bonsai trees while he waited.
"Sorry. Are you sure he works here?"
"Can't you look him up on your computer? I mean, there can't be that many policemen called Carsten Clausen."
"I haven't got any Carsten Clausen's at all. Shall I put you through to personnel?"
"Sure, thanks."

"One moment please."

"Department B. Jacob Lausten speaking."

Out of habit, the policeman still used the dusty old alphabetical reference for the department.

"Hi. My name is Christian Bang. I'm a freelance journalist and I'm trying to get hold of someone by the name of Carsten Clausen. Is that something you could help me with?"

"Just a minute... ...What are you calling about?"

"Have you found him?"

Christian sounded surprised to meet such efficiency.

"...You mentioned that you were a journalist. Where are you calling from and what's your call related to?"

"It's for a series of articles about a couple of high-ranking policemen."

"But, if you know what his name is you must know where he works?"

"Sure, he's with criminal investigations," said Christian lying, and pulled a face. As if it hurt saying it. He hoped he'd guessed right.

"We've reorganised you know, it's not called criminal investigations anymore, but... You're sure his name is Carsten Clausen?"

"Absolutely."

"...Nope. Sorry, can't help you."

"Why not?"

"There's no-one here of that name. Goodbye."

"Okay. Thanks for your help. Bye."

Christian threw down the receiver and leaned back in his chair.

He closed a couple of web pages only to reveal further new sites with pornographic content.

"Fuck it. Fuck, fuck, fuck it."

He decided to forget it. He was damned if he was going to invest that much energy on something that would probably just turn out to be a waste of time. And yet... there was something that still irritated him. Something he couldn't quite put his finger on.

Christian decided to ask one of his colleagues from his time on the paper. The time when he ran around with an unrecognised ambition of making it in a big way as a journalist. A career that had begun at a local paper and had taken him to a national title where initially he'd delivered a couple of brief articles about the the latest high-tech equipment and gadgets. Never writing for pleasure, always in an attempt to earn good money quickly. This was the start of a period where he was attached to the paper's weekend supplement with enough work for at least two articles a week. Just enough to keep the wolf from the door. And if he'd never gone and run into Helena there was no knowing where he'd have ended up. He might even have made editor. He'd only ended up studying journalism by chance. Even though, in fact, it perhaps had more to do with his love of writing than anything else. He had considered taking creative writing courses, but why not earn money whilst learning the trade? OK, newspaper articles weren't the same as novels where you had to make sure you had a finger on characters, plots and tone of voice but it was still words. Written, well-paid words.

His cell phone rang.

"Christian speaking."

"Ah, yes hello. This is Financial Advisor Soeren Christensen from Danske Bank."

Christian rolled his eyes.

"Yes, hello."

"It's about your overdraft application. I'm afraid we can't help you."

More and more porno sites were appearing on Christian's screen.

Completely out of control. He tried to close them whilst concentrating on the conversation.

"I just need to send off this article and then there'll be money coming in again."

"I'm afraid that's not enough. Your finances just aren't stable enough for us to be able to provide you with an overdraft of that scale."

"Well then there's no way out of it then."

"I'm sorry. But you're welcome to make a new application in future. Once you start to achieve a more stable income we'll be happy to provide with a loan."

Christian swore under his breath without really knowing what was more annoying, the conversation or his uncooperative computer that generated more and more open web pages as fast as he could close them. Christian pressed the off button and held it down until the computer shut down with a gentle beep.

"But what's the point? I mean then I wouldn't need the money would I. It's now I need a loan. Now. Urgently. And I've money coming in."

"I'm sorry. Have a good day. Goodbye."

The line was dead and Christian chucked his cell phone away with an oath.

Christian entered the little city-centre café and made directly for one of the tables where a man of about his own age was sat hunched over a shot and the day's papers.

"Hi Henrik."

Henrik looked up and recognised Christian instantly. He sounded surprised to see him.

Christian pulled up a chair and sat down whilst Henrik continued.

"What's it been? Three years?"

They exchanged handshakes.

"Or more maybe."

"Do you still see anything of Helena?"

"No," said Christian lying. "And she doesn't need to know I've seen you today either. Look, I need your help."

"Okay, okay my lips are sealed. Actually we don't see much of each other anymore now she's changed section."

"I need some info. About a policeman. A guy named Carsten Clausen."

"Carsten Clausen? I'll see what I can do. What's it all about?"

"Nothing really. A sort of hunch I need to check out to satisfy my curiosity, that's all really."

Henrik wrote the name down on the edge of one of the papers he'd been reading, tore the page off and put it in his pocket.

"Can it wait? Till next week maybe. I'm kind of busy with some other stuff."

"I see," said Christian and nodded at the liquor and laughed easily while continuing.

"Yeah, yeah. Next week is fine. Have you still got my number?"

"If not I'll find it... What do you say?! How about taking the "*death row*?" It'd be like old times! Boozing till the sun comes up."

"Yeah, lets do that some time... Listen, I gotta go. Thanks for your help."

"No problemo."

Christian stood up.

"I'll call you. And try to stay off the tequila, eh."

"Si, si. Adios amigo."

The sound of lovemaking almost drowned out the tones of Ravel's 'Bolero'. Tones which droned out of a stereo placed in a sizeable, light and airy living room and on to the couple on the bed in the adjoining room.

Helena Madsen panted as she began speaking. Known for talking pretty much all the time. Something that could be tiresome, even though what she said was almost always worth listening to. There was just too much of it.

Helena was a fully-qualified journalist, and a 32 year-old woman who often looked down on those of her colleagues who didn't share her qualifications.

Furthermore Helena was ambitious, quick and sassy. Three very advantageous character traits that had helped her on her way during a very successful career. A career which she herself felt had only just begun. There was no upper limit for her. She could end up anywhere. And there didn't seem to be anybody capable of stopping her, no matter how much they might have wanted to. Helena Madsen was her own woman. A trait she'd got from her father who had always encouraged her to do her own thing and look out for herself. Right from her first hesitant steps she was almost never offered any help when she fell, but was always given lots of praise when she got herself back up.

"I'm off to the Bahamas by the way. All expenses paid... For an interview with Brad Pitt."

Christian stopped moving.

"And you're still surprised that we're not a couple anymore? And... when did you start writing about stuff like that?"

76

Christian had a headache. Mostly because of the long break between drinks. When you'd started it was best not to suddenly stop.

"It was a cancellation. Call it paid holiday... Take me hard!"

Helena reached out and took hold of the tube. She expressed some of the lubricant onto her fingers and rubbed some into herself and Christian in the right places, just before he impatiently and roughly pressed himself up into her.

Helena gasped with both pleasure and pain.

"Ooohh, yeah... And then I'm going to stop off in New York on my way home."

"Shut up a minute will ya."

Christian pushed even harder. Well on his way to satisfaction and a second later they climaxed, both of them, simultaneously.

She was still great sex, thought Christian. You couldn't take that away from her.

He stood up lazily and fetched a joint. Then he sat down on the edge of the bed.

"We could meet up if you like."

"What the fuck would I do in the Bahamas?"

"New York, you idiot. In New York!"

Helena wiped herself with a bit of kitchen roll and grabbed Christian round the neck, as she kissed his throat.

"Uugghh. Do you really have to smoke that crap all the time? It stinks the fucking place out."

Christian ignored her comments and took an extra deep drag. Then he passed it over to her.

"That won't help. Anyway, I can't afford it."

Helena took a couple of drags before passing it back again.

"I'd just be there to hold your hand. And how would you manage anyway on the trip out?"

Helena began picking up her underwear off the floor whilst Christian patted her behind.

"I've had some hypnotism. It actually works."

Christian laughed.

"Of course it does. Have you flown since?"

Helena shook her head.

"No. This'll be the first time."

"As I thought. Have a good trip."

"At least I'll be flying *out* alone."

Christian didn't respond but instead climbed up off the bed and went into one of the front rooms looking for the wine whilst Helena headed for the bathroom.

Most of the walls were covered in books. Shelves and shelves of fiction and non-fiction all mixed up.

Next to the Mac laptop on the desk was a dictionary, a couple of newspapers and a book about international arms dealing.

Christian nosed about a bit but soon lost interest.

Helena's flat was big and well-appointed. You could see she was a high-earner. On the table were a half-empty bottle of wine and a couple of glasses with only the dregs left at the bottom. A wine Christian gratefully drank more of straight from the bottle, whilst looking at a photograph on Helena's desk. A photograph that depicted Helena receiving a journalism award. If you looked closely you could just see a stern-looking Christian in the background.

"You've never considered coming back?"

Helena had just left the bathroom and was now fully-dressed, leaning against the doorway with her arms crossed.

"Back to what? There's nothing to come back to."

"Back to something you can actually make a living doing."

"I still write articles. Just not for you."

"Still jealous 'bout the award?"

Christian turned lazily to Helena, and cast his mind back, briefly, to the occasion on which the photograph had been taken. Taken in the editor's office just after the news that Helena had won the award was released. Denmark's most prestigious journalism award - the Cavling award. It was presented every January to the journalist or journalists (Helena had not shared her award) who had demonstrated particular initiative and talent in the preceding year - as it said in the citation.

"You and your fucking award."

"I won it fair and square."

"Have I ever denied that?"

"I can see it in your attitude."

"Get lost, will ya," he replied wearily - giving up any hope of getting through to her.

He turned away from Helena and moved over to the window that looked out onto the road.

"We made a good couple Christian."

"In your dreams."

"I just don't get why you don't do something with your talent... Your potential."

"What do you know about my potential?"

"I could see how gifted you were back then. I just think... I think it's a shame to waste something like that."

Christian turned around again, his eyes flashing.

"Wait just a minute, what the fuck are you talking about? I'm not wasting a god damn thing. I still write articles okay? And I'm half way through a book, if you hadn't already noticed."

"Your books are good Christian. I've always said that, but you can't just rely on that for a living."

"This is the second time you're on at me about what I can live off. Money isn't everything you know."

"No but it helps. It opens doors... Makes things possible."

Christian laughed scornfully.

"You've never worked as hard in your life as you do now. And you talk about freedom. You, who writes at least seven articles a week, and that's when you're not rushing around the planet. You haven't had a holiday for four years."

Helena seemed to feel the hit and changed the subject whilst reaching for a wine glass.

"Come with me. Meet me in New York. You don't have to pay anything."

"Thanks, but I've got too much to do. And so have you I see. Arms trading. Is it gonna be explosive?"

Helena laughed.

"What do you expect?"

Her mood quickly became serious again.

"I think so. Though... it's a bit of a tricky one. Do you want to hear about it?"

Christian shook his head.

"Some other time maybe. It's time for me to go home."

"You used to be so crazy Christian. I mean in a good way. Spontaneous and impulsive. What's happened to all that all of a sudden?"

"What are you driving at?"

"Come with me! It'd do you good."

He didn't answer, but kissed her forehead. Then he licked her neck and grabbed her bum.

Christian parked his car opposite the block of flats in which he lived. Here he just sat for a while staring out blankly into the darkness before removing the keys from the ignition and stepping out of the car.

Christian locked the car and crossed the road. As he was reaching up to open the main door, someone's outstretched hand all of a sudden took hold of his arm and pulled him back.

Christian turned in surprise and found himself facing the broad jaw of a body-builder type.

"You still owe me for the car, Henry."

Christian relaxed again and sighed.

"Christian. Not Henry. And yes, I know. Now's just not a good time."

"That's no use to me is it... eh?"

"Look I'll get you the money soon... In a couple of days."

"That's what you told me last time."

The body builder sensed something in the air and moved up close to Christian.

"You ought to quit smoking you know. It's fucking unhealthy. Do you know how much of that shit stays in your lungs? And your clothes just stink of it! Man."

The body builder suddenly caught hold of Christian's hands and forced them up to his nose where he smelt them.

"Come on Henry. Do I just smell pussy or what. Mmm, mmm."

Christian didn't answer but remained passive. The body builder released his grip and switched to feeling Christian's clothes. He thrust a hand into his trouser pocket and fished out a warm coin.

"Every little helps. Don't let me down. You know what happens to people who let me down don't you Henry?"

Then the body builder character turned and disappeared surprisingly quietly round a corner.

Christian was alone. He smelt his arm and hand cautiously and smiled to himself.

Holly Burkana got up from the sofa. Still unaware of Alexander Leshenko's death and, therefore, still with the feeling that she had some sort of control over the situation. She picked up her phone and stood a while waiting. Overwhelmed by one last doubt. Doubt as to whether she was doing the right thing.

She dialled the number and shook off her doubt. A second later she was through to her sister.

"Hi it's Holly. I need to see you."

"Welcome back. I was watching on the TV. It looked like everything went well."

"It did..."

Holly changed the subject.

"Isn't it strange. Every time I think of your new boyfriend I end up thinking of Mr. B..."

"What?"

Jodie tried to comment but was interrupted before she could really get going.

"Listen. How about I come and visit this weekend and bring the kids. That'd be real nice. Can we do that? Then we can have a talk... A good talk."

"Yeah of course, but..."

"Great. I gotta go. Friday, then. Bye."

Holly's programme was far from over. Expedition 16 might be over - at least as far as the trip itself was concerned - but the next few days were going to be just as busy as when she'd been in space. There was a long round of meetings and debriefings about everything under the sun to get through. Long intense conversations about what had gone well and what had not gone so well and how they could optimise future missions. There would be discussions about a return to the moon and the upcoming manned mission to Mars. There would be discussions about technical and engineering challenges, about the astronaut's tools, clothing, leisure time, hygiene - everything had to be discussed. And, of course, there wouldd also be time set aside for all the information that was classified. Weekends, however, were still the preserve of family life. Something for which Holly was grateful. It was what kept her going.

Holly fished her car keys up from the table, went out to her vehicle and started off to the mainland. Crossing the swing bridge, continuing on to the local Walmart - the place she preferred to do most of her day-to-day shopping. The fridge was as good as empty.

Though Holly could plan several days ahead and shop for everything they'd need for the kids' lunches, her husband Eric could only manage one thing at a time. And never food, something he first thought about when he, or the kids, were hungry. Which meant that dinner was normally held at the nearest burger joint. A tendency Holly loved to hate.

Holly Burkana left the store carrying a couple of large brown paper bags. She crossed over to her car and began filling the trunk. She dropped a bag and had to pick everything up again one thing at a time. Perhaps that was why she didn't notice the large black *Lincoln Navigator* idling further up the parking lot.

She sat herself down in her own vehicle and began to drive back. Back to Lady's Island. Happy with her decision to visit Jodie and happy to be able to surprise the family with a well-prepared and well-served dinner.

And then, suddenly, everything was turned on its head. At high-speed.

Holly was almost a third of the way across the bridge and had thereby passed the point which functioned as a start signal for the black-clothed man in the big Lincoln. The man fished a small item of electronics out of an inside pocket and held it so that it was facing Holly. It resembled a cell phone more than anything.

The man corrected his impenetrable sunglasses one last time, entered a four-digit number into the display and pressed 'OK'. No reaction. The man shook the device and hit it carefully a couple of times against the dashboard before repeating the procedure. Still in the same calm and controlled manner.

He had to make the attempt a third time before finally achieving a satisfactory result in the form of a discrete beep and a flashing red light from the top of the device.

Discretely and dispassionately the man now followed the events unfolding in front of him. Maintaining a discrete distance behind Holly's car. Holly's car, which now began swerving dramatically from side to side, causing a number of motorists in the opposite lane to sound their horns by way of warning as they passed by.

The man in the heavy Lincoln looked down at the device in his hand and shook it again; this time whilst holding it up to his ear. A rattling noise indicated that the fault with the appliance was internal.

Even though it was customary to work with a safety margin of at least 900 feet in order to protect against unforeseen events such as this one the detonator was not finished with its job yet. Even though it had only just functioned during the first stage, it also had to work during the second and final one.

The man didn't want to draw attention to himself, however, by suddenly pulling over on the middle of the bridge and that meant he had to spend some time getting to the other side. Once there, however, he would be able to adjust the device accordingly.

Holly heard a click from the dashboard. A click that indicated that she would no longer be able to control the car's movement, speed or brakes. Even though she fought long and hard to keep it on the road there was nothing to be done. The car pulled constantly to the right up against the barrier, increasing speed all the time. Each time the car smashed into the metal separating the car from the river the shockwaves passing through her body got harder and harder.

When the barrier finally broke and the car careered over the edge Holly's only thought was that not saying anything to Alex had been a mistake. A mistake not to say that the event they had both witnessed on the space station had been so serious that she couldn't just ignore it. That she couldn't just keep on obeying orders. He deserved that much at least.

Then all of a sudden Holly remembered her years of training. The ability she had worked on to stay calm and make decisions in even the most pressurized and impossible situations. Like the one she was in right now, as she tried, unsuccessfully to lower the side window as she began to remember the last minutes' of radio communication between Houston and the space shuttle *Columbia*. Recordings she had actually spent hours listening to. Again and again and again. Both in order to learn from them and in a sort of reverent fascination at the way the seven crew members had kept their calm right to the very last second. Despite the fact that they must have known several minutes beforehand that they'd never make it back down to earth again. The way they had kept radio contact and shown the greatest possible self-control. Right to the point when the left wing finally broke loose and slung them all to their deaths.

Sparks now appeared from the car's dashboard and Holly now knew that it's electronics were shot. The only thing to do was sit and wait in the cold and the dark. Wait until the water had seeped in.

She released the safety belt anyway and attempted, almost as a reflex to push the door open. But to no avail. The pressure outside the car kept the door hermetically sealed.

Holly Burkana then sent a silent prayer of thanks to Eric and her children. She missed them already.

The man in the big Lincoln rolled into the parking lot and stopped dead ahead of the scene in front of him. A crowd was already gathering. Both on foot and by car. All standing pointing to the point at which Holly's car had broken through and sunk into the water.

A couple of spectators were still shouting for an ambulance, even though the sound of approaching sirens could already be clearly heard.

The man in the Lincoln stepped out of his car and approached one of the spectators as if in a state of shock. All whilst he took the battery out of the device and discovered that one of its wires had worked itself loose.

"What's going on?" he asked, whilst replacing the wire.

The spectator jumped around, clearly excited that something interesting had finally happened to him.

"Wow! Didn't you see it?! It was wild, man. The car just ploughed right through the barrier and plunged into the river. Fuck, man. It was so cool!"

The man nodded in a friendly fashion from behind his black sunglasses, put the battery into place again and entered the four-digit number into the display. The device had one final job to do. A job that would send a sound of so high a frequency down to the car that it would be inaudible to the human ear.

The spectator who had talked to him, had completely forgotten about him as he stood on tiptoes dancing about to make sure he saw absolutely everything.

The man with the black sunglasses lifted the device up to his ear as as if he was listening to a message on his answering machine and pressed the tiny 'OK' button with his thumb.

A second later a dull thud sounded from the underwater explosion, an explosion which, nevertheless, was so powerful that it slung a column of water into the air at the exact spot where Holly's car had disappeared just moments ago.

An explosion which surprised the team behind the technical analysis of the wreckage. Nonetheless, a spokesman later said to the press that what had occurred was a unique event and a result of a number of extremely unlikely circumstances hinging on a defect in the car's electrical systems. He could reassure drivers of the particular model of car involved that such an accident was extremely unlikely to ever happen again. None-the-less a representative of the manufacturer in question subsequently offered all owners of similar vehicles a free safety check. An offer which many people chose to accept.

Even though the accident report seemed conclusive; the matter was not forgotten. Within a short space of time several people had noticed the connection between the two deaths - two astronauts from the same mission. And before long the Internet was awash with conspiracy theories about secret service agencies' attempts to prevent astronauts telling the truth about what had happened during their trip in space. Without anyone being able to agree on what that truth might be.

The only visible change during the last couple of days was a noticeable fall in the stack of handwritten notes. Apart from that the flat looked much as it had always done. There were a few more empty bottles of liquor, take-away boxes and pizza crusts strewn about the place.

Christian turned on the TV, which was showing a repeat of the morning programme as he flicked through the morning post. Adverts and anonymous-looking letters.

He looked up briefly at the female presenter who smiled her standard smile before switching to a more serious face.

He changed his mind and headed out into the messy kitchen and poured water into the cafetiere whilst the presenter droned on. The previous evening's headache was still with him. It had been a really productive evening where he had managed to beat down and overcome his own resistance to getting on with the job. To writing something.

"Every year about 1600 Danes disappear. Fortunately most of them are found again but some are never located. Where do these people end up? Are they the victims of crimes, have they experienced an accident or have they decided to leave it all behind? These are just some of the questions which friends and relatives would like answered…"

Christian returned to the living room and put down the cafetiere whilst ripping open one of the envelopes and reading the letter inside it; already knowing what would be in it.

The heads on the TV continued parrot-fashion in the background. Now they were interviewing a Detective Chief Inspector from Copenhagen Police. A Jesper Bechmann, who was explaining in general terms how missing person investigations were run.

Even though the national Missing Persons Unit no longer existed and the task of finding missing persons was now the responsibility of police forces serving the community in the missing person's last place of residence, many people still laboured under the mistaken idea that missing person searches were coordinated centrally.

The letter Christian had opened was from the Danish tax authorities. A demand for payment.

"What exactly did I do with this 14,000 Kroner they want?" said Christian aloud to no-one in particular.

"With us is Hannah Mortensen, mother of 23-year-old Lars Mortensen, who hasn't been seen or heard of for over a week."

Christian looked up and caught a glimpse of a picture of Lars. The attendant from the gas station. It all came back to him, an event he'd put behind him and almost forgotten.

The presenter continued:

"Even though we, of course, can't rule out foul play, the police's preliminary investigation has uncovered no evidence of a crime... Hannah Mortensen, what's it like having to live with the knowledge that you may never see your child again?"

Christian was now fully and totally focused on the TV screen.

Hannah Mortensen was a presentable middle-aged woman with red cheeks that made nervous furtive glances from eyes that had obviously been crying.

She took a deep almost asthmatic breath before replying.

"It's indescribable. It's awful. And what's worst is the not knowing."

Hannah Mortensen's voice broke, but she managed to hold back the tears as she continued.

"You're just sitting there powerless. Unable to do anything. If I only knew what had happened. Whatever it was, yes, whatever. The worst thing is I've just no idea what's

happened to him. And Lars is a good kid, a lovely kid. He's always kept to his studies and, and he's never been in any trouble with the police or anything like that. So I just don't understand... If only I knew..."

At this point the presenter chose to interrupt.

"Yes, it would appear that it's something that often happens to normal people with a good family background as in Lars' case..."

The TV blanked out. Christian had squatted down in front of the screen with the remote in his hand, whilst he considered his next move. He pulled on a jacket and left the flat.

Christian was well on his way across town as he chatted into his cell phone.

"Any news about Carsten Clausen ...? Okay. But if you could get something this week that'd be really great... Yeah... Thanks a lot. Bye."

Christian finished the call and dialled a new number.

He coughed hard and straightened up in his seat. His voice now had a more optimistic and practised ring.

"Yes, hello. My name is Christian Bang, I'm a journalist working for The Weekly News. I'm researching an article about missing persons... ...Yes, yes, of course I understand. When could you...? ...Of course. Would you be able to talk about it...? ...How about now...? ...Sure I can be there. Thank-you very much, I'll see you soon. Goodbye."

Hannah Mortensen lead Christian politely into the living room.

"Thank-you for taking the time to see me so quickly."

Christian took a seat on the puke-yellow sofa, whilst Hannah Mortensen sat down heavily on the edge of an armchair opposite him. She folded her hands in her lap.

"Talking about it helps."

Christian nodded politely.

"How old is he? Your son?"

Hannah Mortensen looked into the corner of the room several times as if there was a third person in the room together with them.

"Twenty-three. He's our only child. We had him late. We'd actually given up hope of having a child, and then suddenly well, we were lucky."

"And you said he never came home after his shift at the gas station?"

"Well... yes and no. I mean... He lives in town now. At the university campus. You know the building on Noerre Allé."

Christian nodded whilst Hannah Mortensen continued.

"Just past the traffic lights at..."

Christian interrupted gently.

"I know where it is."

Hannah Mortensen smiled apologetically.

"Yes, of course. Sorry."

"That's okay. Keep going."

"He often sleeps here in his old room in the basement when he's been at work. It's easier to come back here than to cycle all the way to downtown Copenhagen. And he's got room for all his computers here."

"Okay. How about his studies? How was he doing? I mean, it can't have been easy if he was working nights."

"No, it has been tough. Especially at the start where we helped him out a bit. Financially, I mean. But things seem to be getting easier for him. He's a smart boy and it's a real passion of his. And it's not every night he's at work, that would've been impossible. Yes, we support him as best we can. He's studying comp... computer science. He'll be starting his third year soon."

"You say we. Where's your husband? Are you divorced?"

"Oh no, nothing like that. But my husband's away a lot. He works on the boats, as an engineer..."

Hannah Mortensen sat quietly while Christian made some notes.

"Do you think I'll ever see my boy again?"

Christian looked up from his notebook and said with conviction:

"I'm sure you will."

They sat in silence for at moment. Then Christian started a new page in his notebook.

"Who have you talked about this to apart from me?"

"Yes, they came crashing in suddenly during the middle of the night. But they were very considerate, the others."

"The others?"

"Yes, they've been here several times... Copenhagen Police."

Hannah Mortensen stood up hesitantly, went over to a bureau and rummaged in a stack of papers. She turned and handed Christian a small business card.

"Detective Chief Inspector Jesper Bechmann."

"Do you mind if I copy it?"

Hannah Mortensen handed it to him.

"No, no of course not."

"But you said they came crashing in during the middle of the night."

"Yes, at first. But Bechmann wasn't with them then. That was the night Lars had been at work."

"Can you describe any of the people that came here that night?"

"Not really. Short-haired well-dressed men. They had a search warrant. And they weren't exactly talkative."

"Why do you think they had a search warrant with them if they were just investigating a missing person."

"Yes, I didn't understand that either. It was only a couple of days later that this Jesper Bechmann suddenly turned up."

"Did you ask them?"

"Yes, but they weren't giving anything away. They just said that I shouldn't worry about Lars, that he'd be fine. But he must have been up to something seeing as they took all his computers away with them."

"Aahh! They'd come to impound his computers...? But you chose to believe that he was all right... Like they said."

"Why would the police lie about something like that? I tried to call him, but I never got through to him. Of course I've left lots of messages on his answering machine but..."

"It seems to me that you're taking this very calmly. First your son is apparently arrested by the police for some unidentified crime, as you say, and then he disappears. How do those two things fit together?"

Hannah Mortensen's expression changed and became unexpectedly firm.

"I've every confidence in what the police are doing and that they're doing the right thing. And if Lars has done something he shouldn't have, then he'll just have to take his punishment won't he?!"

Christian was still irritated when he drove back to town. On the one hand, Hannah Mortensen came across as a scared and worried middle-aged mother, but, on the other hand, she could change, just like that, to a steadfast defender of society, and the rule of law. But how did Lars Mortensen's arrest tie in with his disappearance?

Christian parked in front of a police station and went in to the reception desk. There was a queue so he had to wait until his number came up. He went outside for a smoke while he waited.

The office was stuffed with tatty old filing cabinets and over-flowing shelves - in fact there was just enough room for the two narrow desks. Desks that seemed to be as covered in papers as the shelves along the walls.

Detective Chief Inspector Jesper Bechmann showed Christian in past the assorted junk and ushered him into a rickety chair with thin legs.

A colleague at another desk looked up and nodded busily before burying himself again in papers and case notes.

"You didn't know that Lars Mortensen was arrested the night before he disappeared?"

Christian turned to Jesper Bechmann who had sat himself in the more comfortable chair behind the desk.

Jesper Bechmann took a hasty look at his colleague before answering. A pause that more than clearly told Christian that he was going to be served up a lie.

"Can you just do us a favour and take it from the top?"

Christian nodded patiently, in an almost friendly way. Not as a journalist but as a private individual. And that was how he continued.

"By chance, I was actually present on the night Lars Mortensen was arrested. By some pretty vicious people. Three cars, like it was taken out of a movie, lead by this guy called Carsten Clausen who was a really brutal character. But that's another matter. It all took place at the gas station where Lars was working. I was just in there paying for the gas I'd just put in my tank. Actually it was also time to stock up on beer."

Jesper Bechmann squinted. He exchanged further glances with his colleague.

He coughed and straightened up.

"It's been really fascinating listening to you, and of course if we come across something that can corroborate your account you'll be hearing from us."

Christian shook his head in confusion.

"Is that really all you've got to say? And why is it me coming to you? Shouldn't it have been the other way round?"

"Not necessarily. Cases are often only solved with the help of witnesses."

"If you really think you can get away with just feeding me this crap, to put it bluntly, then you're more fucking stupid than I'd given you credit for."

"Now look, there's no need to be rude is there. We're just doing our job, right?"

"Don't you people ever talk to each other?! Have you spoken to Carsten Clausen at all?"

"What do you take us for? Of course we have."

"And? What about the attendant? He just disappeared? Just like that?"

Jesper Bechmann broke in.

"I think it's time you left police work up to the police okay? Do you think we can agree on that?"

It sounded most of all like a direct threat.

Christian didn't answer, he just stared in amazement. As if the other man was from another planet.

"Thanks for your help. Like I say, if something comes up you'll hear from us."

Christian stood up and made for the exit.

"This stinks to high heaven. And you know it." He slammed the door on his way out.

Christian drove back through town and ended up in front of a bank. He parked the car quickly and rummaged around in his glove compartment after a small stack of papers. He looked quickly at his watch and swore. Within seconds he was out of the car, but dropped a couple of papers and had to fumble around to collect them, before running over to the bank and going inside.

A young bank clerk in a suit and tie looked up with a sour expression when Christian, still breathing heavily, approached his desk and presented himself.

"My name's Christian Bang. It was about the overdraft."

The bank clerk came across as both reserved and arrogant.

"Yes. I believe we discussed it over the phone."

Christian had been standing. He sat himself in the chair opposite. Something that didn't seem to please the young bank clerk at all.

Christian nodded in a friendly fashion.

"And?"

"I do actually have other customers you know. We had an appointment twenty minutes ago."

Christian nodded whilst he looked around. He was already tired and knew what was coming.

"They're good at hiding themselves away, the other customers I mean... But anyway what's the story, how does it look?"

The young man wiped his forehead in irritation.

"I'm afraid we can't help you. Your income just isn't stable enough for the bank to risk taking your business. It's not something we can do."

"It's just until I get it under control. I have the IRS after me now as well. I mean, it's not for me, it's not a loan for consumption."

The bank clerk got up from his chair and looked out of the window.

"You could sell your car. If you're lucky you might get 7 or 8 thousand Kroner for it. I'm not a second-hand car dealer but..."

Christian was now completely certain that this circus was a complete waste of time and that the person opposite him in the cheap suit was a stuck up little twat.

"Nevertheless you get your training from the same place, don't you."

Christian stood up and took the papers out of the young bank clerk's hands.

Christian left the bank and trudged over to his car. As he did so he recognised a couple of crew cutted men coming towards him. Christian stopped and shook his head.

When they reached him the two men took up a position on each side of him.

"If you'd be so kind as to follow us."

"Now what...?"

Christian shook his head again. Resistance would be useless and anyway he was far too curious to protest. He wanted to see where it was all heading.

The two men shoved him into the back of the waiting Ford and headed off at high speed.

In the car Christian turned on the back seat and watched his wreck of a VW Polo disappearing behind him.

He was about to make a comment when his phone rang. The display showed the name 'Henrik'.

"It's Christian."

"I've dug up some stuff about Carsten Clausen."

One of the crew cuts reached out after Christian's phone.

"You can't speak on the phone in here."

Christian moved further away.

"I'll call you back Henrik. Thanks for your help."

"Are you okay? You sound strange... Well that Carsten Clausen guy is a high up in police intelligence. One minute he works for the security division the next..."

One of the crew cuts reached out for Christian's phone again, and this time he managed to get hold of it. He took it away from him, turned it off unceremoniously and returned it to him with a satisfied nod.

Christian smiled back at him.

"You guys are something else."

They turned into a parking lot just before a major intersection, and continued up a ramp before disappearing completely into a concrete building.

Carsten Clausen was sat back relaxed behind his desk whilst reading through some files. He didn't even look up when Christian and the intelligence officers entered the room.

Only after Christian had stood in front of him for several long seconds did Carsten Clausen turn his attention to him. He nodded curtly to the two crew cutted men who exited the room quietly shutting the door behind them.

"Sit down."

He nodded towards a chair in front of the desk, indicating that Christian was to sit down.

Christian remained standing though.

"Am I under arrest?"

"No, no. You haven't done anything wrong have you?"

Christian didn't answer and Carsten Clausen continued.

"There were just a couple of questions I wanted to ask you."

Christian remained silent whilst Carsten Clausen looked more closely at him. As if he was trying to judge Christian's motivation just by observing him. He sighed and put on a charming smile.

"I'd just like to know why you're so interested in our young friend Lars Mortensen?"

Christian nodded slowly.

"Because I saw on TV that he's now missing all of a sudden. And because I happen to know you took him into custody immediately before he went missing. It's a bit of a coincidence wouldn't you say?"

"Are you a family member?"

Christian was still on the offensive and smiled with deliberate friendliness, as he continued undeterred.

"How do you think people will react when they find you've been caught out? Not to mention your boss and the politicians' reactions."

If Carsten Clausen felt threatened by what Christian was saying he was very good at hiding it. He must have something up his sleeve, thought Christian.

"Ah, now I get it. You're a detective?"

Christian ignored the sarcasm.

"Other people would probably call it journalism but okay. How can a person suddenly disappear with all those police around?"

"I thought you were an author. Can I see your press card?"

"It's in my car."

"Really? And me who thought you hadn't had one for years."

Christian didn't answer, and the whole thing was starting to bore him. Unless something started to happen soon he was going to walk out. They didn't seem to have anything to go on apart from some absurd harassment. And Christian couldn't see what they could have on him anyway. He smoked pot. Yeah, so? So did the Minister of Justice by all accounts.

Carsten Clausen took a case file down from a small pile of other case files on the table in front of him and started to thumb through it.

"Let's have a look shall we...?"

Carsten Clausen started reading.

"...High school, the military. An officer no less. Do you like ordering people around Christian...? Studied Danish at university, dropped out and took a degree in journalism, and dropped that without graduating and took a job. Okay, okay, okay, first with some local papers and then some nationals. Wow! You've even received a number of awards for journalistic excellence. Hmmm... And so fucking what. And what happens next? Gives up a promising career just like that? And you've started to drink - right?"

"If I'm not under arrest I'm leaving. You know as well as I do that you've got problems. As soon as the papers get hold of this your career is over. You can't touch me and you know it. I've still got friends in the press, you know."

Carsten Clausen mouth turned down theatrically.

"Well, well, well. Here's a man who really believes in himself. Impressive."

Carsten Clausen lowered his voice still further and whispered slowly.

"There's just one small problem. A detail if you will. A twist... A twist in the tail."

Christian sensed approaching danger, but had no idea how immediate the danger was.

"And that is?"

"The simple fact that I actually have the power to have you put away for a very, very long time. There's Chapter 12, paragraph 107 of the penal code - and there are others but I won't bore you with those now - a person researching or distributing information which is classified in order to protect the interests of the Danish state can be punished for espionage by a prison term of up to 16 years. And this irrespective of whether the information in question is accurate or not. And if that isn't enough then there's always Chapter 13, Paragraph 114, subsection b., for example, relating to terrorism. Do we understand each other?"

Even though Christian had considered the likelihood of a response of this kind he was shocked and had difficulty taking it seriously.

"Terrorism?! How the fuck could you pin a charge of terrorism on me?"

"Up till now you've been a significant hindrance to our enquiries, for example."

"You must be kidding. Just by asking a couple of questions about how good you are at losing people who are supposed to be under arrest? Someone, who, as you've just told me yourself, is a national security risk. Get the fuck out of here."

"Believe me, I'm very good at putting together a charge. And if you ever, ever cross me again I'll make sure it hurts much more than your finger. And you have my promise on that."

Carsten Clausen's voice had turned icy cold and his stare showed very clearly that he meant everything he said. He closed the case file with a snap and stood up abruptly.

A movement that made Christian take a step back despite himself.

"I can't interpret that as anything other than a threat."

Carsten Clausen smiled again. This time more easily; he seemed satisfied with Christian's reaction.

"Not at all. Look on it as a friendly warning... Have a good day, and if we see each other again you'll have really disappointed me."

Carsten Clausen extended his hand, and Christian chose to ignore it. Then he headed for the door.

"I'll keep and eye on you."

Christian turned in the doorway.

"Yeah, as you say... Remind me do I stand up or sit down when I wipe my ass? I can't seem to remember."

Christian slammed the door as he left. Leaving a laughing Carsten Clausen behind him.

Christian sat on the back seat of a very full bus. Just the sort of place he really hated. Being so close to other people. Breathing their smells, hearing their words seeing their bodily bulges. No, he'd rather drive himself poor in his car.

He kept an eye on the bus' progress as he reviewed the content of his conversation with Carsten Clausen.

Christian wasn't really all that shocked. The misuse of power wasn't exactly unheard of, and threats to shut up or keep out were also familiar. Something he, despite everything, had already learned from his time as a journalist. It wasn't so much what had happened that was scary. Rather, it was the man behind the words. That there was actually a man like Carsten Clausen in a position like that was in fact the scariest part of all. What a man like that could do - had, evidently, already done - was actually just as great a threat to society as genuine terrorism, Christian concluded to himself.

Christian pulled out his phone and dialled a number.

"Hi Henrik. Look I'm sorry I was a bit abrupt before. I got interrupted."

"That's okay. Anyway as I just about managed to say the guy in question works for police intelligence. It seems he works in operations. It's limited what you ever get to know about people like that but apparently he has been involved in some funny business..."

"And?"

"Fairly precarious, but he made it through due to a lack of evidence." Hernrik was obviously trying to build the suspense.

"Come on spit it out," answered Christian, almost irritably.

"Okay, okay. Easy now. Here it comes, here it comes. He's alleged to have been bribed by right wing nutters. To look the other way. It was actually two of his own colleagues that tried to bring him down. But when the witness suddenly started to recant one by one, they had to drop the case. And, as if that wasn't enough, his colleagues were demoted and transferred to normal police duties."

Christian nodded to himself. He was obviously up against quite a character, even by the standards of his own department.

"Okay. Thanks."

"I hope you can use it. It's not much to go on, but every little helps as they say."

"Thanks, Henrik. Really. See you soon, all right? And hang tight. Bye."

"You too. Bye."

Christian put the phone back into his pocket, just as he recognised a building. He was uncertain as to whether this was the right stop or not but took a decision and stood up quickly, pushing a couple aside who didn't move out of the way quick enough. Then he edged his way to the door and jumped off.

Christian spotted it from some way away and swore to himself. *Fuck!*
When he reached the car he pulled a parking ticket off, threw it onto the
seat next to him and started the engine. Then he drove out into the traffic
and headed home.

The flat stank, and there were piles of trash and stuff all over the place.
He swept the worst of it to one side, opened a window and sat down
at the computer. He trawled through the papers, but only found a brief
mention.

Christian felt tired and rubbed his neck. He was hungry. He got up from
his chair and looked out at the evening sky before moving out into the
kitchen. There were a couple of dry slices of bread in the fridge and some
cold meat that was past its sell-by date. He smelled it and decided it
would do - at any rate he'd take a chance and eat it. It wasn't as if there
was much to choose between. His kettle clicked, telling him that the
water had boiled and that he could make himself a cup of powdered
coffee. He reached out and grabbed a half-empty bottle of bourbon and
shoved it under his arm whilst balancing his way back into the living
room with coffee in one hand and his sandwich in the other. He put
everything down next to the computer and tried the coffee. Strong - just
what he wanted. But not so strong that you couldn't taste it.

Christian reflected on what had taken place. The only thing he'd got at
the moment was some mild harassment - not enough for a story. He
needed something more substantial. Proof, someone who was prepared
to go on the record. But about what? A boy who gets arrested only to
disappear a couple of days later? Interesting, but not interesting enough

for a story.

Christian's thoughts were disturbed by his cell phone. He put down the coffee. It was a text from an ex-directory number: *'Are you home?'*

Even though he'd no idea who'd sent it to him he decided to answer. *'Yes.'* A minute later a new message ticked in. *'Are you alone?'* A question he answered a little more cryptically. *'Aren't we all?'* Then silence.

Christian waited five more minutes with the cell phone in his hand. He drank his coffee and looked out into the night sky. The storm clouds were gathering and rain had already started to fall. Then he spotted it.

A Bordeaux-red Dodge van waiting in the shadows cast by the weak street lighting.

A car that stood out so much that you couldn't help seeing it. Which was perhaps also the point.

Christian positioned himself in the window and stared demonstratively down at the darkened windscreen whilst gesturing with his mug.

The lights went on, the motor started and the car pulled away far too slowly.

"Uggh. Very scary," said Christian aloud and shook his head in disgust.

It had finally got properly dark. The rain was falling harder and harder on the roof and windows. A noise from the intercom pulled Christian out of his thoughts and he stood up and moved reluctantly away from the computer without putting down the receipt. The receipt from the gas station.

"Yeah?"

"Will you let me in?"

The voice was a woman's. It wasn't a voice Christian recognised.

He hesitated whilst he speculated as to who it could be. One of his flings?

It wouldn't be the first time. He pressed the button that opened the door and let the woman in.

Christian opened the door to the flat and stood waiting, excited to find out who it was. When he found out it actually came as a bit of a surprise.

"I guess you finally understood the sincerity of my approach."

"Won't you invite me in?"

"Sure, come on in."

Christian opened the door and let Sofie and the discrete smell of her perfume glide past. On into the hall where she took off her damp jacket. She continued into the living room with arms folded.

Christian studied her body in greater detail whilst he considered whether or not it was for his sake that she was wearing perfume. It was at any rate a more distinctive odour than the one she'd been wearing that day they'd met on campus.

"Why are you ex-directory?"

Sofie wandered around the living room, and lifted up a couple of books.

"I'm not. I just hid my number to arouse your interest."

Christian smiled arrogantly behind her back.

"It worked. I'm aroused."

Sofie turned.

"I guess you know that Lars has disappeared."

"Yes. I saw it on the news. I'm very sorry. I never got to interview him either."

"I don't think that was why you came."

Christian was taken aback.

"Okay?! And why don't you think that?"

"A real journalist would never have behaved like you did."

"So you're an expert on journalists now or what?"

"No. But I'm really good at spotting liars."

"Am I to understand that you think journalists never lie. You've obviously never opened a tabloid."

Sofie's reply came hesitantly.

"What I meant was, that I could sense that you were being dishonest."

"You're right. I lied a bit. As far as I remember I said something about you needing some adult company. That was a lie. What I should have said was that some sex would do you good."

Sofie took Christian's comment completely in her stride and continued pacing the living room.

"That's not why I'm here."

"I was just trying to be honest."

Christian could sense the tension. The immediate attraction which he sensed intuitively was mutual. She hadn't just come to talk, he thought. This didn't make Christian pompous, however. Actually he was never pompous. It was just an observation.

Sofie turned and walked towards him, as she began to relax. There was less tension in her carriage and her arms had found their more natural place by her sides.

"That same evening you came I went into Lars' room. We had planned to meet, but he never showed up and I let myself in with a spare key. I could see that something was completely wrong. His room wasn't like it normally was. It felt most of all as if someone had turned it upside down in an attempt to find something or other. It wasn't chaotic, just untidy. I mean, Lars was a stickler for order, having things in their proper places.

And I know he'd never leave his room in that sort of state."

"It didn't cross your mind that he might just have been busy?"

Sofie stopped next to a couple of sizeable works of reference and looked at the page they were open on before answering. Then she directed her gaze at Christian.

"No. And, actually I think it has something to do with his disappearance."

"That sounds pretty dramatic. You don't think he could just have changed his habits a bit?"

"Lars isn't the sort of guy to just flip. It took forever just to get him to speak to me. He's very reserved and definitely not the sort of person to do things spontaneously. He's smart and he knows a lot about the things he's working on, but if he's not surrounded by order he has difficulty in pulling himself together to do anything at all."

"I've noticed that beautiful women often make people reserved."

Sofie ignored Christian's comment and went off on a completely new tangent.

"By the way... that series of numbers you showed me. The ones and zeros. It's actually a word, written in binary. A word that means..."

Christian interrupted her before she could finish.

"Nibiru. I know."

Now it was Sofie's turn to be genuinely surprised, whilst Christian nodded in the direction of his computer.

"The web. I've actually just checked it on the web."

He waved the receipt and shrugged his shoulders indifferently.

"There are programmes for that sort of gag. Programmes that can translate to and from binary using ascii code."

"I guess you also know what it refers to then."

"I know enough to say that 'Nibiru' seems to be a term from Sumerian mythology that functions as a name for the planet Jupiter."

"That receipt. Did you get it from Lars?"

"What makes you think that?"

"Several things. First and foremost because Nibiru is actually something Lars and I have spent a lot of time talking about recently."

Christian was unsure how much to reveal, but decided to say no more than was absolutely necessary. He was the one pumping Sofie for information not the other way around. She was quick and smart so he'd have to be on his guard.

He put the receipt back in his pocket and removed a couple of jackets and a jumper by throwing them into a corner, thereby revealing a worn armchair.

"Why don't you have a seat? How about a drink? I've got some wine. Bourbon? Water?"

Sofie sat herself in the chair. At first she just sat, but then she pulled her legs up to her chest and wrapped her arms around them.

Even though she looked to be almost frozen, it seemed as if the position was a sort of comfort to her.

"A small bourbon then. But not too much. I have to get up early."

Christian went out into the kitchen and searched unsuccessfully for a clean glass. He took a dirty one and rinsed it - drying off the remaining spots with an old dishcloth.

Back in the living room he found his own glass by the computer. He picked up the bourbon and the two glasses with one hand and pulled the office chair over to Sofie with the other one. Then he sat himself down to pour the drinks and passed her her glass.

"Santé."

110

"À la votre."

"Basalamati."

"What does that mean?"

Christian smiled easily as he answered.

"Cheers. The only words of Farsi I know."

Sofie nodded and looked intently at him, whilst they both sipped their drinks in silence. Then Christian coughed.

"Was there any special reason to mention Nibiru?"

"I'm doing religious studies. In fact I'm just finishing my thesis. It's about the Babylonian creation myths."

Sofie's gaze was unfocused and her thoughts were obviously elsewhere. Christian tried to help her on her way.

"And? You say you're a religious studies student."

Sofie became concentrated again.

"Yes, that's why Lars, asked me."

"But Lars is studying Computer Science, isn't he? Why the sudden interest in mythology?"

"I don't know. He never said. I just told him what I knew."

"And what do you know?"

"Actually Nibiru has a number of meanings. But you're right the term does stem from Sumerian mythology..."

Christian smiled weakly, slapped his forehead lightly and pointed to one of the reference books on the table.

Sofie returned his smile as she continued.

"...used in Babylonian astrology, where Nibiru refers to the god Marduk..."

Christian nodded slowly and interrupted.

"Marduk is the head deity, the Babylonian equivalent of the Greek god

Zeus, and Roman god Jupiter. Which leads us back to the planet."

"Exactly. But did you also know that Nibiru is also said to be a planet?"

"I don't get it."

Sofie took a further swig of bourbon and continued.

"Lars was completely put out when I told him that. Actually I think he was scared. He hasn't really worked on anything else since I told him."

"You say that Nibiru is also a planet in it's own right. I don't get it. Where is it then? I mean, if it's a planet then we should be able to see it right? I mean we would have heard of it already wouldn't we? As far as I know there's no planet in the solar system called Nibiru."

"That's the whole point. It's also often called the secret planet for that very reason. Or Planet X. At the moment it's just a theory. Pseudo-science I encountered when researching my dissertation. It was a guy called Zecharia Sitchin who started it and he's become very popular. Especially on the Internet. And that despite the fact that academics have murdered his theory. And I agree it's nonsense. At best it's a massive misinterpretation, at worst just speculation in an attempt to make money. To me he comes across as a wind up merchant but he sells plenty of books, and, like I said, he's very popular. Lars seemed to swallow it hook, line and sinker."

"Can you fill me in on the details?"

Sofie continued.

"Sitchin studied economics at University of London. He worked as an editor and journalist in Israel before he moved to New York. He's a full time self-promoter now. He's also started speculating about a host of other things, all based on his own totally inaccurate translations of the Babylonian or Mesopotamian creation myth Enûma Eliš amongst others. Sitchin swaps the gods' names with the names of planets. And in that way he's introduced two new planets to our solar system: Tiamat and Nibiru. Tiamat, which no longer exists is supposed to have been somewhere between Mars and Jupiter. A planet with water, snow, forests you name it. However as a result of the gravitational pull of another planet, Nibiru, which was a planet that was actually on its way through the solar system Tiamat was thrown off course and collided with one of Nibiru's moons. An collision that created asteroids, the moon and... ta da... The earth."

Sofie made dramatic gestures with her arms as she sounded her little fanfare.

Christian sat. Then he swallowed the last of his bourbon.

"Right, I see... Wow. Where is this Nibiru supposed to be now then?"

"The idea is that Nibiru will return at some point as it evidently moves in and out of the solar system as a result of it's enormous elliptical orbit."

"And what's that supposed to mean?"

"Depending on who you ask, it can mean everything from the end of the world in 2012 to heavenly enlightenment. Sitchin also claims that Nibiru is populated by a technologically advanced race. A race that once visited the Earth looking for gold, but, while they were about it they also planted humans as a sort of experiment - that way humans could dig the gold up for them. It's all in the Bible if you know where to look, most of Genesis Chapter 6 is about how the sons of God made sport with the daughters of men."

"Today you'd just call it mass rape, but okay it's just a detail," commented Christian drily.

Sofie continued unperturbed.

"And when God saw that everything was developing the wrong way he made a few changes. First a life limit of 120 years and then a flood to exterminate all life on Earth. Noah was the only one to survive, Noah who, lest we forget," at this point Sofie lifted her finger and paused, "was also the offspring of a woman and one of the sons of God."

"And this is what you think scared Lars?!"

"He seemed scared. And it was the only thing I could get him to talk about when we met."

"You do seem to know quite a lot about it I have to say."

Sofie shrugged her shoulders.

"It's my thesis."

Christian looked at her. Studied her delicate snub nose, the slightly round cheeks, the long blonde hair and high forehead. The narrow shoulders and slim arms. The taught bust and the long fingers with well-groomed nails.

"How long have you two actually been seeing each other?"

"I'm not sure," she said, strangely hesitant.

Sofie stood up. Slightly red in the face. Maybe it was the drink, or maybe because of the frankness of Christian's stare.

"Can I use the bathroom?"

"Sure."

Christian withdrew his gaze and pointed in the direction of the bathroom, whilst stretching behind him to gather up the bottle.

Sofie left the room quickly and headed out to the bathroom, which gave Christian time to do some thinking. That Lars - a computer science student - had been arrested by police intelligence could only really mean one thing. That he'd hacked into something confidential. But why would he then suddenly disappear and why scribble coded messages on a receipt to a man he'd never met. God knows. And why Nibiru? Where did that fit in exactly? The Babylonian creation myths probably weren't top secret. Not as far as Christian knew anyway.

What about all the alien intelligence stuff? No way, too far out. Christian definitely didn't believe in UFOs. There were even times when he didn't believe in his own existence. And even if UFOs existed, how interesting was that? There could be all sorts of accounts of this and that - but so long as there was no actual proof like a conclusive video or a direct and official visit from beyond - well... As far as Christian was concerned it was a waste of time and most of it was plain nonsense.

Far better to spend your time on something more earthly - women, for example.

Sofie came in from the bathroom just as this thought crossed his mind and stood a moment later. Just standing in the middle of the room.

"I'd better be getting home."

Christian just stayed in his chair whilst he stretched lazily. He looked at her body again with renewed interest.

"As you wish. And there wasn't anything else you wanted to talk about?"

Sofie looked at him in confusion.

"Like what?"

Christian smiled his most charming smile.

"I was just thinking why you came? I mean, we could easily have talked this through on the phone?"

He knew he was being nasty now. But it wasn't as if he was known for being diplomatic.

It seemed to hit her harder than he'd intended though, and Sofie seemed lost for words. Christian felt it was up to him to help her.

"Forget it. I'm glad you came."

She wavered, and of course he knew full well why. The fact that he hadn't sprung up and tried to persuade her to stay had made her unsure of herself. An attractive young woman who was used to being pursued, found it difficult suddenly being ignored. A classic that worked every time.

"Don't you want to follow me out?"

Christian got up slowly and emptied his glass on the way.

There was something about her. Something unusual. The green eyes with the fixed look. The sharp intellect. Not just her body, though that was of course the main thing. No, something deeper, even though that sounded clichéd.

In the hall Sofie began putting her jacket on. It was still wet.

"How did you get here? By bike?"

Sofie nodded.

"Yeah."

"Well, it'll be quite a trip then. Enjoy it."

"He's not really my boyfriend."

Sofie looked him straight in the eyes when she said it.

Christian was about to deliver some trivial answer when she interrupted him.

"He's really, really cute, and we're really, really good friends. But that's it."

Christian suddenly became serious.

"I think it's time you went home now. Have a good trip."

Sofie went right up close to him. So close that he could feel the warmth of her breath against his chin.

"Don't you want to kiss me. Just once?"

"Yes, but I don't want to hurt you."

"Why would I be hurt?"

Christian knew that if he let her go now she'd spend the next few days cursing herself and her childish behaviour. Acting so directly without her feelings being returned would cost her countless recriminations. On the other hand, he had actually meant what he'd said.

Fuck that, he thought. She must be old enough to take care of herself. So he grabbed her hard by the arms and pulled her to him whilst cursing his own predilections.

Next morning most of the living room was tidy. Even the kitchen was starting to look inhabitable.

Christian emerged from the bedroom and drowsiness and headed straight to the desk in the living room and found himself a cigarette.

Sofie was fussing about in the kitchen - apparently in the process of dishing up a mega-brunch.

"I thought you had to get off early?"

Sofie turned surprised. She hadn't heard him.

"Oh, I didn't mean to wake you. It was meant as a surprise."

"It already is," answered Christian emphatically. "I don't think this place has been so clean and tidy since I moved in. And that's a long time ago."

Sofie kissed him on the mouth - repeatedly. So many times that in the end he decided to gently push her away.

"The hair suits you."

Christian looked around after a mirror in surprise.

"Don't say you've given me a haircut."

Sofie laughed.

"No, no you fool. You've a bad hair day... It suits you."

"I thought I had those every day."

Christian made for the coffee machine which had nearly finished brewing. Something he hadn't actually used since his parents gave it to him for Christmas some years ago.

"Just have a seat and I'll bring everything in."

Sofie pushed him back into the living room as she bustled around.

Christian bent forward just far enough to be able to see up the t-shirt she was wearing - one of his. She wasn't wearing any knickers.

Christian smiled and took a couple of extra drags on his cigarette. Then he went back to the living room and turned on the TV.

"Listen did you actually go to bed at all? You must have worked all night tidying this up."

Everything in the living room had been tidied up into neat piles and the table was in fact so tidy that it would have been possible for several people to sit round it.

"When are you leaving?"

Her question put Christian on the back foot and he scratched his neck sleepily and turned down the volume on the old TV.

"What do you mean?" he answered loudly.

"I saw the corner of a holiday catalogue - USA. Are you off on holiday?"

"Prying eyes."

Christian had pulled it out.

"What did you say?"

"I said yes. Maybe."

Christian searched in vain for an ashtray. He wasn't going to use the bonzai trees' pots. He, therefore, ended up throwing his but out of the window.

"There are so many great places in the States. Have you been there before?"

118

"Yes, a couple of times... It's a long time ago now though."

Sofie brought some breakfast in on a tray he didn't know he owned.

And she'd been really inventive. Given the severely limited resources at her disposal it was close to a miracle that she'd been able to fix up any sort of breakfast at all. Perhaps, though it was all down to the way you served it. The sliced rye bread cut into rounds, just like the sliced bread - she'd even toasted it golden brown.

Jam in the bowl which she, luckily, didn't know he sometimes used as an ashtray. It was clean of course and he didn't care, but she would've if she'd known. The butter on the white side plate, the milk in its little jug, the clean cups and the fresh coffee. Nothing less than a gastronomic miracle.

And after breakfast there was nothing better than sex. Especially with a really curious woman like Sofie.

Afterwards, well, actually also during the performance, Christian began to feel a little guilty. Something that rather surprised him. It wasn't like him at all to have moral scruples. He was happy living alone and he'd gotten used to it. The thought that he'd have to break this to Sofie at some point was going to be hard. And would hurt her feelings. He could just see it coming. Not that he didn't think well of himself. Just not here. Not now. No this was something else. Even though they actually hardly new each other and had only spent the previous night and this one morning together.

Christian put it out of his head and tried to think of something else.

"How old are you actually?"

"27."

Christian nodded.

"I'm thirty…"

Sofie interrupted and completed his sentence.

"36. You said."

"Did I? I might have been lying."

"It's what I would've guessed."

"You don't think I'm the youthful type then?"

"Not in that sense no."

Sofie laughed whilst Christian let his stomach relax, which was a bit on the big side though he was a thin man and puffed out his cheeks.

"In what way then?"

"Are you really a journalist?" she asked, suddenly serious.

"I used to be. In the real world I'm an author."

Sofie brightened up.

"Wow. Cool. What have you written. Something I should have read?"

"Hardly. A couple of small and very personal books that never sold very well at all. I'd be very surprised to learn you were one of the three people who'd actually bought one."

Christian looked across to the TV screen in the background. Time was passing. If he was going to get any writing done today at all he'd have to start soon. He heard a snippet of news about some supposed UFO sighting in China. Actually in Shanghai's Xinzhuang suburb where a number of independent sightings were recorded of a large object hanging in the air for several minutes whereafter, and to everyone's great surprise, it suddenly left at amazing speed. Two Russian-made *Sukhois SU-30MKK*, fighter planes from the Chinese air force had been dispatched to intercept it but had no chance of getting anywhere near it.

A TV cameraman who happened to be working on something else nearby had managed to film the final and most dramatic events. The point at which the fighter planes turned in pursuit of the object. An object that resembled, more than anything, a little white tennis ball, and one which, with the greatest of ease, seemed capable of accelerating to impossible speeds and disappearing into the heavens.

"I'm going to have to get some work done," said Christian.

Sofie looked hurt. She had obviously expected more of her day with him.

"I'm sure you've got things to do to. You have a dissertation to write, wasn't that it?"

Sofie pulled herself up.

"Yes, you're right. I've just lost all motivation. There are so many other things I'd rather be doing."

Even though Christian could easily have followed this admission up with a couple of interesting questions, he did his best to stick to his own goal. One thousand words every day. Just like Jack London. You could always delete it all again afterwards. A method which, up till now, had worked well. Some days he even managed to write several thousand words.

"You're going to have to go now."

"Will I see you again?"

That was too much. Christian couldn't pull himself together to discuss it now, and answered evasively. Yet again his consideration surprised him.

"Call me."

Sofie was already dressed and went out into the little hall where she put her jacket on.

"Thanks for... a wonderful night and for this morning."

Sofie stood on tiptoes and found Christian's lips with her own.

"And the same to you," answered Christian and opened the door on to the stairs.

"See you 'round."

Sofie kissed him quickly a couple more times before tripping of down the stairs.

When Christian closed the door behind him he was relieved and satisfied to find his old familiar feelings returning. Relief at saying goodbye to a woman he'd spent a night with, was an emotion he knew well. He was pleased to be himself once more.

He turned on the computer and began to write. To work on a story that was based around Shakespeare's 'Hamlet' and which for that reason was set in and around Hamlet's castle: Kronborg.

He was fighting with a tricky character. A character that was constantly disturbed by the the thought and the image of Carsten Clausen.

Christian's phone beeped. It was a text from Sofie. A text with her home number followed by a smiley.

Christian smiled darkly and shook his head weakly a couple of times. Then he looked round his living room. Maybe he should keep her on as a skivvy, Christian thought to himself. She could certainly tidy up. The sex was average though. Not that she wasn't active. She was just too ordinary. A bit too perfect. Something he'd be able to change he was sure but which would take a lot of time. And was that really what he wanted to do? No, he thought. Rather a trip to New York with Helena, even though he'd decided ages ago not to do it. Inviting your ex away for the weekend to somewhere on the other side of the Atlantic could only mean one thing. She was trying to get him back. That hadn't stopped him thumbing through a holiday brochure of course. The trip itself was tempting.

Women! Wonderful, fantastic creatures - from a distance. As soon as you started some sort of relationship with them they tried to change you.

Next they would try and do something about just the very things that had actually attracted them to you in the first place. He had seen it before - with ex-girlfriends - and now, of course, with Helena. That strange need that women seemed to share. Where could it come from? Perhaps they were actually just worried that one of their friends would run off with him. As if he was just another collectable object that anyone could pick up and use at will. As if he himself had nothing to say in the matter.

Christian forced himself to think of something else and continued to plug away at the text, whilst looking forward to the time when he could shut down the computer and grab some more bourbon. What was left swilling around at the bottom of the bottle was nevertheless just enough to wet his lips. He needed something else. Something with more of a kick.

Wedlock asked the taxi driver to pull up at an intersection some distance from his destination and walked the last bit of the way.

He changed pavement several times without even thinking about it. Used every reflection as a mirror and looked over his shoulder constantly. All actions that were so routine as to be automatic.

When he finally reached the embassy he took the stairs in two quick jumps and nodded in a friendly manner to the guards on duty outside. Poorly-trained personnel who'd never be able to defend or prevent anything. But then that wasn't the point. The staff from the Danish security firm were of symbolic value. They showed that the US looked after itself and its allies.

There were, he reflected, a whole lot of things that were only of symbolic value. Airport security procedures, for example. In the real world they couldn't prevent anything if someone was really determined to blow up a plane. The only thing you needed was the will power. Just think 9/11.

Wedlock, who officially was an agricultural attaché, showed his ID to the American marine behind the bullet-proof glass and continued through the metal detector and onward into the embassy complex.

On the first floor he made his way into a small office that looked out over Dag Hammarskjölds Allé. He walked straight through to the balcony on the opposite side of the room.

Only here - on American territory - did he finally relax and light a cigarette. Even though official American policy was that smoking was totally prohibited for all employees Wedlock couldn't give a damn. They were welcome to sack him, he thought, as he blew smoke right into the face of the man who had just come in. The colleague that Wedlock was closest to: Bob Harris. Both of them had been called in to carry out this particular job. Both of them had previously worked for the CIA.

"Do you remember Camp Avalanche? Abu Ghraib? That was where you talked about it first."

"What?"

Wedlock didn't know what Bob was getting at.

Bob Harris. A tall slim man in his mid-fifties with greying hair and a pock-marked face, and with a scar just visible across his throat. Despite his piercing grey-blue eyes he still managed to look friendly. Over-friendly even. And kind of perplexed. After a roadside bomb had injured him he'd changed. Not that he couldn't still do his job, but something had happened to him. Something his friend Wedlock had already noticed in the hospital.

Maybe it was because Bob Harris lived with a woman, even though both Wedlock and Harris were officially unmarried. In fact they'd being together for 8 years now. Something that was extremely rare for people in their line of business where divorce rates were sky-high. As for kids, they had a seven-year-old daughter together, and Bob was even step dad to a boy of ten.

"May 2004 was the first time you started talking about quitting smoking and you haven't done shit about it."

"I probably won't then will I?"

Bob moved over to the railings to escape the trail of smoke.

"Why haven't you reported before now? It's over a week ago."

"You of all people ought to know how fucking hard it is killing someone like that. I needed a bit of time to myself. Anyway, I reported to Susan straight away - the same day."

Harris smiled disarmingly and leaned against the railings.

"Sorry. Are you okay?"

Wedlock nodded curtly.

"Sure. What've you found?"

"We've found out why the Danish secret service were after him."

"And?"

"That's how he came in."

Wedlock couldn't help laughing. He was impressed.

"That's pretty cool. You mean he used the Danish secret service's network to hack his way into ours?"

"Exactamundo. The only thing they found out was that he'd been having a little look around. They haven't found his onward traffic to us. The young Lars Mortensen was too good for that, he hid his data flow very effectively. First between the Danish secret service and InterPol, and then on to us via other intelligence agencies. He was good - you have to give him that."

"And no-one else is after him?"

"Not as far as we know. So no, there isn't."

Bob Harris stood a while before continuing.

"The only problem now is that the Danish police have seized his computers. And we can't exactly go knocking on the door asking for them."

Wedlock nodded and interrupted impatiently.

"Look, don't tell me you haven't actually read my report?"

"There's been other stuff."

"Okay. Then let me inform you that there's nothing to worry about on the computers that were at the mother's house. He'd erased the lot by the time I got there. And that was before the Danish police. What about the material I submitted? That's been sent for analysis right?"

Bob Harris straightened up from his position leaning on the railings and looked Wedlock in the eye.

"Actually I was just coming to that. Come on, let me show you what we've found."

Wedlock sighed.

"Don't you just love your work sometimes? All that sniffing around in other folk's dirty laundry."

"Is that a rhetorical question or are you actually being serious here?"

Wedlock smiled weakly.

"I dunno. What does rhetorical mean?"

Bob laughed and patted Wedlock on the shoulder as they left the balcony and went back into Bob Harris' office.

He opened his laptop and put the DVD into the open drive.

"We had to spend a lot of time decrypting this - a lot of time, so there's no doubt that he knew what he was doing. Plus the disk was all scratched up... A fucking shame. That's the sort of guy we really need working for us. Waste of talent. Waste of a life if you ask me."

Wedlock waited impatiently to see the contents of the DVD.

"Here it comes."

The DVD was ready and Bob entered the access password. Seconds later a number of video files became available and Bob opened the first of them.

"As you can see our young friend had some other... More juicy interests..."

The video started to play. Sofie was visible on her way into the bathroom. Naked and ready to take a shower.

The angle from which the footage was taken showed clearly that it had been shot with a wide angle lens from the corner of the room, and that

Sofie had no-idea she was being recorded.

"At first I didn't know why he ran away from the Danish police. But then, I wouldn't be proud of having to admit I'd been filming my female neighbour like that. Even though…"

Wedlock moved closer to the screen.

"She looks kinda hot."

Bob Harris remained serious and turned off the video.

"We need to be 100 percent-certain that this breach has been sealed. Once and for all. There's a lot at stake here."

"Do I look like a fucking amateur? No I don't. So you don't have to tell me what's necessary, all right?! If there's something to find I'll find it. And the source is something you don't need to worry about at all. He's gone for good."

Bob Harris continued insistently.

"He's been downloading things we can see that, so there's no question the system's been breached."

"I'll look into it, okay?!"

Wedlock's answer was unusually aggressive. A tone which was like water off a duck's back to Bob Harris.

"What about friends? A girlfriend? The girl on the video maybe?"

Wedlock rubbed his eyes tiredly.

"Do geeks have girlfriends? I don't think that girl's his bit of stuff. I mean if she was he wouldn't have had to put up cameras to film her in the shower. And if they *were* an item he'd have filmed them at it and uploaded everything to *YouTube* years ago."

The two men considered each other intently as Bob Harris continued.

"There's one thing I'm completely certain of anyway, and that's that he took a copy of the material before he wiped his computers. And no, don't ask me how I know. I just happen to know. And since it's not on this DVD, it must be somewhere else. I'd like to get Susan to take a look at it."

"Susan?! She's not experienced, she's too easily influenced. I don't think she's ready for this sort of stuff yet."

"Look, Danish is her first language, she's a woman. She can do things we can't."

We, thought Wedlock. *We* meant him: Wedlock.

"I think you're making a mistake."

Bob Harris shrugged his shoulders.

"Friends or not - you shouldn't question my judgement."

Wedlock and Harris glared at each other in silence. Then Wedlock turned on his heel and left the room.

Wedlock was back out on the street in front of the embassy. Furious at the way he'd been treated. *I bet he's screwing her. Why else did he want her in the field?* Harris, who otherwise always let Wedlock make his own decisions. Not that he had anything against Susan Johannesen, it was nothing personal, but she just hadn't got what it took to do field work. You needed much more preparation and as it was she just hadn't received the necessary training.

He would just have to make the best of it and hope it didn't all screw up. Did she, for instance, know anything about the unwritten rules? Rule number one, for example. Stick as close to the truth as you can. That way you didn't have to lie as much, and what you said was more plausible. If not, then he'd bloody well make sure he told her. It'd be his job to brief her on the operation's current status. *Damn!*

Christian opened the DVD drive on his laptop and inserted a disk. He set the system to play it. Moments later the living room was full of the sound of '*Trois Gymnopédies*' by the, fairly eccentric, French composer Eric Satie.

A suitably peaceful work given Christian's unruly mood. He'd spent the night chatting and drinking. As his drunkenness took over he had become more and more mean, and had ended up viscously insulting every single woman he'd chatted to.

In reality there had only been two of them but they had become so important in his addled brain that there might as well have been twenty of them.

According to their profiles both of them were highly sexed, and whereas one was an s/m fan in a small way the other was just gagging for it - a borderline nymphomaniac. Two different profiles that worked just as they should and appealed to the majority of men.

Both women had chatted with countless men, as far as it was possible to see without anything coming of it. It wasn't because Christian's approach was all that different, apart from the fact that many women seemed to like the paragraph where he'd described his work as an author - something which women seemed to find particularly interesting. Anyway. It was certainly the first thing both of them had asked him about after he made contact with them.

Christian had had a plan in chatting to both girls at once. Given that they both seemed reasonably attractive and both seemed to be without too many inhibitions he'd thought of bringing them together - so that the three of them could spend some time together. A suggestion that one of them was definitely not pleased with and which left both of them feeling particularly let down. To which Christian replied that they should just pull themselves together and look on it as a challenge and a new sexual adventure - very modern it was too. But as their answers got more and more sharp Christian became more and more rude, which, of course, culminated in them both ignoring him completely. Which again left him just sitting there, very drunk, laughing at himself and his view of the world.

Christian got up from the chair and wandered over to the window. The Bordeaux-red van was gone. Actually, after that night he hadn't seen it again, and it satisfied Christian to know that all they'd been doing was trying to scare him. It hadn't worked.

Sofie had rung early. Far too early. And asked whether they couldn't meet up - go to a café or... Christian hated meeting people in cafés so he suggested a park instead, though what he really wanted to do was to go back to sleep. A park where he spotted her almost as soon as he turned the corner of the path.

Christian studied her profile, whilst he speculated as to why she was so keen to see him. She had been very insistent and Christian had decided to say yes so that he could put an end to the whole relationship thing. Not that they had any relationship, he said to himself. But he thought he knew how she felt. He was therefore trying to get in first, before everything developed to the point where it wouldn't just hurt her in a superficial way, but would actually cause genuine distress.

Sofie was sitting bent forward looking out at the water in the lake whilst she texted a colleague about swapping shifts.

When Christian reached her she straightened up, put her cell phone in her pocket and stood up meeting him with a broad smile, a deep kiss and a long hug.

Sofie spent her time working in a bar when she needed money. A job she enjoyed and found inspiring as she met a large number of wacky, fun types. It did mean that she had difficulty finding the time to get her dissertation finished, even though it was all she needed to complete to graduate. She'd completed all the other obligatory courses long ago, and even though her tutor had repeatedly stressed that it would probably be a good idea to just sit herself down and get on with it, now that she had actually, finally, agreed a title, there were other things she'd rather be doing. And as time passed, so her conscience began to complain louder and louder.

Should she really just have stuck to anthropology, instead of changing to Religious Studies after completing her Bachelor? And why had she chosen to specialise in the history of religion when there was so much interesting material in, for example, the sociology of religion.

The thing that was really preventing her from finishing was probably the unconscious fear of finishing. For what would happen then? More likely than not she, like several other graduates she'd talked to, would fall into a deep depression from which she'd struggle to ever escape. And what about her career opportunities? Who would want to employ an anthropologist? The only alternative she could face was a Ph.D. But how realistic was that? It wasn't as if there were that many grants available, plus you had to be amongst the best students to get one. And in her heart of hearts, Sofie knew she wasn't one of them.

And then there was love. All the partners she'd had had let her down. After a stormy and passionate relationship where everything had just been fun and games and dreams and reaching for the stars - together - the house of cards had suddenly collapsed. From one day to to the other. And every time it happened she was just as surprised as she'd been the last time. Suddenly the guy wouldn't want to stick around because he'd suddenly realised that she wasn't the one for him after all. Or it was just because, as he said, they'd grown apart.

She hadn't actually been dumped yet by someone leaving her for someone else. But could people sort of just grow apart, just like that in the course of an evening? She must be doing something wrong. But what? She was a pretty self-aware person and wasn't anymore or less naïve than her peers. That was her own opinion anyway, when she thought about such things. So what could it be? Not her looks at any rate. There she was confident. And it pleased her, even though she didn't like to use it. And now there was Christian. This time things just had to work out - nothing was to go wrong. With a man that was eight years older than herself and that bit more mature and sensible. Kids, there'd be kids too.

Sofie considered him out of the corner of her eye whilst they sat on the bench together. On a warm sunny day with birds on the lake and happy people all around. Several shouting playing kids jumping and running around on the grass. Children. She wasn't getting any younger. In fact soon she'd be thirty.

A woman of Eskimo ethnicity approached Christian and Sofie on the bench as she rummaged in the rubbish bin. Then she straightened up and started talking into a brown paper bag. Seemingly disturbed.

Christian caught her eye and she began speaking to him. Directly. She looked at him with a light in her eyes that marked her out, either as completely crazy or, at best, as someone with an unusual and spiritual insight.

"When Saquasohuh Kachina dances on the square in front of the children and throws off the mask the time will have come."

The woman began to dance an Indian ritual dance. Slowly. With slow, slow-motion movements. Surprisingly fit and subtle, whilst she chanted and sang in a language that neither Christian nor Sofie understood.

None-the-less Sofie grabbed Christian's arm and whispered to him - almost alarmed.

"Do you know what she's saying? Do you have any idea what she's talking about?!"

"Not a fucking clue. And I couldn't care less."

Christian thought it was time the woman found herself a bottle with something in it, instead of a bag which was evidently completely empty. Even though he could, of course, sense that Sofie found her scary Christian was more irritated by the woman's intrusive behaviour than anything else.

The woman's hoarse voice became more and more insistent and she came closer and closer. Only when she'd reached the very bench where Christian and Sofie were seated did she pause in her dance and hissed.

"The time is... 2012."

Christian shook his head and put his arm round Sofie. They came to their feet, and began to walk away. As they did so the woman behind them began to scream. So loudly that it attracted the attention of several people.

"Nibiru! Nibiru!!"

Christian stiffened at the words and turned and stared at the woman as she laughed hideously from a mouth full of bad teeth. Christian was about to approach her, but Sofie began pulling him insistently away.

"What do you know about Nibiru? Do we know each other?" asked

Christian.

Sofie pulled Christian even harder and managed to drag him away. The woman simply stood coughing and laughing at the same time.

Christian was shaken, even though he never wanted to be. What the woman had said. The way she had said it. It gave him the creeps. Something that very rarely happened to him, so there could be no doubt that the woman had hit a nerve.

Even though Christian, like many other people, had heard of the Maya Indian's so-called Long Calender, he had never taken it seriously. The belief that the world as we know it would end in December 2012, was on a par with believing in Father Christmas. Or Nostradamus for that matter. There was no doubt, of course, that the Mayans had developed calendar systems that were both sophisticated and precise, but as far as he was aware the end of a calendar simply marked the end of yet another cycle and was a long way from the thousands of judgement day predictions that the Internet was overflowing with. So it wasn't what the woman had said that had scared him. Rather it was the way she had said it. Her performance had been almost witch-like.

From a position on the other side of the lake Susan Johannesen was keeping a close eye on proceedings. She had erected a *D3*, a digital Nikon SLR camera on a tripod from which she was shooting nine pictures at a time. All taken with a 400 millimetre super-telephoto lens and all of Christian and Sofie. Sitting, standing, walking.

Christian and Sofie wandered down paths that led them out of the park - only then did they begin to breath more easily. With cars rushing by and cyclists passing the threats were more mundane and predictable than women who spoke in tongues about things they had no way of knowing about.

Christian needed a drink - a strong drink. And invited Sofie into the nearest café, contrary to his usual practice. This would have to be the exception that proved the rule.

First when he was sat at the table and had downed a double Fernet Branca with its characteristic flavour of myrrh, rhubarb, aloe and saffron, did Christian feel comfortable again. Comfortable enough to have a normal conversation at any rate.

Sofie was drinking too. An ice-cold Baileys. When Christian went to the bar a third time he settled the tab. Her asked for 500 Kroner cash back, but this wasn't available.

Christian swore. He knew that he'd almost got through this month's money - and the month was only just starting.

Sofie looked up at him when he returned to his seat.

"You never answered my question."

"When, what question?" answered Christian disorientated.

"I asked you in the park whether you knew what the woman was talking about."

"But you already know I guess. It's almost getting predictable. Every time there's something I don't understand you're ready with an explanation."

Sofie licked her wound and felt a bit superfluous. She wasn't sure if she really understood what it was Christian was getting at. She chose not to let it bother her and just continued in the same vein.

"Do you want to know?"

"Sure. Go ahead. I can see you're burning to tell me. Eager to show off your fantastic knowledge of myths from all around the world. Right?"

Christian had lost it and was angry with everyone and everything. Especially Sofie who now just sat squirming on the chair opposite.

"What's with you? I just wanted to tell you what the woman said. It was actually pretty scary. You weren't the only one to get a shock you know."

Christian relaxed and cursed himself again for not just saying what it was he actually wanted to say. To tell her not to call anymore. That he didn't want to see her again.

"Sorry. I don't know what came over me."

He grabbed her face between his hands and looked her deep in the eyes.

"I'm sorry. Come on, tell me."

"No, now you're pissing me around. Do you really want to hear it?"

"Please, tell me," he said, this time with more conviction.

"It was pretty mixed up. *Saquasohuh* means blue star, and *Kachina* is just the name the Hopi Indians give the personification of the divinity - or a *'life-bringer'*. And there are lots of those. The myth is that a blue star will be seen in the sky and that one of the performers at one of the traditional Powamu dances will take off the mask. That's the final signal that judgement day is at hand. But it's just a fairy tale children's story like you'd find in any other culture. In the west people understood it literally and many people consider it a prophecy, despite the fact that Saquasohuh Kachina was never part of the Hopi Indian mythology. It was just for kids and I'm sure many of the Hopi Indian elders still get a good laugh out of the white man's total naivety."

Christian tried to concentrate and listen whilst watching a female guest who'd just entered the café.

"Hmm, hmm. Okay. What about 2012?" he asked, now obviously not really listening.

"That's something very different. One of the Maya calenders - the most recognised and the longest stops at the year 2012. The exact date it stops is a bit unclear but most researchers put it at 23rd December. What's supposed to happen next is less clear. At any rate if you understand it as part of Mayan mythology. A lot of researchers think that, as with other calendar systems, it's just the end of a new cycle - and thereby also the beginning of something."

"Okay, I could have told you all that," answered Christian. The newly-arrived woman had sat down with a guy without looking at Christian at all. Not once.

"And you don't think it's pretty weird that it's just the sort of thing Lars had interested himself in?"

"You've heard of Jung right?"

"Jung? You mean the psychoanalyst?"

"Yep. Freud's colleague. Carl Gustav Jung. He was actually a pretty smart guy. Anyway he had this thing he called 'synchronicity'. And that's what's happened here. No more than that."

Sofie's brow furrowed. She didn't quite get it.

Christian continued.

"It's like the times when you think of someone and then they call you right after. Pretty weird, eh?"

"Yeah."

"Well that's all there is to it. It's just a coincidence. Perhaps closely related to the fact that you always remember dropping your toast with the jam side down and never remember dropping it with the jam side up. Even though it's actually just a question of probabilities. If you carried out a trial you'd find that it'd fall jam side down just as many times as jam side up. But we choose to only remember when it falls the 'wrong' way - making it a minor miracle when it falls jam side up. Our memories are selective because they are still rooted in religion and mythology. There's still so much we don't understand and that makes us uncertain - makes us yearn for an explanation. And when there isn't anything else to explain something we usually fall back on occult explanations and superstition. Without explanations of the world and the things in it there are lots of people who'd be constant nervous wrecks."

"Did you study Religious Studies too?" said Sofie laughing, but she sounded surprised too.

"No. Perhaps I should."

Sofie turned serious and took hold of his hand.

"I've had a visit from a woman. A woman who claims to work for the police."

"And?" said Christian curtly, but he let Sofie leave her hand where she'd put it.

"It's just all so strange. I mean, she visited me at work, but I never told any of the police where I worked. At least I don't think I did."

"Well you must have."

Sofie continued unperturbed.

"And another thing, all the stuff she asked me was stuff I'd already told them the first time they visited me... ...I think she was lying."

"You said that about me too."

"Well I was right wasn't I?"

"What did she ask about?" Christian wanted to get back to the matter in hand, even though it was hard to imagine being more bored than he was right now. His head still hurt. A dull pain over his left eye that even alcohol couldn't do away with. Not yet anyway. Still there was plenty of drinking time left so there was no need to give up hope just yet.

"Well, one thing was, she asked whether I had any pictures of me and Lars. Even though I already told them once that we weren't going out. It was as if she just kept at it. Without listening to any of my answers at all. Just round and round the same questions again and again. It just seemed like she was anxious to pull some spectacular revelation out of me. And then she suddenly began to ask me about whether he'd ever given me presents."

Sofie stopped right up and just sat and looked at Christian.

"Yeah? Well, has he ever given you presents then?"

"I said he hadn't. But it's not exactly true. I'm not sure if you'd call it a present though."

"Why did you say no?"

"I only remembered it later. After she'd gone."

"And you haven't called her?"

"No, I got her number but..."

"Did she say what her name was?"

"Susan... Susan something."

"Hmm. Okay, what was it Lars gave you then?"

Sofie smiled easily as she answered.

"A flash drive. With room for two gigabytes."

"How romantic."

"Yeah."

Christian quickly thought things through. You did not need to be a brain surgeon to see that taking a look at the flash drive might be a good idea.

"Have you got it on you?"

"No it's back at campus. Why would I go around carrying a flash drive?"

"What do I know? Maybe you needed to insert it into something or other. That something I'd need to do every once in a while... For example."

Even though Christian had managed to hide his rather rash question behind some rather obvious sexual innuendo, he'd actually just wanted to lighten the conversation up with a joke. Making a reference to sex wasn't actually the smartest thing in the world just now.

"Yeah, well you're a man," said Sofie with a knowing look.

Christian turned serious again, and didn't quite know how he was going to get her to let him have a look at the flash drive without having to tell her all sorts of things he didn't want to.

"You know, you're right. How about we go back to your place?"

"Actually, I feel kind of like I'm being watched. Maybe I'm just paranoid, but I just have this feeling. And I've only had it these last couple of days. Can't we go back to your place instead?"

"Relax will you. You live on campus just round the corner where there are loads of people. And now, you've even got me with you."

Sofie hesitated, but changed her mind when Christian leaned forward and planted a long slow kiss on her lips. The things you can make yourself do, thought Christian, as the bile rose in his throat.

They had bought a few luxuries. Both food and a bit to drink. A couple of bottles of decent wine - well, actually four, even though Sofie had tried to insist that two would do. Steaks, potatoes, garlic. And it was all going to end up simmering away in the big frying pan in the kitchen at the end of the corridor.

Christian pulled yet another bottle of red wine out of the bag and poured them another glass each.

Sofie had just gone off to take a shower in her room. The afternoon actually hadn't been that bad, even though she'd filled most of it with anecdotes from her time as a student. The potatoes were bubbling away in the background.

Christian was adding the final touches whilst Sofie poured the rest of the first bottle of wine into her glass. Then she wandered drunkenly out of the kitchen and just avoided walking into another student who was on his way in. She laughed goofily towards Christian and then straightened herself up and tossed her head back proudly.

Christian had shrugged his shoulders and smiled weakly by way of response, he hadn't really understood what her gesture had meant though it was obviously meant to be funny.

Christian separated the cloves of a garlic and chucked them into the frying pan with the melted butter whilst he completed a thought. He would finish this thing - it hadn't even begun really, and he was going to do it this evening. After the food and... yeah. He could just go home, he thought, and patted his pocket. The flash drive was still there. It was one one of the first things he'd made sure of when they got to her room. Sofie carrying the bags out to the kitchen had given him just enough time to recover it.

Christian threw the student at the other end of the kitchen a glance. He was sitting reading a book whilst eating something indescribable. God they're so young, thought Christian.

"Do you fancy a glass of wine?"

Christian waved one of the bottles and smiled.

"Are you asking me?" the student replied in some confusion.

"Can you see anybody else?" answered Christian with a smile as he thought of the other residents who were probably still lying around sweating on the beach or one of the town's parks. Eagerly reading or discussing yet another obligatory text that they just had to get their heads round before the upcoming exam.

"Errr... no, thanks. But thanks all the same."

The guy obviously had difficulty making his mind up. Was it time to give in to temptation or should he just trudge on through his book.

Christian nodded weakly and went back to his cooking.

He took the sizeable steaks and hit them with the bottom of the empty wine bottle. When he was finally satisfied he took a slug of wine and put the steaks on to fry along with the garlic and the boiled potatoes that had already been chopped into slices of just the right thickness. A bit of salt and a bit of pepper and now he could just leave it for a couple of minutes, just as long as it didn't get too hot.

Why on earth was he standing here cooking when he could hardly be bothered to boil himself an egg when he was at home? Women, he thought. They could actually get you to do almost anything.

Only now did Christian hear the sound. The sound of screams. From Sofie.

Christian put down everything he was holding. At first he just stared questioningly at the young male student who stared back at Christian just as surprised.

Christian ran out into the hall and on to Sofie's room at high speed. The door was already open when Christian got there and the room was empty. The general state of disorder showed that someone had just been here. A stranger, someone Sofie had evidently caught in the act.

Christian ran out of the room again in momentary confusion. Then he caught sight of the stairs and ran over to them. He looked up and just managed to catch a glimpse of Sofie's arm before she left the staircase.

What was worrying was that there was someone else hot on her heels. Christian threw himself up the stairs and took the next couple of flights two steps at a time, but had to slow slightly as he neared the top - it was exhausting.

And when he finally got to the top he knew that it was too late - way too late. In fact, he could already hear the sound of approaching sirens in the distance.

Christian went right to the edge of the roof and held on tight to the railings as he looked down. Down at the ground where Sofie's body was clearly visible as more and more people began to gather around her.

Christian stood for several long seconds before deciding what to do next. Realised that the attacker must still be on the roof and looked around him. Nothing. The person must have made it down to the top floor before Christian had reached the roof. Next he went quickly down to the stairs and along the landing to Sofie's room and recovered his jacket.

Christian had to find some shade from the sun that still stubbornly refused to set. Just shade. On his way back to his flat he sweated like never before. He even found himself wanting water. *Water?!*

He had made a concious decision to leave the car at home. First of all because of the ridiculous total lack of parking, something that had now become the norm in the centre of town. But also just so as to get a bit of exercise. It was a long time since he had gone jogging as a matter of routine, and hangovers and fresh air weren't good friends.

These had now been replaced by a different and more pressing pain. The pain of just having witnessed a murder. That was what it must have been. And even though he didn't feel that he had known Sofie for what she was deep down inside, he'd known her well enough for her to confide in him.

No to mention the fact that they'd been to bed together.

Christian moved back into the shade. The image of the dead woman below the eight-storey building wouldn't go away. And though that was more than enough on it's own, the most unpleasant thing of all was the fact that someone had taken it upon themselves to kill her. But for what? And why?

Christian let his hand run down the outside of his trouser pocket. Just to make sure that the little flash drive was still in it's proper place. When it came down to it, there couldn't really be any doubt as to that being the cause of Sofie's death. Still the question remained - *why?!*

Because someone had been caught in the act? Christian thought back once more to the image of the ransacked room and the glimpse he'd caught of Sofie's pursuer on their way up the stairs. *But that wasn't a good enough reason to kill someone!* Not unless... Unless you were improbably cynical and quite determined not to be found out at any cost.

Whatever it was that the young Lars Mortensen had got his hands on it was something that other people would kill for. Maybe they'd also killed Lars Mortensen? But who were "they" then? It couldn't be the Danish secret service could it? No, that was just a step too far. It just wasn't believable - it was simply too far removed from the Danish way of doing things. In any case, it seemed most unlikely to Christian that the Danish state was in possession of secrets that were worth killing for. No something else was up - something more sinister. *Foreign intelligence agencies?!* There were plenty of them. But why then would the Danish secret service be interested in the young attendant?

If Christian was going to stand any chance of making any progress he was going to have to find out what was on the flash drive. If there was anything, that was. Could it all just have been a diversion that Lars had planned? Or just a totally harmless present given to the woman that, it seemed, Lars was crazy about? Only time would tell. Christian was certain of one thing, however, he wasn't going to involve either the police or the secret service. Not yet at any rate. Because right now he had no proof of anything. Not before he'd had a look at the flash drive.

When he got home, Christian spotted a couple of cars that he didn't like the look of. A couple of almost identical dark Fords with their engine's idling. The shadows cast by the lights in his flat told him that there were at least three people in there. And unless he was much mistaken one of them was Carsten Clausen.

He stood still a while watching, still not quite aware of what was wrong with the picture in front of him.

It was still just light enough for him to be able to see a couple of hundred feet in front of him without any real difficulty. And thought here were no obvious signs of a disaster, like a fire or a fallen tree, there was something or other that just didn't fit in.

Then he suddenly realised what it was. It hit him like a hammer, at the same time as a deep frustration welled up in him.

"Fuck," whispered Christian.

All four wheels on his car had been removed.

"Fuck!" he whispered again, at the same time as he tried to get a grip on himself and make sure that he didn't do something he'd regret. He took a couple of deep breaths and made his way across the street and waved in a cheery way to the two drivers.

The flat's door stood wide open and Christian had to straddle a couple of bags that had been knocked down across the hall on his way into the flat. Carsten Clausen spotted him straight away. Not that he reacted.

146

Sitting in Christian's office chair rocking back and forth with a half-empty bottle of bourbon in his hand he smiled tellingly and nodded his head.

"We were just passing."

Christian tried to close the door behind him but discovered that it had been broken open and the lock was ruined. He looked briefly at the silent men with their crew cuts who were busy rummaging through his bedroom.

"Who's going to pay for the lock?"

"If you win your court case then we have to. Otherwise it's up to you."

"I'm assuming of course that you've got a judge to issue a warrant for this."

"Oh, we only do that when we think we've got time for it. Most of the time we just go with our gut instinct where the warrant gets issued after the fact."

"What happens when you make a mistake?"

"Then it's our problem - but we never make mistakes."

If Christian had ever considered, even fleetingly, handing over the flash drive to Carsten Clausen, there was no way he was going to do it now. A mixture of anger, stubbornness and - he had to admit - a certain professional curiosity and desire to get to the bottom of things removed any doubt in his mind. Plus, of course, the immense pleasure it would give him to bring Carsten Clausen crashing down.

"I thought the idea was that our paths weren't going to cross again."

Carsten Clausen avoided answering Christian's sarcastic comment directly. Instead he continued in a more neutral tone.

"We've had a report that a certain Sofie Breinholt was found dead at the bottom of a building a couple of hours ago and a witness identified a person in her company who fits your description. Fortunately for you, that witness also confirmed that you weren't directly involved, as apparently you were both in the kitchen when the accident, or whatever it was, occurred up on the roof. The question is now - actually there are plenty of questions, so many that it's starting to get on my nerves - what were you doing in Sofie Breinholt's company and why did she suddenly decide to leap to her death. I'm sure it's got nothing whatsoever to do with our friend Lars Mortensen has it?"

"Have you come to arrest me?"

"No, no not all. Why would I want to do that? You weren't directly involved were you? No, I'm just here to ask you the question I've just asked. But don't think that things will end here. When we've finished the case will be turned over to the relevant authorities. That'll be the murder squad, if I'm not mistaken, where the case will probably be closed and considered as either an accident or suicide. But all that doesn't stop us having a little chat now does it? You know, for old time's sake."

"If you've got nothing on me why are you ransacking my flat?"

"Well, you know how it is. Seeing as we're here we might as well take a little look around. And don't worry. We won't be taking you in for your dope. You can smoke that in peace."

"Thanks."

If Christian had the capacity to hate that was what he felt right now. Being totally subject to another person's whims and unable to put up any sort of resistance. And Christian new that Carsten knew it. And that he was enjoying his position.

When, eventually, it was all over and when Christian had signed a document which stated that he had given the secret services permission to search his flat - he made his way to his laptop and turned it on. As the machine booted up he collected his notes again. Notes that had merely been skimmed and then thrown to one side with no attempt to keep them in any sort of order.

When the computer was finally ready Christian put the flash drive in the socket and opened it.

"Come on. Come on baby. Show us what you've got," he said aloud.

Nevertheless he already knew that it probably wouldn't be as easy as he had hoped it was going to be. In fact, if it turned out that Lars Mortensen had just transferred everything onto a flash drive and given it to a friend without the slightest form of data protection then Christian would be disappointed, seriously disappointed.

Despite the fact that the data was password-protected he was disappointed anyway though. As well as some folders which obviously contained documents that belonged to Sofie there was one which had clearly been left there by Lars. At any rate one which had been put there by a person with the same perverted tendency to name files using the binary system as Lars had. The folder was named '0100001100110010'.

He was a bit of an original, thought Christian, as he shook his head and double-clicked the folder. And just as he had expected the computer generated a little dialogue box requesting a password.

Okay, so Lars Mortensen hadn't just popped everything onto a flash drive just like that.

Christian took the flash drive out, put it back in his pocket and turned off the computer. The he made his way to the sofa and lay down, suddenly and unexpectedly disinterested. He just didn't care anymore, even if the world's future was tied up with the information on the flash drive. His reaction to Sofie's death now suddenly began to take over and washed in over him now with great force. So violent was his reaction that he could do little else than let it take over. In waves. As he repeatedly whispered the same word over and over again:

"Fuck... ... ...Fuck."

Then he shut his eyes. Suddenly he was completely exhausted and seconds later he was asleep.

Slam!

Christian woke suddenly and turned in surprise at the noise. Still befuddled by sleep after his rude awakening.

He didn't know what the time was but it didn't feel as if he had slept more than a couple of hours.

Slam!

It was the front door. The front door that was blowing about. Someone had gone out of the street door and the change in air pressure had made Christian's ruined front door bash back and forth in the draft.

Christian sat up abruptly on the couch. Heavy and with an aching head after a long day filled with more drama than many a life. He began once more to think about Sofie's violent death.

Perhaps it was time he began taking things a bit more seriously thought Christian. Flippant comments and superficial relationships didn't seem like the way forward now death had touched him so closely - and death in the form of a murder too. Be that as it may, Christian was aware that, as much as anything, this attitude was a form of self defence. He was sufficiently self-aware to recognise this. That is why there was no question of forcing himself to act any differently than he did.

He got up from the sofa and made his way to the kitchen in an attempt to find something to drink, whilst he tried to force his completely dry mouth to generate some moisture. As he did so he suddenly noticed an unusual whistling noise and stopped at the foot of the step out to the kitchen. It could still be the wind from the stairs he thought.

He chose, just in case, to continue out to the kitchen window where he looked out. Just to be on the safe side. And he was very lucky he did.

Reflected in the kitchen window he could clearly see someone stepping noiselessly forward through the doorway to the living room behind him. A man Christian didn't know. A man who was known as Wedlock. Standing no more than thirty feet from him.

Even though Christian's heart was stuck in his throat he knew instinctively that he would have to keep calm and act quickly and efficiently if he was to get out of this in one piece. He understood, just as instinctively that the man behind him was almost certainly connected to Sofie's murder and probably hadn't popped by for a chat.

Christian crept over to the back stairs and realised that the chain was on.

He pulled a face as he realised that he was going to have to get it off with small slow movements and as quietly as possible. A circumstance that unfortunately also meant he'd had to turn his back on the living room.

Christian held his breath as he took two short steps over to the chain. Then he removed it without making a sound and opened the door. Which made the front door slam with yet another bang.

Christian did not wait to see the other man's reaction but ran out onto the stairs taking them in massive jumps so that he was almost flying. And on. On into the yard. Out of the gate and into the street, where another painful memory hit him. His deformed car.

Nonetheless it gave Christian just the kick he needed to get moving and get away.

The little summer house on the South Harbour was cute and well kept and boasted both a flower garden and a vegetable patch.

By the edge of the house, on the little paved path that lead to the back garden was an equally well looked after and newly-polished Harley Davidson. A five gear red/white *Softail FXST*. Custom-built with a rebuilt 1550 cc motor kit including, amongst the most obvious alterations, expanded intake ports, a 50 mm SE throttle body and *Screamin Eagle* Roller Rocker Arms. A full-blood machine which you couldn't come close to owning unless you had five to six hundred thousand Kroner to throw around.

Christian walked up to the thin glass door and knocked on the pane. Something which immediately, and rather unpleasantly made a large dog jump up from it's position behind the door where it had been lying hidden. Just waiting for someone like Christian to come past.

Christian jumped back in surprise whilst looking for something to defend himself with.

"Ludo! Quiet, Ludo. Quiet!" It was a woman's voice. A voice that belonged to a young woman with prominent breasts and a pretty low-cut blouse.

Very suitably she bent forward and caught hold of the dog's collar. A thick spiked steel collar that was almost more scary than the dog itself.

The woman straightened up again displaying the most perfect set of white teeth Christian had seen for a long time. They were perfectly set off by a deep tan. She opened the door a crack.

"Hello?"

"Is Bazman home?" Christian tried hard to maintain eye contact but his gaze kept wandering down, quite of it's own accord.

"Baz?!" shouted the deeply-tanned woman. "It's for you!"

"Christian. Just say it's Christian," tried Christian in a friendly fashion whilst he wondered to himself why she had referred to him as 'it'.

The woman ignored him completely and was already on her way back into the living room, this time pulling the dog after her. Christian was suddenly aware of the sound of a TV in the background.

"You're bloody lucky we hadn't gone to bed... How's it going Henry? You look like a man who's lost a couple of wheels. Come on in!" The powerful body builder moved out from the living room dressed in a T-shirt that was far too small for him and beckoned Christian inside.

"We're just watching the end of 'X-Files'. It's a repeat but it's actually fucking good. Do you want a beer?"

Bazman didn't wait for an answer but opened up a couple of beers and handed one of them to Christian.

"Cheers. The first beer of the day, and the last." Bazman drank a toast to thin air.

Christian nodded silently and followed his example. It tasted good.

"Liz, this is Henry. Henry, Liz."

"Christian. My name is Christian."

"Your name's Henry till you pay me the money you owe me, okay?"

Christian couldn't help laughing. Things couldn't possibly get more bizarre.

Liz smiled again and this time she didn't withdraw her gaze. In fact she looked him right up and down, from top to toe. With such intensity that it was almost unpleasant.

"But perhaps you've come to pay?"

Christian looked at Liz and then turned his gaze on Bazman whereafter he raised his head slightly in a little angled nod. A movement that Bazman understood straight away. Nonetheless he stayed where he was. More interested in the climax of the TV series than anything else.

"Arh! No, look it doesn't matter. Just spit it out. She can take anything. Right up the ass why not," answered Bazman, grabbed his crotch demonstratively and rummaged around.

Liz gave him a gentle slap across his arm, but said nothing.

Bazman pushed at her feet. She was lying curled up on the sofa with one arm one the armrest. Liz made room for Bazman who sat down heavily and pointed to a leather chair on the other side of the new glass table which was the living room's centrepiece.

"Have a seat."

Christian sat down, as he tried, unsuccessfully, to follow the show's plot.

"That laptop you got hold of for me... You don't by any chance know a programmer do you?"

"Do I look like an IT consultant to you?"

"What about a hacker then?"

"I don't know shit about computers. What is it you're up to?"

"I need to access a file that's password protected."

Bazman shook his head.

"Sorry mate."

"What about Mikkel?" This time it was Liz who spoke.

"Naah." Bazman looked doubtful.

"Doesn't he owe you a favour?"

"Who's Mikkel?" put in Christian.

"Mikkel is a wanker who works out at Symbion. The sort of guy you only ask to do something if you really have to."

"Then listen, this is really, really important."

"Why the fuck should I help you? You haven't even paid me the money you owe me."

"I only came here because there's nothing else I can do. I think you know that really."

"That was what you said about the car. And the laptop and all the other stuff I've got you."

"Other stuff? What other stuff?"

"Yeah, all that pot you smoke, for example."

"Look, this time I really need help..." Christian hesitated, uncertain of how to proceed. "I'm close to getting a handle on a... well, on a policeman."

Bazman and Liz looked at each other. Then they laughed out loud.

"A policeman?! What the fuck Henry? Have you turned into a gangster or something?"

"And I wanted to ask you if I could stay here for a couple of nights."

Bazman's expression changed dramatically. From a gentle look to something almost frightening - exactly the side of his character Christian had been hoping to bring out.

Liz looked at Bazman, as if she expected an answer. Then she pushed impatiently at his thigh with her foot.

"You can use the house opposite. That's what I bought it for."

Bazman got up quickly and went into the small adjoining room only to return seconds later. This time he was carrying a pistol that was so small it was almost possible for him to conceal it in his huge fist. A 6.8 inches long *Kimber 1911 Ultra Carry II/Night Sights*. It weighed only 28 oz when fully loaded. One of the best guns available that you could conceal about your person.

"Easy, easy, easy, easy. There's no need for that," said Christian alarmed.

Bazman ignored him and nodded quickly to Liz.

"I'm just going to show Henry round. Is there any bed linen in the cupboard?"

"Yeah, sure. There's a duvet in the chest."

"Come on."

Bazman was already on his way to the door, as he beckoned Christian to follow him.

"I don't want to know anything about it, okay? And if you get caught then we've never met each other. Is that understood...? Here! Take it."

Bazman handed him the little short-barrelled pistol.

"And be careful. It's loaded."

"Wait a minute will you. I don't want your gun all right. This isn't the States, you know."

"You'd be surprised. That sort of thing's more common than you'd ever imagine. Take it."

But Christian stuck to his guns. Even though he was tempted, just a little bit, he still had his wits about him. He knew that he would never, under any circumstances, actually use a weapon like that. Notwithstanding the fact that there might be people out there who wanted him dead. No, there must be other ways of solving your problems than killing people.

They had reached the house next door. A cold and dark little house that had been left to itself for some time. The paint on the façade had long since started to crack and fade.

It looked like one of the water pipes needed replacing too, and the felt roof needed some attention where it had been pulled about by the wind.

Inside everything seemed to be in good order though, in fact all the

156

furniture seemed to be as good as new. There was even a 22 inch flat-screen television that looked like it had just been taken off the shelf in the store.

Bazman put the pistol in one of the kitchen cupboards.

"Well now you know where you can get help if you need it."

He pulled a light cotton duvet out of a small chest.

"Look, let's talk it over tomorrow, all right?! I need to get some sleep. Have to follow my work-out schedule. There should be a toothbrush and stuff in the bathroom. Sleep well."

Bazman was already on his way out of the door when he thought of something.

"Do you want Ludo over here?"

"No, no. There's no need really. I'll be fine."

"Are you sure? He goes for people if you let him."

"Yes, I can imagine... I'll be fine, but thanks."

"And if there's anything you need just help yourself." Bazman closed the door behind him and Christian could hear the gravel crunching under the big man's feet as he made his way back.

Christian knew that he was safe here. He didn't like to think what he would have done if he hadn't had this place to hole up in.

Bazman's world might be an immoral and to many people an unpleasant one but he definitely stood by his own. Virtues that many people seemed to have forgotten all about. Even though this of course didn't make the crime which Christian knew went on right he couldn't help but feel a certain respect. They took care of their own. And right now Christian was one of them.

He walked over to a low cupboard that lined the wall. The cupboard that housed the TV and a little stereo. He kneeled down and opened one of the doors, and smiled almost happy at the site of a number of bottles of spirits. Smuggled, all of them.

But that wasn't all. In one of the cupboard draws there were several clear plastic bags full of the finest organically grown marijuana.

I could get used to this, thought Christian with a smile.

He dug out a pack of rolling paper and hummed to himself as he rolled the first of several joints.

The next morning was as sunny as the previous day had been. Bazman's whistle was louder than Christian would have liked as he and a barking Ludo made there way up the gravel path that lead up through the garden to the house.

Christian who had heard them coming several feet away was sitting up straight, when Bazman knocked on the window.

"Breakfast time!"

"Thanks, I'll just take a shower and I'll be with you."

"There should be a pair of shorts and a T-shirt in the cupboard. And some clean pants!"

Christian crawled out of bed. He had slept surprisingly well. Even the usual hangover had left him to himself.

The table was laid for a big breakfast. And everything was organic. Freshly-squeezed juice, a gigantic shake - which turned out to be for Bazman, and Bazman alone! - slices of apples, pears, bananas and strawberries and fresh-baked bread from the local bakery. No butter.

"You can't taste it anyway," said Bazman. "And anyway it just goes straight onto your waistline. Which is no good when you're on a diet."

"I didn't know you were on a diet."

"The national championships are in a month. And I'm gonna be pumped. Like I'm cut out of iron."

"This'll be your year honey," said Liz as she came out. With cold milk, boiled eggs and a low-fat cheese.

"They suit you, those shorts - pretty sexy."

Liz smiled and fluttered her eyelashes.

Christian looked across nervously at Bazman who had ignored her flirt. Instead he consumed the gigantic shake in one go. Then he took a couple of raw eggs up out of a bowl and broke them against the edge of the shake glass. He poured them in and shook everything around so that the last of the shake was mixed in, and then poured it all straight down his throat.

Christian had to look away. It was one thing to eat a boiled egg, even a soft boiled one. Yeah, or in omelettes and pancakes for example. *But raw?!* There were limits.

"And I assume you got up several hours ago to go training, am I right?"

"Four and a half mile of country road and a few weights to loosen up and get my body working. But I'll be going over to the gym once we've sorted out our business. Have something to eat man. You look like you could do with it!"

The black five-door Mercedes rolled heavily out of central Copenhagen and passed the campus area on the left hand side.

Whilst Bazman sat singing along to some crappy pop song, keeping time by knocking on the side window Christian had a clear view of most of the all too familiar building. It was not easy for him, and he shook his head as he reflected on the unnecessary loss of human life. Over the loss of Sofie. Over the shock. It was not every day that he witnessed a murder. And for what? A few secret documents that probably weren't worth more than a couple of paragraphs in the local paper, if anybody ever bothered to cover them.

Bazman saw Christian shake his head.

"What's up Henry? You look worried. You okay?"

"Yeah. It was just a thought."

"You said you could bring down a cop. What did you mean by that? And spare me the details please. Just so as I know I'm not wasting my time here. I know we're in a Mercedes, but I'm not a taxi driver."

"If I can prove that the police have... have screwed up and haven't done their job then heads will roll."

"And you need a hacker to do that?"

Christian just looked out of the windscreen without answering.

"You're not very talkative this morning, eh Henry?"

"Well, like you said... The less you know the better."

"Uuhh. Tough guy, eh?!"

"That wasn't why I said it."

The black Mercedes turned left and drove on before turning into the last street before their destination.

Mikkel sat hunched over a height-adjustable desk. The first of three occupants of a cold blue state-of-the-art office environment. Mikkel didn't notice Bazman and Christian standing in the doorway. And it wasn't before Bazman knocked on the glass dividing wall that Mikkel turned around.

The two other men in the room, who sat facing the door, had noticed and acknowledged the two guests some time ago. Both of them came across as friendly and open.

Mikkel recognised Bazman straight away and stood up. Smiling he held out a friendly hand and shook both their hands briefly. Then he rolled up the sleeves of his perfectly ironed shirt and loosened his tie. His jacket was hanging neatly from a coat hanger on the wall.

"How's it going, Bazman. What brings you here?"

"Are you busy?"

"Very. With customers breathing down the back of our necks? Constantly? Yeah, you could say we were busy yeah."

"Perhaps this is the wrong time then," said Bazman.

"For the right person I expect it's a two minute job," said Christian drily and looked Mikkel straight in the eyes.

"What's this about?"

Mikkel seemed confused that Christian had suddenly taken over the conversation.

"Can we go somewhere else?" continued Christian.

Mikkel stood a while hesitating. Then he turned to one of his colleagues.

"Thomas, do you know if the meeting room...? No, sod it. We'll go outside. I need a smoke anyway."

Thomas didn't even look up when Mikkel spoke his name. Mikkel showed them out into the smallest of two connected back yards with a number of tables and benches.

When they'd found a quiet corner Christian continued.

"I need your help to access some files. Files in a particular folder."

Mikkel raised his eyebrows and looked accusingly at Bazman.

"Look I'm not into that sort of thing anymore. Anyway, I haven't the time."

Bazman broke in.

"It wouldn't take long surely. Not for a pro-hacker like you."

"Whatever I might have done once it's history today, okay?! Everything that's going on now, is happening in the here and now. Including what we're talking about."

Mikkel looked about. Just to be quite sure that no-one was listening. Then he looked at Christian with an angry expression.

"What is it then?"

"Just one little folder."

"What, on the net or what?"

"No." Christian shook his head.

"What then? What media?"

"Media?"

"Yeah, DVD, flash drive, CD... floppy disk. Blu-Ray?!"

"Oooh. It's a flash drive."

"You got it with you?"

Christian nodded but didn't hand it over.

"Yeah."

Christian and Mikkel looked at each other for a brief second. Then Mikkel took a decision.

"I'm going to book a meeting room. Twenty minutes tops, okay?!"

Christian shrugged his shoulders without answering.

Christian sat dozing in a chair, whilst Bazman wandered around outside, where he either sent texts or made phone calls. Pretty much non-stop. To whom was something Christian never found out. And actually he didn't care. He knew that the form of business or activity Bazman was engaged in was a *business* you did not ask questions about.

Meanwhile Mikkel, undeterred, was working on his laptop. He was into his second hour. And every time he thought he'd succeeded he shouted out still more enthused than the last time he thought he had cracked it. Christian had tried looking over his shoulder but what he was doing seemed totally chaotic with a number of programs open and running simultaneously and a command prompt in which he was writing continuously. He also seemed to be using an operating system that Christian wasn't familiar with - at any rate it didn't seem to be Windows.

Then Mikkel gave up. Temporarily. But he was so turned on, you'd think he was having sex. Perhaps that was what it was as far as he was concerned.

"This can only have been done by one man. Condor Deuce. C2."

Christian shrugged his shoulders whilst Mikkel continued.

"Actually, there are some people who say he's from round here - from Denmark."

"And?" answered Christian baldly.

Mikkel stood up and handed the flash drive back to Christian.

"I have to go now. But I promise! I promise! I'll come back and look at it at your place tonight, okay? There's no fucking way I'm going to let him do this. Fuck, it's just too much man! Fuck!!"

Christian wondered whether anyone could actually get turned on by doing this sort of thing. And if so whether Mikkel could.

Mikkel, who was almost euphoric. Totally wild at the prospect of cracking a hacker. It was a good thing that there were people like that around, thought Christian. Good for him at any rate.

"Do you know him?"

"Not directly. But in hacker circles Condor Deuce is known as one of the two inheritors of Kevin Mitnick. The guy the FBI got hold of in 1981. That's why he's called Condor Deuce," said Mikkel and raised two fingers by way of illustration. "Kevin Mitnick called himself Condor. So that's why."

"If you say so I'm sure it's true."

"It is. Tonight, okay?"

Mikkel reached out his hand and showed Christian out to Bazman. Then he followed on behind.

"Well?" asked Bazman as he finished his phone call.

Christian waved his hand despairingly.

"More time. Tonight. At your... our place."

Then Mikkel was gone and the two men returned to the black Mercedes.

"You could go to the gym with me if you like. You could use it. I'll show you what to do."

They were on their way back through town.

Christian smiled in a friendly way but shook his head.

"No thanks. I, eh... I'd rather you showed me how to make money. That's something I could really do with."

Bazman turned silent at that.

"You've bought a new car I see. You didn't have this one last time anyway."

Bazman shot him a serious glance.

"I haven't bought anything. And I don't own anything either. Everything you see is Liz's. I'm on the dole."

"Maybe it's Liz I should be propositioning then?"

"Yeah just try, I'll even help you if you like. With a baseball bat."

That made them both laugh.

"By the way. Do you think I could pick up some stuff from my flat?"

"Of course. I'll call Klaus. He can fix it... I'm going to have to get on with my training, so I'll drop you off here okay?"

"Super, thanks. I've nothing better to do without a computer and they say exercise is good for you."

"Do you want me to lend you your fare?"

"No, no. Don't worry. I've still got my credit card."

"Well then you take out that money you owe me."

"I haven't got that much... For fucks sake, you made off with my wheels."

"Yeah, well I reckon we're about quits then," answered Bazman laughing.

"Can I have my name back then?"

"Actually, I think it kinda suits you... Henry."

The black Mercedes pulled in to the curb and Christian stepped out on to the cycle path, after which the car immediately set off.

It was in the house, where Christian was now staying for a second day, that Mikkel spent most of the night accompanied by a large white Russian. A drink which he hardly touched.

When he finally succeeded everyone had been up to the table at least once to look over his shoulder. Bazman, Liz and Christian. Even Ludo had had a sniff.

When he finally succeeded Mikkel was silent. Silent and serious. As, like some modern Pandora's box this was just the start. The start of something which Mikkel had intuitively understood he would never be able to finish. He just wasn't good enough, though it was a great comfort to him that he'd got as far as he actually had.

Mikkel stared at the screen in front of him. Stared fixedly at the open folder, which, of course, contained another folder. A folder named *Bingo* - and a film clip. And, as was standard for hackers of that calibre the layers just got harder and harder. He knew that. It was all part of the game. Just the way it was. But given the trouble Mikkel had had getting passed the first layer of security he knew that there was no point in trying any longer - he was never going to be able to tackle the next hurdle.

Mikkel leaned back in his chair and sat for a while rubbing his face. He was tired. Then he took a deep swig of his drink and called to Christian and Bazman who were sharing a joint in the garden. A good joint if you asked Christian. Though he, as was the case with alcohol, always seemed to be able to cope with the intoxication. The only thing that happened was that he could become a bit abrupt and harsh. And that was only when he had been drinking. Never when he smoked. Hash just made him calm; lovely and calm.

"That's what there is," said Mikkel and pointed at the screen.

Christian and Bazman stood a while as it sank in.

"Hey, is that porn?" asked Bazman enthusiastically. "And what about the Bingo folder?"

"I'm guessing that's password protected too?" asked Christian cautiously.

Mikkel nodded.

"I think we should take a look at the film," answered Mikkel. "I have a feeling that it'll help us find out what to do next."

"Lets do it. There's nothing else for it."

Mikkel double-clicked the icon and a second later Lars was visible. A very different Lars to the one Christian had known. A Lars Mortensen totally at home. Totally cool. And with total confidence radiating from his body, and his speech; a confidence which suited him extremely well. The recording had clearly been made whilst Lars was alone as he could be seen starting and stopping it:

"Congratulations. You made it past the first stage. The second stage is this video where I'm going to explain the rules of the game: the folder - yes, that one. The folder you really, really want to get at - is protected such that the third time the incorrect password is entered the file will be erased. The same of course holds for any attempt to copy it. If you don't open the folder in time the contents will be destroyed. And not just destroyed, gone *forever*. If you're really stupid enough that you're asking why? - well, a stupid question deserves a stupid answer: Because I can! I couldn't give a flying fuck for public interest or about the consequences of making this material available. If I did I could have just released it on the Internet. No, I'd rather that this was a trophy in its own right, a trophy that only the very best can win. Someone who can prove that they're actually better than me. Do you think that person is you? I can promise you you won't be disappointed if you do succeed. Three attempts. Three attempts. Best of luck."

Lars held three fingers up demonstratively and then folded two of them leaving his middle finger as the only one raised. Then he stood up and moved towards the camera. Seconds later the film ended.

The three men in the little house were silent.

"Have you any idea what's in there?" asked Mikkel and turned towards Christian.

"No. Not apart from the fact that it's very, very important."

"Well, shall we give it a try?" Bazman broke in.

"Wo, wo. Easy," answered Christian calmly.

"Agreed. I'm not going to try my hand at this. This bloke is far too good for me. It took me most of a day just to get this far. And I'm actually bloody good if you want to know."

"Yeah, people can say what they like, but you're bloody good," said Bazman, backing him up.

"Well, what next?" asked Christian ignoring Bazman's comment.

"You'll have to take it to someone else. To the best. That's if you can find him."

"Who is it?"

"Talon Karrde. Well that's his alias anyway. It's from Star Wars. They say he's the one who won the money from the FBI."

"FBI?!"

"Yeah, yeah. It's not like you think. The Feds held this competition where the prize for cracking their code was 70,000 dollars. And for each day that passed the value of the prize fell from 60 to 50 to 40 and so on until it hit 10,000. After which the competition would be over."

"And?"

"Well legend has it that Talon Karrde took the 70,000 after just two hours' work. And he hadn't just broken the code, he brought down the entire network to boot. A real whiz kid evidently, but I guess you couldn't not be. There's no-one who really knows who he is. Most hackers think he's part of the *Cult of the Dead Cow* group - cDc - for short. At any rate that's a name that crops up repeatedly. They're based in Lubbock, Texas."

"So what do you suggest?"

"That we contact cDc. Or rather that *I* contact cDc. I'm still in contact with one of the boys. At least I think I am. I can try now if you like?"

Mikkel turned to his laptop and activated a chat program. He began writing avidly straight away. Twenty minutes later he turned to them.

"You should be able to contact Talon Karrde using this e-mail address. But you'll have to travel over there and remember to write '*Condor Deuce needs help*' in the subject field. I'll write it here so as you remember."

Mikkel wrote Talon's e-mail address on a scrap of paper and handed it to Christian.

"I think that's about all I can do for you folks. I should have been home two hours ago."

Mikkel nodded to the two men facing him.

"I have to admit I've met my match here. But I'd like to know if Karrde can crack it. Yeah, I'm kind of curious. Especially when you know there's something really top secret hidden in there. Still, we got through the first part okay."

Mikkel got up and stretched his aching body. Sitting hunched over a computer for hours on end left it's mark on your physique.

"Yeah. Thanks for your help. I don't need to ask you to be discrete do I?"

Mikkel turned serious.

"There could be just about anything in that file. It could be that you'll be sorely disappointed. What do I know? A gimmick. A trick. It wouldn't be the first time. But you can rest easy. I'm used to keeping secrets. Do you realise how much money I could make if I went to a competitor with some of the information I have about what my customers are up to? Sooo. Anyway, it was a pleasure - best of luck with it."

When Christian and Bazman were alone Christian speculated as to what his next move should be. He was going to have to go to the States, and if he was going to do that he needed money. More money than he had.
"I'm guessing borrowing from you is out of the question, right?"
"Do you believe in Santa Claus? No, you've got a knotty little problem there. One thing is helping you with a place to stay but this isn't a free for all. I'd never get it back, it'd be giving it away."
Christian had already come to the conclusion that even though he didn't want to he was going to have to accept Helena's invitation. He didn't have any other options.
"But if you're going to have any hope of returning to something resembling a normal life you're going to have to do what it takes and get this nut cracked."
"Yeah, thanks for that. Do you mind if I make a few calls?"
"It's a free country... Until further notice anyway."
Christian caught his meaning and looked at him with raised eyebrows.
"Yeah, yeah. Take it easy. If something's up you know where we are. Goodnight."
"'night."
Christian made sure that Bazman had left the gravel path before entering the number into his cell phone.
"Helena speaking."

"Hi, yeah. It's me."

"Hi, Christian. I'm just packing."

"Yeah, I guessed as much. Are you on your way tomorrow then?"

"That's right, the plane leaves at 7 o'clock tomorrow morning."

"I guess you won't be wanting company then?"

"Are you asking me?"

"Yes."

"You should have rung a couple of hours ago. Was there anything in particular?"

"You talked about inviting me to New York. Does the offer still stand?"

"Aaah Christian, for fuck's sake!"

"Look just answer my question will you?"

"How do you expect me to organise that now? It's half past ten. If you'd just had the sense to ring a bit earlier."

"Can't you just leave me a ticket in the airport?"

"Why's this suddenly all so important to you anyway?"

"Well I thought maybe it would be a good way for us to get back together. Start afresh."

There was complete silence from the other end of the line. It went on for a long time.

"Do you really mean that?"

"Yeah. I think it could be really something. Especially as you're paying."

"That's the Christian I know. You had me worried... The hotel's called the Crown Plaza, it's on Times Square. I'll be there Friday afternoon. You can just turn up. I'll get the airline to do you an open ticket and you can just pick it up from the desk in the airport... You surprise me Christian. But it's a nice surprise. I'll look forward to it."

Christian shook his head and ground his teeth. It's a good thing it wasn't a video phone, he thought.

Even though Klaus - whoever he was - had made sure that there were clothes and toiletries available he'd no way of knowing that Christian was going to need his passport, and perhaps his laptop. Since it was three days since Christian had been home anybody watching the place must surely have given up and found something better to do. Christian was prepared to take the chance anyway. And what could happen? In broad daylight. He was an adult in the prime of life.
Christian managed to convince himself and took a train from the nearby station without informing either Bazman or Liz of his intentions. Just thanked them for their help and for putting him up. After all, this is Denmark he thought, as he remembered Sofie.

Back at the flat all seemed to be well and Christian found himself questioning his own paranoid tendencies. Just until, that was, he stepped out of the street door again. On the other side of the road, where the Bordeaux van had been parked there was a racy little coupé. A Hertz rental model which Christian thought he recognised from somewhere. His thoughts soon changed when a tall presentable man with swept-back black hair and dark glasses got out. Without doing anything else he stood with his back leaning against the car. It was abundantly clear from his attitude that he only had eyes for Christian.
Christian had to think fast. He stopped to give himself time, lit a cigarette and started walking. He crossed the street and began walking away from the car.
When he reached the corner he stopped as if he had forgotten something and turned on his heel. Then, seeming to change his mind again he turned

once more, shook his head and went into the bakers.

About three hundred feet down the street Wedlock increased his pace and reached the bakers within half a minute. By that time, though it was all to late. He stopped in front of the window and looked in. All he could see was an empty shop. The only person inside was the baker.

Wedlock followed the street to the corner and took a look around. Well-knowing that he'd been spotted and that Christian had tricked him and had disappeared.

Wedlock was professional enough not to let this affect him. It was just a matter of time before Christian slipped up again. And when he did Wedlock would be ready, very ready.

Wedlock went back to his car and sat himself behind the wheel. He lit a cigarette and leaned back in his seat whilst he thought things through. What had happened to Sofie had been a mistake of course. A regrettable mistake. Human error - literally. Sending a new agent out into the field like that - that was a real screw up. Just as he had feared and just as he had warned. And, even though Bob Harris had decided to stick to Wedlock from now on, even for the simple stuff, it couldn't alter the fact that Harris had made a mistake.

That irritated him. Because it hadn't been necessary. In actual fact it wasn't so much about the fact that Wedlock had been reprimanded. The issue was more that Harris had made an error of judgement and had chosen to completely ignore Wedlock. That he had more faith in Susan's ability as a field agent than he had in his own friend and colleague. *Shit!* When a new agent was starting work normal procedure was to start them gradually with simple and uncomplicated tasks. Like shadowing and stuff like that. And as they did their job better and better, the agent in question got more and more practised and the tasks got more and more difficult. These might include discrete searches at locations where there was a risk of being caught in the act, and where the ability to think on your feet and stay calm were exceedingly important.

As it was, Susan Johannesen was off active duty. In other words, she'd been shipped off to headquarters for a full debriefing on what had gone wrong, why it went wrong and how such a situation could be avoided in the future.

Taking another person's life, especially in another country, was always a last resort. Each time you killed, whether correctly or incorrectly, there were almost always complications, plenty of complications. Not least the local police force's own investigations. So if you could avoid it you did. A rule which all agents had learnt to respect and take seriously. But, of course, it could still happen. Errors, bad-luck, panic, anything. And in this case the agent had overreacted, acted in haste and had lost control of the situation. She'd grabbed hold of the girl who, in pulling herself free had fallen from the roof. *Fuck!*

A waste of time, a waste of precious resources. And all because of Harris' stupid mistake. They were going to have to talk about this. When Wedlock had time, that was.

Wedlock's phone rang.

"Yeah."

"The system should work now."

"I'm assuming it works at all locations?"

"Both of them, yes sir."

"You know what I mean."

"His cell phone and his laptop."

"Okay. Thanks."

Wedlock started the car, turned on the stereo and put the volume up.

Another *Black Eyed Peas* song. This time *'Pump It'*.

COPENHAGEN AIRPORT

After a picking up his ticket from SAS without any fuss, Christian now faced the awkwardness and unpleasantness of the security check. A security check where they'd put you straight in the slammer if you happened to say 'bomb.' Completely hysterical and utterly pointless, thought Christian. What clown dreamed up all these regulations anyway? Some civil servant who thought he knew what was what and how things worked perhaps. Just because they had spent 5 years at university - not that they learned about explosives and hijacks there. People are easily duped, he thought.

Duty-free cigarettes were some compensation, however.

Christian misread the display and it wasn't before he reached gates 34-35 that he realised he should have been at gate 24.

He sat himself at the front of the right aircraft and travelled to London/ Heathrow, where he changed flights and continued to New York in a 747.

Relief. That was the word. He was relieved. Both literally and figuratively. Relieved that he had got away, had put it all behind him. Especially after his recent meeting with Wedlock.

Christian knew two things though. Things he had become more and more sure of after he fled his home the first time.

For one thing he knew that they were after him - and that "they" weren't the Danish secret services. The other thing he was now certain of was that he would now be able to recognise the guy he had seen this morning. Both from the way he dressed and the particular way he moved.

But, for now, he was free.

Christian's hand strayed to his trouser pocket - it was still there. The little flash drive.

New Jersey, New York

When Christian reached Newark Liberty Airport he accidentally got the address of his hotel wrong. An error that the immigration official took very seriously, even though Christian tried to explain that he had just misread the address. But there was nothing to be done and the man took Christian's papers and placed them in a red file as a clear indication of how seriously he viewed the situation. Christian was then transferred to a sort of police station where he had to sit waiting beneath a tall counter for what seemed a very long time.

They really understand how to put pressure on you, thought Christian indifferently whilst a handcuffed and shackled prisoner was lead past. For a moment he began to be concerned: *Did they know who he was? No, come on. That was just the sort of thing that happened in crappy novels.*

As he had thought, it turned out to be nothing more than a formality, and after he had chatted a bit with the guy behind the counter about the exact address and why he was in the country in the first place Christian could, finally, get on with things. Which meant taking an Olympia Express bus to Port Authority on 8th Avenue.

He had deliberately only packed what was absolutely necessary and he was, therefore, able to go straight from the bus and on to the hotel Helena had mentioned. Crown Plaza Hotel on Times Square which was actually just a short distance from Port Authority.

Helena had told reception that he would be coming and he had no trouble in getting a key card to their room.

A bell boy lead him past the down escalators and on to the lift and seemed to be about to accompany him all the way up to his room.

"That's fine. I'll take things from here. Thanks."

Even though he smiled it was clear that the man had been disappointed at not receiving a tip.

Christian had not come to New York to waste his money on such pointlessness, and in any case he did not have any money to waste. Actually Christian was not quite clear about how much Helena had had to fork out for the trip. Christian thought most of it would be covered by the newspaper. That's the way it always used to be when he was on the paper anyway, and he found it hard to believe that things had changed radically since then.

So Christian felt no compunction in calling reception and ordering a large *Porterhouse* steak, a couple of chilled cans of *Coors* and a double bourbon, *Old Grand Dad*, before changing his order at the last minute to a bottle.

Next he turned on the heavy old-fashioned TV which reminded him of the one he had at home and made himself comfortable on the bed. A single bed which meant they would be sleeping very close. A thought that vaguely irritated him. He liked to have plenty of room when he slept.

Christian zapped between the myriad different channels but was soon bored. Then a news item on CNN Headline News caught his attention. There was a great deal of media interest in a story about some UFO that had just been spotted above O'Hare international airport in Chicago.

Several witnesses described a disk-shaped vessel that had hovered above one of the terminals before suddenly disappearing into a thick layer of clouds.

The witnesses, primarily represented by 'Joe,' a *United Airlines* aircraft mechanic, were all professional airport staff and were well used to flying machines. Nevertheless, even though there were plenty of them who were prepared to go on record neither the flight operator or the *Federal Aviation*

Administration - FAA - thought it worthwhile investigating the matter. More likely than not it was just a highly unusual weather phenomenon, said an FAA spokesman.

Christian thought the story somewhat bizarre. He reached across and grabbed a pack of cigarettes from the carton in his bag. Then he stood up and went over to try and open the window. A seemingly impossible task until he found the knack.

The room was equipped with enervating smoke alarms that prevented him from simply smoking in his room, he wasn't going to resort to vandalism in order to disassemble them.

He was just about to light up when someone knocked on the door. It was the the food, and not least the drinks.

Whilst he ate Christian speculated as to how he should get hold of Helena and let her know that he had arrived.

It was obvious why she wasn't at the hotel. With time on her hands in a big city like New York her credit card would be itching in her pocket. And if he knew her right she had already bought the first jacket, the first pair of trousers, the first top and the first dress. This despite the fact that it was only just gone 12 noon.

Christian decided not to send her a text and satisfied himself by drinking the last of the second Coors. It called to mind a sign he'd once seen: '*Beer - the reason I wake up every afternoon.*' Then, finally he lit his cigarette and thoroughly enjoyed every single drag.

There was nothing like a cigarette after a good meal. And he had his favourite drink to hand.

He had not yet worked out what his next move was to be. He stood for a while considering various possibilities. He couldn't just take off and go wherever he choose. And for at least the 117th time he cursed his pitiful income. Was it ever going to improve? *Fuck*. It was no use thinking about it.

Christian looked across to Broadway, but was far from impressed. It had been just the same the first time he'd visited the city many years ago. Everyone he knew raved about Manhattan but as far as Christian could see he could just as well have visited the red-light district of Copenhagen. It was chock-a-block with bums, junkies, prostitutes and other people whose purpose in life was equally obscure, all defiling around between each other like characters in an outlandish freak show. But, eventually, it had crept over him anyway. The city's pulse and rhythm. After the fourth day it was hard to explain to himself why he didn't simply up sticks and move over here. Especially the area around Greenwich Village and TriBeCa which managed to combine the best of both continents. From both cultures. American and European in the best possible way, dripping with art and liberation plus an inbuilt ability to make money and think big.

Christian sat down at the table with his laptop, but couldn't access the Internet. He called reception, only to be told that their network had just gone down. They expected, however, to be online again within the hour.

Christian didn't have much else to do so he decided to find a net-café. There must be one somewhere nearby.

Christian found it harder than he had expected but succeeded at last in finding what he wanted in another hotel.

He fished the piece of paper out of his pocket that Mikkel had given him and wrote a quick mail with the title: '*Condor Deuce needs help.*

Hi Talon. Someone recommended you as a person who might be able to help me access a password-protected file. Christian Bang.'

A mail to Talon Karrde who answered almost immediately.

'Welcome to New York. Welcome to the Sheraton Manhattan Hotel :-) I didn't think Condor Deuce needed any help.'

Christian considered his words carefully before sending his next mail:

'Condor Deuce has disappeared. The file I need to access was encrypted by him.'

A long pause where there wasn't much else for Christian to do than update his webmail. Then the message came. Brief and to the point:

'Give me your cell number, I'll give you a call when I can.'

How the guy knew where Christian was, was as incomprehensible as it was scary. The digital age. Where were they heading? And when would the Internet take control? If the human brain just consisted of a mass of synapses between which individual packages of information were exchanged, what was the difference really between the human brain and the Internet? Would the Internet one day become concious? Would the total quantity of available information break some unknown barrier at some point? A tipping point? A meme? Like the Myth of the The Hundred Monkeys from the Japanese island of Koshima? Christian shook these thoughts off him and concluded that in the real world anything could happen. Wasn't it Michel Foucault who said that events were constantly at their own limits? That events and incidents became all the time in a never-ending process? Or perhaps it was Bourdieu. He couldn't recall...

Christian was almost back at his hotel when his phone rang. It was Helena.

"Did you have a good trip?"

"Yeah. I only just got here."

"Where are you? Have you made it to the hotel?"

"Yeah, yeah. I'm just admiring the view from the room," he lied.

"Did you get any sleep... in the plane?"

"Yeah sure. I'm fine."

"Well let's meet then? In the red sofa maybe? In the bar in the lobby?"

"Fine by me," answered Christian easily as it would give him a natural opportunity to continue his alcohol consumption. He felt more and more in the groove, more and more devil may care. *Maybe it was the city after all?*

Christian had just sat down when Helena came waltzing in. But to Christian's complete surprise she was not alone. Helena was accompanied by an American woman of about her own age. A woman who, as luck would have it, was attractive. Attractive in an unusual way. Maybe it was the faint shadow of a scar on her cheek? Something that at any rate made her otherwise completely regular features more personal and appealing than just a pretty face, whatever it covered.

'*There is only one true temple and that is the human body. We touch heaven when we touch each other*', he thought. Though the quote came from a 17th Century German philosopher, Novalis (that was the philosopher's name) must have had a woman in mind like the one Christian was now about to be presented to.

Christian stood up, pleased at his sudden philosophical turn of thought and kissed Helena on the cheek whilst keeping his eye on her friend.

"Christian, this is Jodie. Jodie, Christian."

Christian and Jodie shook hands and could both sense a simultaneous, mutual and natural attraction.

"Nice to meet you."

Christian smiled welcomingly.

"And the same to you."

Christian's immediate unease at Jodie's presence was long gone and he made no subsequent attempt to hide his interest.

Helena noticed the steady gazes, but was preoccupied with introducing them to each other.

"Christian is an author and he's already written two really fine novels. He hasn't really hit the best-seller lists yet but it's only a matter of time I'm sure."

Christian was surprised at this positive account of himself. It wasn't exactly a hot topic of conversation when they talked together privately. But perhaps she just couldn't stand the thought that Jodie might find out she was spending her time hanging around with a loser. A man who had once been well on the way up the greasy journalistic career pole, but who, as a result of some pathetic lack of self awareness, had suddenly made himself believe that he'd be a much more successful author. If Christian remembered rightly that was exactly the description she'd given of him the last time she'd attempted one. Okay it was during an argument but still.

Helena continued her description as they made themselves comfortable on the sofa and Christian ordered a mineral water for Jodie and a Cola Light for Helena.

"Jodie is a journalist on the *New York Times*."

Christian smiled knowingly.

"Ahh, a colleague. Where do you know each other from?"

Even though he had asked Jodie the question it was Helena who answered.

She was quite impossible today Christian decided, giving up. It was going to be a long weekend.

"It was back in 2003 when I was in Texas covering the space shuttle accident."

Helena looked at her friend for a brief second.

"Terrible story. Terrible."

A dark shadow passed briefly across Jodie's face as she nodded silently. Helena extended a comforting arm to Jodie.

"Oh, I can be so stupid sometimes!"

Jodie smiled weakly but genuinely.

"It's okay. Don't think about it."

Jodie took a sip of her mineral water whilst Helena stroked her arm repeatedly. Something that obviously made Jodie feel awkward. At any rate she took hold of Helena's hand in a friendly fashion and removed it as she patted it.

"It's okay really. I'm fine."

Even though Christian could clearly sense something unspoken he still had no idea what it was. Apart from it obviously having something to do with space shuttles. He was going to have to ask if he wanted to know more as neither of the two women opposite seemed to be prepared to elaborate.

"Why so serious?"

Jodie's brown eyes changed their focus and she considered Christian again.

"It's my sister, she died in a traffic accident."

"Sorry. I'm sorry to hear that. But…?"

Jodie kept her gaze fixed on Christian whilst she answered quietly.

"She was also an astronaut. She had two young girls and a husband. Actually, her youngest is just six. So it's been a big blow. Not least for the kids who have to make do with just having a dad… Perhaps I'm not being fair but..."

"And this happened recently, am I right?"

"I've just come home after the funeral."

"It's amazing how a life can just... *'Death is one moment...'*"

Christian deliberately didn't finish the quote, which he had intended more as couple of comforting words than anything else. Jodie accepted the invitation to finish the sentence.

"*'...and life is so many of them.'* Tennessee Williams. Yes, it's true. But I feel for the kids."

"Do you fancy something stronger? Drink is often really good for taking the edge of thoughts like that."

"Not now, Christian." Helena sent him a killer look.

But Jodie nodded seriously.

"Is that what it takes? A night on the tiles to get it out of your system? Like when you were young and could do anything."

"Well I thought perhaps the three of us could go out for a meal together in any case."

Helena tried to get a foothold in the conversation again and the others helped her along.

"That sounds like a good idea," answered Christian, even though he was feeling pretty full after eating an excellent steak in the hotel room.

"You must know plenty of great places to eat?"

The question was directed to Jodie who nodded accommodatingly.

"Yes, '*Colors*', for example. That's a great place. It's run by the people who used to own '*Windows on the World*'. A restaurant that was on the top floor of the World Trade building. I'll call and get us a table and we can meet up there. It's between Astor Place and East 4th Street. On Lafayette."

Jodie was still in a serious mood when she got her things together and the two friends stood up and kissed each other on the cheeks. Finally Jodie gave Christian her hand.

"It was nice to meet you," said Jodie and smiled graciously.

"And you," answered Christian, whilst considering a cheeky answer. A thought he dropped as soon as it crossed his mind. It would have been too unsuitable. Even for Christian.

Then they went their separate ways and Christian and Helena went up to the hotel room where Helena turned suspiciously quiet.

"Is there something up?"

Christian had laid himself down on the bed and turned on the TV again whilst Helena walked around with measured steps and took her purchases out of their bags. A blue-white blouse which, if you asked Christian was rather dull and a couple of *Goffredo Fantini* high-heeled shoes. They were nicer.

"No, no, why do you think that?"

"The way you're walking around chucking things about, says to me that something's up."

Helena abruptly stopped what she was doing.

"I'm not chucking things around."

Christian sighed and gave up.

"Okay."

He turned back to the TV and attempted to ignore Helena's gaze.

"Are you planning to just lie there all weekend?"

Christian didn't look up at her as he answered.

"No. We're going out to eat aren't we? And I'd kind of assumed we'd be going out to play tourists at some point."

Helena answered weakly.

"I don't know."

Christian wasn't going to turn off the TV, even though he understood perfectly well that Helena wanted his full attention. But if she wasn't able to give a clear answer then he wasn't about to start playing her games. Despite this he could see the sense in trying to keep the peace as far as possible and he stretched his hand out to her.

"Come on. Come over here."

Helena remained standing in the middle of the floor. Christian stood half way up, caught her arm and pulled her down on to the bed next to him.

"What's up? What's troubling you?" He ran a hand through her hair and held on tight and lovingly to her neck.

"It just seemed like you weren't very glad to see me. And that was why I invited you along. So we could have a couple of good days together like you said. Like we used to."

"Why shouldn't I be glad to see you?"

"I don't know. I'd just expected something else. You hardly even kissed me."

Christian removed his hand from her neck and straightened up in bed. He looked serious.

"I think it's great that you've invited me to New York. I really like spending time with you, and I like kissing you every once in a while. But that doesn't make us a couple. It's not as if we haven't talked about this before." Once again Christian went for the brutal and direct approach. Knowing, as he did, that he sometime soon was going to have to tell her that he wasn't coming back with her, he couldn't really see a better way of tackling the situation.

"I know, it's just me. Come on let's leave it at that." Helena was obviously disappointed but was trying to make the best of things.

"It's important to me that we understand each other. Otherwise it's better that we just don't see each other. I don't want to go around feeling guilty about not having given you the relationship you want. That's also something we've talked about before."

Helena sighed. She now wished she hadn't brought it up.

"Yeah, I know. And it's not because I wanted you back. It was just that… it would be nice, maybe."

"What?"

"Well, you know, to play at being a couple for a weekend."

"Isn't that exactly what we're doing now?" Christian asked quietly.

"Yeah, yeah. It's just me. Well…" Helena sighed. "I think I'm going to take a shower."

Helena stood up slowly and wandered around a bit before undressing while Christian just lay there admiring the scenery.

"How was your interview anyway?"

"It was cool. Really cool. Everything was just 100% tip top. I got ten minutes with him and then I just hung out at the hotel for a couple of days. He's actually really, really nice. Very charismatic. And smart. He even knew a bit about little old Denmark. Especially furniture design and architecture."

Christian snorted.

"Yeah, I can imagine. Are you in love?"

"With Brad Pitt?! Who isn't?"

"And you got a good story out of it?"

"Yeah, yeah a great one. I've already filed it."

Helena was now quite naked and on her way out to the bathroom where Christian could hear her turning on the tap. A couple of minutes later she was humming a happy tune.

He wanted to give her time to wash herself before taking his own clothes off and surprising her in the shower.

Christian changed channels and had just got himself comfortable with a pillow to support his back when the phone rang.

"Hello?" answered Christian with a voice that was suddenly rusty. Something that often happened when he was thinking about sex.

"Hi, it's Jodie. I just wanted to tell you that I've booked a table for 20:30. Is that okay?"

Christian had to cough before answering.

"Yeah, sure. That sounds fine. Where did you say it was? Lafayette?"

"Yeah. 417 Lafayette Street. See you. Ciao."

"Bye."

Jodie's voice sounded different on the phone. More inviting. Sexier. Christian was suddenly unsure whether he should go out to Helena and decide to drop it. He wasn't in the mood.

Whilst they ate their tapas and Helena and Jodie chatted Christian had the opportunity to study Jodie more closely.

She was wearing a red dress with small glassy sequins and she'd let her thick black hair down and was wearing discrete matching make up, matching, that was if you ignored the flame-red lipstick. At the hem of her dress you could just sense the contours of a tattoo on one of her expansive breasts. When he looked up again he saw directly into Jodie's eyes and their gazes met. Christian smiled gently and raised his glass. "Cheers."

The two women raised their glasses and returned to their conversation. Christian turned his attention to Helena. She was wearing a close-sitting beige two-piece with her new high-heeled shoes, and she looked really good. And, just like Jodie, she was wearing a dash of discrete make up. Christian's gaze shifted again. He had to admit that Jodie's lips were very inviting.

After their meal was over they continued to *Bleecker Street Bar*. A pretty trivial joint with dart boards, a jukebox and round wooden tables all of which was much more Christian's style. When Christian and Jodie had had a couple of drinks they went outside for a smoke. It was a warm night, and actually quite pleasant. As the evening wore on, they spent more and more time outside and stayed there longer and longer. Finally Helena joined them. Now accompanied by one of Jodie's male colleagues - Bill - who, fortunately, was capable of drinking just as much and at just as great a speed as Christian, who was now getting pretty seriously drunk.

It had happened earlier, but more discretely. This time there was no mistaking it. Jodie's warm hand closed around Christian's, as he, for perhaps the sixth or seventh time lit her cigarette. She looked at him without speaking whilst she inhaled and blew blue smoke out into the night air.

"I never asked you... How come you're single?" asked Christian and worried that she would suddenly turn out to be a lesbian.

"Why do you assume I'm single?"

Christian shrugged his shoulders.

"If you had a boyfriend wouldn't he have been here tonight as well?"

"Well, he might be out of town," said Jodie, her eyes sparkling.

"When the cat's away the mice will play, or what?"

Helena had been standing yawning for sometime as she chatted with Jodie's colleague. Even though she'd done so discretely, and had, of course, apologised, he hadn't been able to hide the fact that, as far as Helena was concerned it was getting late and would soon be time to turn in.

Helena went over to Christian and threaded her arm through his, and laid her head on his shoulder demonstratively.

"I'm getting tired. Is it okay if we go back to the hotel?"

Christian stood and tried to think what to do next. He was more drunk than he'd been for a long time. The looks that he and Jodie had been exchanging throughout the evening and the way she now, completely openly, had touched him, meant that Christian had no desire whatsoever to head back to the hotel. He formulated a witty remark. One that would be both unusually flippant and totally direct. So that there was no way of misunderstanding his desire for immediate satisfaction. But Christian never got the words out. Jodie got there first:

"Well, it's been a pleasant evening. I hope we can do it again some other time... Bill?"

Jodie's colleague, a tall guy with a bum chin, smiled behind a canopy of smoke revealing perfect teeth.

"Shall we share a taxi?"

"Yeah, it's getting late," answered Bill with a smile.

Christian sent Jodie a flattering look. A look that was answered by a relaxed and natural smile. Then he nodded curtly in disappointment as he understood that this was unfortunately neither the time nor the place. He changed focus, and squinted at Helena.

"Okay. Shall we go?"

They said their goodbyes and exchanged cheek kisses, whilst Helena continued to insist that Jodie should take a trip to Denmark sometime soon.

Christian hailed a taxi and held the door open for Helena. Then they were on their way back.

Out of Bowery and on across 3rd which took them pretty much straight to their hotel.

They were silent for most of the journey, with just a couple of remarks about what a nice evening it had been. Then he felt Helena's warm hand on the inside of his thigh.

"Where did you go?" she asked quietly.

Christian had been about to tell her that his night wasn't over and that he needed a few more drinks. Especially now Jodie seemed to have changed her mind. Helena's touch was more a disturbance, as far as he was concerned, than anything else.

"What do you mean?"

"Today. In the shower. Why didn't you come out and visit me?"

Her hand continued further and further up his leg towards his crotch and finally he had to take hold of it and hold it.

"Look, I think I'm going to head back."

"What? Back to what?" Helena was genuinely surprised and didn't seem to have any idea what Christian was talking about.

"Back to the bar. I really need to get drunk."

Helena took her hand to herself.

"You don't think you're drunk enough? You should see yourself."

"Don't you ever have that feeling? That you just want to drink yourself into oblivion."

"You're not trying to tell me you're going to head off into town on your own. You know you really can be an asshole sometimes Christian. Don't you have any honour or duty or respect for others? Is it all just you, you, you? And everyone else can just fuck off if they don't fit into your plans?"

Christian didn't answer but if he was perfectly honest he could see there was something in what she said.

His head was spinning. Perhaps it was a bad idea after all?

"Why did you come here? You don't seem to want to fuck me, or even to spend time with me? What have I done to you Christian? Why do you absolutely insist on punishing me like this?"

"Easy girl. It's nothing like that," was Christian's best attempt at an answer.

"What is it then?"

As always when she was angry, Helena didn't raise her voice. It just changed tone, became hard and cold.

"Okay. You're right. Lets just take a bottle to bed instead."

Christian had changed his mind. It hadn't been easy, in fact any form of thought was becoming difficult.

Maybe it was the heat in the car, it's air conditioning seemed very temperamental.

Helena didn't answer. Instead she just stared out of the window.

Back at the hotel, Christian took a couple of deep swigs from the bottle of bourbon, whilst Helena got ready for bed. Without talking. Without even looking at him.

She went out to the bathroom and when she came back ten minutes later Christian had passed out on the bed. Fully clothed and stinking of alcohol and smoke.

Helena lay down in the bed and pushed him aside, so there was room for her.

Then she lay down with her back to him and cried quietly to herself. Cried at her own disappointment at having invited Christian to New York.

She was upset that the naive hope she had had, that they might be able to reawaken their former intimacy and all the pleasure they used to have in each other's company. It upset her that he was still, still so bloody immature that he could get completely and utterly hopelessly drunk only to pass out in a hotel room.

Helena dried away the tears for the last time and found that she could now take measured and deeper breaths. She'd made up her mind. Even though, it had actually really been Christian that had made it up for her. No, now it was definitely over. And unlike the other times when she'd felt the same only to end up doing the complete opposite she could feel that this time she really meant it. Her love for Christian was gone.

Helena closed her eyes and her final thought as she fell asleep was the pleasure she'd taken in taking the full credit for the journalism award that they had, if truth be told, really deserved to share.

Christian had to find a place to stay. Soon, somewhere cheap. That was his first thought when he opened his eyes to yet another day. A hot and sunny day, so it would seem, though his headache was almost unbearable and his eyes shut on reflex to keep out the worst of the light.

The last time he'd been in Manhattan, he stayed at a youth hostel on Upper West Side. It was probably still there he thought as he sat up.

Then he noticed that the room was completely quiet - Helena wasn't there. Christian stood up and fumbled around with the phone in his jacket pocket. He dialled her number and got through to her.

"Hi, it's me. Where are you?"

"In the airport."

"Okay?!" Christian was surprised, despite himself.

"Don't worry. I paid the bill. Including your food and your whiskey."

"Wasn't it... Wasn't the plan that we were going to play tourists?"

"I'm going home," said Helena quietly.

"Would it help if I apologised?"

"Yes. But I'm going home anyway. And, by the way..." Helena hesitated.

"What?" asked Christian his curiosity roused. He knew her well enough to know that something was up.

"You were right all along. We should really have shared it."

"Shared it?" asked Christian, though actually he knew perfectly well what she was talking about.

"Yeah, the award. The Calving Award. I guess I'm lucky that you're too proud to complain, but do you know what?"

"No."

"It actually suits me now. Suits me fine. Have a nice life. Goodbye."

"...Helena?"

It was too late. The call was over.

On the one hand he was fortunate that he had been saved the discomfort of having to tell her that he was actually going to stick around in New York. On the other hand he felt a certain sadness mixed with a degree of irritation and disappointment that he had been outdone. *Fuck the fucking Calving Award!*

Christian took a very long shower, stole the hotel soap and the little extra bottle of shampoo and went out looking for somewhere cheap to eat his breakfast.

Wedlock woke at the first beep and lifted his cell phone to his ear. "Yeah?"

"Activity registered in New York. Manhattan. Crown Plaza Hotel. Local unit activated."

"Okay, thanks. Ask them to just keep him under surveillance until I get there."

"I'm sorry, but we can not do that, sir."

"And why is that?"

"You don't have the authority."

"Well just ask them to remain passive, okay?"

"I'm sorry, but that sort of order has to be authorised at a higher level, sir."

Wedlock put the phone down with an oath. He dialled a new number.

"Hello?" answered a sleepy Bob Harris in the other end.

"It's Joe Blow..."

"Wedlock?! We're still in the same country aren't we? I mean the same time zone. Just in case it'd escaped your attention I can tell you that the time is now... twenty-two minutes past four. In the morning!"

"We've got a report of activity in New York."

"Fine. That's good. I assume they've already put a local team on to it then?"

"Exactly. And that's just where the problem lies."

"I don't follow. What problem?"

"They're not prepared to wait for my arrival."

"Well, why should they?"

Wedlock sighed.

"I just want to complete this assignment. Anyway, they know even less about what's going on than we do."

"Which is standard. We all work to the same code. On a need-to-know-basis. You know that."

"Look, just pull the strings okay? It's important to me to follow up on this one and finish it personally. There've already been too many slip-ups, way too many mistakes. I just want to make sure that there are no more fuck ups."

"Hey, you just crossed the line there, pal. That was unnecessary."

"Come on Bob. For old times sake."

There was a long pause. No-one said anything.

"What do you want me to do?"

"Just ask them to wait till I get there."

"And that's all? I still think we should just take him out as soon as we can."

"We need to let him think he's got away and that he's safe. That'll make it easier for us to find out where he's headed. He'll get careless and drop his guard. Then we'll be able to go in and take whatever it is he may be carrying around with him with no fuss, discreetly. That's what we do."

Another pause, where all Wedlock could hear was Bob Harris' tired and laboured breathing.

"I'll have it fixed by tomorrow morning."

"Thanks Bob. I'll get going straight away."

He dialled another number.

"Transport to New York. ASAP."

"Check. Route via Thule Airbase - departing from Copenhagen in two hours."

"Thanks."

198

Wedlock stood up, feeling pleased with himself. Now he would get a chance to go home. Finally. Back to his own country where he knew the ropes and away from this backwater miniature USA where they all spent their time adding more and more crappy English to their phony little language. In what other country were the two most common words of English 'computer' and 'fuck'? Or what about 'corn flakes,' 'hot dog,' 'shit,' 'dating' and 'single', 'Mickey Mouse' or 'okay'? And there were more. Where everyone seemed to spend their entire time sitting down. On chairs, railings, garden furniture - anything! And if they weren't sitting around they were lying around. In parks, on benches, at the beach. The only thing Wedlock was going to miss was all the tall hot blondes with the smoking blue eyes.

He shrugged his shoulders. Or would he? When he thought about it there were plenty like that state-side. Now he'd be able to go see that woman who still thought he worked in the agricultural sector.

Christian took the subway - a number nine heading uptown. Up to 103rd. The hostel was just across the street from there, on Amsterdam Avenue.

He went in and got himself a bed in a five man room and they gave him some bedding. All for around thirty dollars.

Back in reception Christian left his luggage in a locker he'd rented for that same purpose and went out looking for a shop that sold phone cards.

He got himself an AT&T prepaid SIM card and a copy of the New York Times which he carried under his arm.

Once he was back on the street he replaced his Danish SIM card with the new one. He wouldn't be needing the old one for a while.

Christian looked across the street and a man in black caught his eye. Not that there was anything particularly peculiar about wearing black, it was more the shoulder bag the man was carrying. A brown check imitation leather effort that just seemed too feminine for a tall muscular man in dark sunglasses. But on the other hand, New York was such a wacko hangout that someone with poor taste in clothes was probably not so exceptional anyway.

Christian reached the subway stairs and jumped aboard a number one heading toward *South Ferry*. Then he spotted the man again. The man with the check bag.

Christian smiled to himself, but could sense a growing unease. His innards were starting to churn in a most unpleasant way.

His thoughts turned to other things, however, when a woman with long blonde hair, who seemed only to be wearing a thin cotton black two-piece of some sort with a white shirt came and stood to his left.

The train was full and her buttock was just next to his hand. Each time the train stopped and started she leaned against him more and more.

Christian left his hand where it was and couldn't stop himself from playing along, slowly and gently, and no more than that it could still be taken for chance movements.

At 59th Street, she looked back over her shoulder and smiled warmly.

"Have a nice one," she said and before he had looked about him she had got off and disappeared into the crowd.

Christian stayed on the train as far as Rector Street, where he got off and wandered on. He needed to get some exercise and get the blood away from his groin. He needed to think clearly again. There was nothing like a woman to distract you. The women he didn't seem to be able to live with or without.

Christian wandered downhill and passed a small park with a fountain in the middle, *The Bowling Green*. He decided to find a bench where he could sit and have a smoke. Despite it's size the area had a long and extensive history, but now it was just a public park. According to a stone tablet it was the town's first park, and dated from March 12th 1733.

Christian looked about himself and wondered when the so-called Talon Karrde would contact him. Then a thought struck him. He'd sent the guy his Danish number. Shit, thought Christian. He'd have to mail him the new one. Which meant he'd have to find a net café some place. But not before he had finished his cigarette though.

Christian stretched out and continued smoking whilst performing his exercises. Exercises with which he was so familiar that they more or less took care of themselves. Exercises whereby he considered people and buildings and retained an impression of them for use later in descriptions in his books.

A couple of benches to his left a black man was sitting and sleeping. Unless you looked closely you'd just have thought he was leaning forward slightly over his paper. A paper he'd spread out on his lap. But he never turned the pages and when Christian looked more closely it became obvious that the guy was in fact just having a nap.

A couple of bums slightly further down the row of benches were busy with something, and to his right three well-dressed business women were sitting and sharing a joint.

A man walked over to the bench nearest Christian's and started to read a paper. A man that Christian didn't really notice initially as he was busy studying a large white building on the other side of the park. A building which called itself *National Museum of the American Indian*. On the huge entrance pedestals Christian managed to see two of the four large sculptures - seated female figures. Figures with two kneeling and standing children by their sides. Not quite identical, although they were very much alike.

The sleeping man with the newspaper woke up and stood up to be replaced by a woman who was smoking a cigarette. Just sitting looking at the fountain.

Every now and then a couple of drops from the fountain reached Christian but it didn't bother him, busy as he was studying the woman more closely. She was drinking coffee, was wearing short brown boots a black dress and dark grey jumper. On her lap was a greenish corduroy jacket. She didn't appear to be married, at any rate she wasn't wearing a ring. Her hair was shoulder length and the colour of local government. She'd brushed it back in the middle. Her lips were a natural red and she smiled sleepily and blinked in the sunshine.

Christian couldn't see the colour of her eyes, but they were probably dark. They had a sparkle at any rate - perhaps it was just the sun.

The woman stubbed out her first cigarette and then lit another one. And as she did so Christian spotted the man with the check bag once more, he'd come to sit next to her. This was the third time Christian had seen him, and that made it at least two times too many.

Christian stood up a little too abruptly and remembered Sofie's paranoid imaginings. The one's she had just before she was found dead at the base of a building. How likely were you to run into the same guy three times in a row? And under these circumstances? Small. In fact so small as for it to be inconceivable.

Christian took a deep breath and decided to try and achieve some clarity instead of this pointless paranoia. He headed up Broadway, and turned left into Morris Street and then on to Greenwich Street whilst looking repeatedly over his shoulder. Not too obviously but enough to see if there was anyone following him. Nothing. *Ha!* Christian breathed more easily and laughed relieved. It was all a bit too far-fetched he thought as he approached the corner of Liberty Street where he turned round one last time. And then he stiffened.

About 150 feet behind him he spotted the man again. There could no longer be any doubt about it. He was being followed.

Christian forced himself to keep calm and he kept on walking without altering his gentle pace. Until, that was, he reached the corner where he speeded up as soon as he was out of sight.

Even though he was completely out of shape he managed to run the entire stretch, right down the street and ended up in a small stretch of park down by the waterfront. From here he took a sharp right which brought him out into an open area near the marina. The *North Cove Marina* behind WFC - World Financial Center.

Only now did Christian pause to assess the situation:

There were lots of people milling about. Business people and tourists. Christian focused on them one by one:

A young oriental couple posing for each other and filming with a video camera. Newly weds, or so it seemed, and very happy.

Down by one of the ferries a black man was playing the music from *Saturday Night Fever* from his ghetto blaster whilst mumbling inanities to himself.

A ferry!

Christian had no idea what the black guy was rambling on about. He only had eyes for one thing. The *Liberty Park Water Taxi* in front of him from which a constant stream of men in suits and women in skirts, many of them wearing sneakers were filing in and out.

He pushed his way in amongst the crowd and paid his five dollar fee at the last possible opportunity. He was lucky, the water taxi set off straight afterwards.

Christian looked around nervously to try and spot the guy who'd been following him and eventually caught sight of him standing with a crestfallen expression on the quay. His expression made Christian want to jeer and wave.

But he quickly became serious again. Some organisation was following him. That meant that they must know where he lived. He'd have to get back to the room as quickly as possible and find an alternative. But he couldn't just head off. He didn't know what direction to travel in. *Damn phone number!* He was going to have to find some way of getting on the Internet.

The water taxi docked and Christian was the first to come ashore.

He didn't really know where he was, beyond the fact that it was somewhere in New Jersey. He walked upstream and arrived at a main road: Audrey Zapp Drive, where he flagged a taxi. He asked the driver to take him to the nearest Internet Café and he was dropped off at Bergen Avenue.

After sending his e-mail, Christian headed back out and found his way to Journal Square after asking a passer-by for directions. From here he made his way to the station and caught a train back to Manhattan. Then he changed to another line and headed on to Amsterdam Avenue. When he got there he could see straight away that the locker with his bag in it had been broken open.

Christian heaved his bag out and discovered to his horror that his laptop was gone. There couldn't be any question who was responsible and there seemed to be no point in reporting the theft. At least they hadn't got what they really wanted. The flash drive which was still in Christian's trouser pocket. But the computer - and the manuscript for his next novel - was gone. Almost certainly forever. And he couldn't remember when he'd last run a backup. It must have been well before all this kicked off though. Well, at least he hadn't written all that much. On the other hand, this meant that they now had access to all the other stuff on his computer. Documents, sketches, diaries, commentaries, draft articles, e-mails, e-mail addresses, web profiles, dating profiles and, what was worse, his bank data and tax returns. His entire fucking life was in that data. Data which they'd be able to exploit with the greatest of ease. *Fuck, fuck, fuck!* Christian kicked the locker's door in frustration whilst cursing like a madman to himself. Now he was really hyped up. Hyped up and even more determined. Determined to reach his goal. Whatever it was that was on that flash drive it must be of such importance that all the bastards who'd been out to get him would lose their jobs and be publicly hung up by the balls for all the world to see. That, at any rate was what Christian would enjoy most of all.

Christian took what remained of his luggage, not that he'd had much with him in the first place, and headed back outside. He made his way to an ATM but it declined his credit card.

Christian didn't move. Then he started to laugh. It was all he could do - all that was left to him. Laugh at the whole ridiculous state of things.

He took the flash drive out of his pocket and held it up to the light.

"You'd better be worth something. Or I'm fucked - I mean really fucked."

A passer-by stared at him as he thrust the flash drive back into his pocket. Christian hardly noticed as he searched his other pockets for money. Money he now gathered in his fist.

He had exactly 165 dollars. One hundred and sixty-five dollars. Then he reached for his inner pocket. Yes, the ticket back to Copenhagen was still there. He could get home if he wanted to. And perhaps that would be the best option. Give up and go home. But home to what? Then a thought struck him. He hauled the copy of the New York Times from his back pocket. He was just about to dial a number when his cell phone beeped indicating that he'd received a text.

"Mail me, when you reach Los Angeles. T.K." The number was ex-directory, so there was no way he could answer.

Los Angeles?! How the fuck was he going to get to Los Angeles?

Christian made his phone call. Got through to reception and then to the person he wanted to speak to.

"Green."

Silence.

"Hello?! Jodie Green."

"Cat or mouse?"

"I'm sorry? Who's this?"

"It's Christian. Christian Bang."

"Christian?! Nice to hear your voice. Are you with Helena?"

"No she's headed back."

"Okay? Why?"

"It's a long story. Look, how would you like to meet up?"

"Aarh. I'm pretty busy at the moment..."

"I wasn't really thinking right now. How about later."

"Are you suggesting a date?"

"Yeah, a date."

Jodie hesitated.

"What about Helena?"

"What about Helena? She's gone home. She's not my girlfriend anyway. And we're adults after all, aren't we?"

"I just feel kinda awkward going behind her back."

"Okay, what if I asked you to help me with something. Not a date, something more business-like?"

"Sure, that'd help a lot," Jodie laughed.

"Well, lets say that then. When would it suit you?"

"Do you have a cell phone? A number where I can get hold of you? It's just, I don't know when I'll get off."

Christian gave her his number and hung up. Then he realised that he hadn't had anything to eat since morning.

Christian found a little Mexican joint. '*Senor Swanky's Mexican Café and Speakeasy*' on Columbus Avenue, west of Central Park where he could sit outside.

He ordered a *Giant Mission Style Burritos California* with beef, rice and beans, cheese, guacamole and sour cream and a large beer. He enjoyed the food whilst watching the traffic and listening to the other guests.

A young couple arrived on roller skates and sat slightly apart from everyone else. Almost immediately the girl began having a go at her boyfriend because he had a bit of a habit of drinking too much every now and then. Just like home, thought Christian with a smile.

To the far left there were two other couples and to the right of him sat two stout women, but they were too far away for Christian to be able to hear what they were talking about.

Closest to Christian, who'd chosen a strategic position up against the wall in the right-hand corner of the restaurant there was another couple. A man with an oriental appearance and a woman who looked almost Italian. Their conversation was even less interesting than the argument, and Christian shut it all out and went back to his food with his thoughts elsewhere. The thought that, if he ever got out of this he was going to write a book about it.

When he'd finished his meal Christian was uncertain of what to do next. He decide to look for a place to sleep. After that his money would be gone.

His cell phone rang.

"Mouse."

"Cat." This was getting fun, thought Christian.

"Buddha Bar, eight thirty. I've booked a table. I hope you like sushi. Do you like sushi?"

"You can't be a cat and not like fish."

Jodie laughed. "Okay. It's on 12ᵗʰ Street. West 25. See you later."

Christian looked at his cell phone. There were several hours to go yet. Plenty of time to find another place to stay. He asked a random passer-by who advised him to try *The Big Apple Hostel* on 45ᵗʰ Street, which was just round the corner from Times Square.

On his way there Christian chose to take a number of detours and looked back over his shoulder repeatedly. After his extremely unpleasant morning he was beginning to feel that it was time to be extremely cautious about what he did and how he did it. Especially if he wanted to get out alive.

When he arrived a thought struck him: If they knew that he'd been staying at Amsterdam Avenue, they'd soon find out that he moved on to 45ᵗʰ Street. It was just too risky.

So he spent the rest of the afternoon as an unwitting tourist, mostly just wandering about, though he did wander through *Central Park* as well as taking a trip up the *Empire State Building*.

Christian had now realised that he was in a very, very precarious position. Without a realistic chance of finding a place to stay the night and without any money. He was going to go all in. All or nothing on Jodie, where nothing meant taking the first flight back home to Denmark.

Christian had never been to a *Buddha Bar*, and even though he knew that the chain had spread to a number of western cities and must therefore be fairly successful, he found himself surprisingly impressed by the state-of-the-art décor.

From the outside it had looked much more unprepossessing. However, as soon as you walked through the big double doors, you encountered a number of life-size figures standing in niches along a curving golden entrance which opened onto the restaurant proper; a restaurant that consisted of several rooms. With oriental masks on the walls, a gigantic bamboo garden, a throned Buddha sitting at the back behind the dining tables, and bars in each of the two adjoining rooms, it was definitely out of the ordinary. A place where they really took interior design seriously - and it worked and made a nice accompaniment to the pleasant lounge music in the background.

Christian and Jodie had actually managed to arrive at the same time and almost walked into each other on the pavement. Now they'd been shown to a table in the middle of the restaurant nearest the large Buddha. They were both seated with their *Kirin Ichiban* beers in front of them and a warm jug of *sake* between them as they waited for their food.

Jodie looked even better than he remembered and Christian made no attempt to hide his interest. He could still come across as relaxed and at ease, despite a nagging and rising desperation.

"You've some business to attend to here I assume. I mean, as you came along with Helena."

Christian coughed.

"You could say that yes."

"You sound secretive."

Christian knew that he was going to have to tell her everything. It might not be a good idea to put all his cards on the table at once, but he'd have to show her enough of them for her to help him. He decided to start with something more personal, and therefore, for him, less important. He chose to start by listening rather than speaking and chose a subject about which she had shown some weakness.

"Were you close, you and your sister?"

Jodie sighed and took a deep breath.

"We were more than close. We were good friends."

"And she was your only sister?"

Jodie nodded without saying anything and it was obvious that it was difficult for her to get going. Difficult to say any more. He was going to have to help her in some way.

"It must be difficult. Losing someone you care about."

"I'd rather not talk about it if that's okay," answered Jodie.

"I'm sorry. Of course... Now, how is it you're supposed to do this? Oh yes, you pour me a glass and I return the favour. The Japanese way. Kanpai."

Christian smiled his most charming smile and lifted his little cup of steaming sake.

"Did you say kanpai? I thought it was Kampai."

"Lots of people just have difficulty in pronouncing the 'n' because it comes before a hard consonant."

"You sound very convincing. Are you sure?"

"Waiter? Waiter?!"

Jodie laughed and tried to catch hold of Christian's hand before the waiter spotted him. Without success.

The waiter, who was oriental in appearance approached their table and bowed politely.

"Yes?"

"Are you from Japan?"

"No sir. Only from Korea, sir. North Korea. Unfortunately."

"Okay. How do you say 'cheers' in Korean?"

"Cheers?"

"Yeah, you know. When you're drinking. Cheers!"

Christian lifted the sake cup in his hand by way of demonstration.

"Aahh," said the waiter and smiled: "Kong gang ul wi ha yo!"

Christian and Jodie both looked rather surprised.

"Okay?! Can you run that past me one more time. Kong gang... you what?"

"Kong gang ul wi ha yo," repeated the waiter. This time more slowly.

"Kong gang ul wi ha yo," repeated Christian. "Okay, thanks. That was a lot to have to say just for a drink."

The waiter bowed politely and disappeared again.

Jodie took a long look at Christian. Smiling at first. Then her expression changed gradually until she was almost frowning.

"We used to borrow each others clothes. Like... sisters do, you know. Or... Well actually it was mostly me stealing the stuff Holly didn't want anymore. We were very close. Much closer than siblings normally are I think. We went on holiday together. As adults. Before Eric. Her husband. Before she had children. We used to go up to our parent's summer house. At Sandy Neck near Barnstable, Cape Cod. The only place we could just be ourselves and share our little secrets. About boyfriends, you know and just generally. I had a boyfriend back then who was a bit wild and not really the easiest of guys to get along with. But when I was with Holly, I could be confidential in a way that I couldn't be with others. It was also her who protected me when I was a child. She's four years older than me and she's always been there for me for as long as I can remember. The perfect big sister... ...And now she's gone... Just like that... I really miss her. What about you?"

Christian nodded imperceptibly.

"Yeah... I have an older brother. But we don't see much of each other. In fact hardly ever. The last time must have been when our parents... I don't know what you call it in English ...When they'd been married for fifty years."

"Golden wedding."

"Almost the same as in Danish then."

Jodie poured some sake into his glass.

"Do you really need my help?"

Jodie's question took him aback a bit and he hesitated before answering.

"Yes. yes, actually I do." Christian tried to find the right form of words, the right formulation before continuing:

"I need to get to Los Angeles."

Jodie frowned and looked disappointed.

"Money. You just wanna borrow money."

"Yes, but, but it's about more than that. I don't know how to say this, but... It's about... hmm... It's that I've come into possession of some material that seems to be so compromising that people are prepared to kill to get hold of it."

Jodie swallowed slowly before answering. Still with a disappointed look in her face:

"That sounds kinda dramatic. Why don't you just go to the police then?"

"It's a bit more complicated than that. I need to get in contact with a particular individual, before I can tell you any more. A person who, unfortunately, lives in Los Angeles. The problem is that I don't have any money. Someone has made it their business to block my credit card. Probably someone from the same group that have stolen my laptop and are tailing me everywhere I go."

Jodie studied him more closely and tried to judge the sincerity of Christian's words by looking him deep in the eye. Given the thoughts she'd been wandering around with recently what Christian was telling her didn't seem as fantastic as you might have imagined.

"Does that mean to say that you still don't know what this material consists of?"

"Exactly. I've just come into possession of it. I was given it by a woman. A woman who has just been... Who has just been murdered."

"Murdered?"

"I know it sounds like a crappy movie, but... but it's actually true. She was pushed to her death."

"And you don't know who killed her?"

"No. It could be anybody. But, whoever it is they're very efficient. They've managed to track me to where I am now. To the States. And it was here they stole my laptop and blocked my credit card. It suggests to me that they're not just highly professional, they're a bit better connected than just plain criminals... I'm afraid that they're probably connected to some government agency. They can carry out operations in different countries. I mean who else could it be if not the CIA?"

"And there's no chance that the material you've got hold of is actually none of your business? And that what you're actually engaged in is spying; damaging not only your own country's interests but also those of the United States?"

"It's possible. And of course I wouldn't use it if that's really all it is. But I just have to know. So many strange - and highly illegal - things have already happened that I'd be very surprised if all it turned out to be was a floor plan of the Pentagon or some such. There's gotta be more to it than that. And I have to find out. Especially when it concerns the death of someone I know."

Jodie sat for a while and considered what Christian had told her. Then she looked at him. Determined.

"Okay, I'll lend you the money. How much do you need?"

"Unfortunately, I can't just take a plane. I'm going to need a train ticket or a car. And I can't just pull up at a hotel to spend the night either. Anywhere where I've got to supply my name, use my passport, anything like that. I'm not safe."

Jodie nodded resolutely.

"We'll sort something out. That last question... did that mean you want to spend the night?"

Christian smiled.

"Fuck. Look I know it sounds crazy. But I just can't give it up now. Do you have a couch I could sleep on?"

Jodie answered his smile and lifted her glass.

"I've every respect for a man who doesn't give up. I trust you. And yes, I have a couch. Kong gang ul wi ha yo!"

Christian shook his head resignedly. Things were starting to get really weird. In fact now it was almost too much. Whereas he, a few minutes ago, had been scared - if not terrified, he now felt an almost dangerous sense of irresponsibility. It was all so crazy anyway, he just couldn't take things seriously anymore. Not right now anyway. Feelings which he sensed that in some way or other, Jodie shared. Why, he wasn't sure.

Christian lifted his own glass and in appreciation of the beautiful woman opposite him.

Even though the civilian airport in Tune, just a few miles outside Copenhagen, only handled a few scheduled services a day it was still popular with special operations and so-called VIP-flights. Flights like this one. And when it came to VIP transports there was no better choice than a *Challenger CL-604* aircraft from the Canadian aircraft manufacturer Bombardier. With a cruising speed of 529 mph, a length of just over sixty-eight feet and a wingspan of almost sixty-five feet, this type of plane was well suited to the upper atmosphere and heights of around thirty-nine thousand feet. As now, where the plane was heading due north east towards Thule airbase in Greenland.

Wedlock sat in the front separated from the plane's three other passengers. Three men from the embassy who he had never met and didn't talk to. Apart from the four passengers the only other people on the aircraft were the captain, a co-pilot and a technical crew member who also performed the duties of a cabin attendant.

When they had covered about half of the almost 2388 miles they had be travelling, one of the passengers stood up, made his way over to Wedlock and sat down. A big man of around fifty. Very well looked after and with a gigantic chest which clearly indicated that he'd have no trouble with a 330 pound bench press.

Wedlock looked up in a friendly way as the big man sat down.

"Hi?"

"Edward. Edward Armstrong. But just call me Armstrong."

"Sure. Nice to meet you… Armstrong," answered Wedlock, as he studied the man's muscular biceps.

"The nature of the task has altered. You've been granted additional powers so that you can act more effectively."

"Huh?"

"The target has disappeared."

Wedlock sat up straight in his seat.

"Say that again."

"You heard what I said the first time."

Wedlock shook his head and sighed deeply.

"Okay am I supposed to issue a wanted notice? Like the fucking stupid Danes?"

"You know best. I just expect one thing from you."

"And that is?"

"That you get the job done."

He handed Wedlock a thin folder stamped '*Above Black*' and bearing the operation's title '*Operation: Nibiru 2012*'. Then the man got up without making any further comment and returned to his seat where he made himself comfortable and closed his eyes.

He hadn't smiled once or given any sort of welcoming or friendly indication at all. He was expressionless. But there was no mistaking his words. Brief and to the point and without any doubt. Calmly articulated and well thought out.

Wedlock looked back at Ed Armstrong, whilst he wondered where they got hold of people like him. At the same time he was very pleased. Pleased that now, finally, he was moving up the ladder. He now ranked as Bob Harris' equal. The fact that he'd been Bob's subordinate had irritated him from the very beginning where it had always been Bob who'd been in the know and who'd delegated the assignments, despite the fact that there could be absolutely no doubt that Wedlock was both smarter and faster, as Wedlock concluded to himself.

He had already proved that on a number of occasions. And now someone had finally taken notice. From now on, everything would be different. Very different. Things would be done better and with more precision. Both the planning and the execution.

Wedlock was already looking forward to it, and smiled to himself and to the folder he had just received.

The dawn was slowly breaking outside Jodie's apartment on 72nd street. Christian was almost asleep and only barely sensed that Jodie had snuggled right up to him. Only when she sniffed did he react. Jodie was crying.

"Why are you crying? Was it really that bad?"

"I'm crying because I'm lying here feeling so good, and my sister has just died."

Christian turned on to his side and rested his weight on his elbow. Then he stroked her hair delicately, whilst she enjoyed the smell of tobacco from his long slim fingers. It reminded her of her youth. The time when she had dreamed of marrying and having children. From the time when her boyfriend had been studying psychology at New York University whilst she studied journalism, and where children were just around the corner. Where his, and later their, experiments with ayahuasca - a sort of herbal LSD - sent them both into some of the deepest corners of the mind. Where she'd spent a lot of time with some of the most radical students and had ended up running away from everything. On a motorbike right across their great nation. They ended up on the west coast more dead than alive, like a couple of delayed pranksters from the ecstatic days of Ken Kesey and his revolutionary debut novel 'One Flew Over the Cuckoo's Nest'. Where they just flipped more and more out with only the thinnest of instincts for self-preservation. And from where Holly - and god knows how she did it - had finally dragged her back home. Home to start afresh. Home to the abortion of the dead twins in Jodie's now infertile womb.

They lay there silently for a while. The feeling of loneliness was stronger now than ever and Jodie had to really get a grip on herself so as not to start crying again. And who was this man lying next to her? A stranger she hardly knew. A slim, dark-haired and unusually charming Dane with a talent for women. She could see that. She'd spotted that straight away. That sort of indefinable masculinity that radiated from him which Jodie knew instinctively that most women would fall for. Not that Christian was attractive really, if you considered things objectively. His crooked teeth and unhealthy complexion were far too prominent for that. But he wasn't ugly either. Far from it. His features were regular and even though he would have looked better with a bit more muscle he was naturally well and harmoniously built.

"You quoted Tennessee Williams earlier. How about '*Mendacity is a system that we live in. Liquor is one way out an' death's the other.*' Are you familiar with that?" asked Jodie.

"Now you're talking about death again. Was it a beautiful funeral?" asked Christian seriously.

The fact that Christian was still a relative stranger seemed to make it easier for Jodie to open up more than she might otherwise have done. The fact that she could sense that she didn't have to justify her feelings, was, in any event, a great help. It meant that she was now about to say things that she had sworn she would never tell anybody. But she'd had to rethink that. There was just too much going on in her head for her to be able to simply return to her everyday life without at least talking it through with someone. And that someone could just as well be Christian. She still had her friends of course. But it was hard being single when almost everyone she knew had settled down to raise a family long ago. When almost everyone else had no real need of company beyond their immediate family. When confidential conversations were almost always just about work and gossip. About who was what and why. This had meant that she started keeping herself to herself some time ago. She worked as hard as she could stomach working, and, of course, that made her a well-liked reporter. But, just like everything else in life, it had had its price: loneliness.

"It's a very strange thing to take part in a funeral when you know that the coffin is empty. To have to grieve and to be upset, and of course everyone was really devastated, but it feels strange anyway when the person you've lost isn't there. In fact there wasn't much left of her at all. Just like with the *Challenger* space shuttle in '86 I expect."

"It must have been some car accident. How can that happen I mean that there was nothing left of her?"

"The explosion was so powerful that everything was blown to bits. And the... bits that were left were carried off by the current and ended up as... ...fish food. Either for the sharks or for the crabs."

Jodie laughed in an unusually harsh way. Even though there were pauses between her words and even though Christian sensed that she was fighting to get them out.

"The car ended up in some water somehow?"

"The car evidently had some sort of electronic fault that resulted in my sister losing control. The car ended in the river and then the fuel tank exploded."

"That sounds pretty dramatic. Were there any witnesses?"

"Sure, plenty. And there's nothing to indicate that what happened was anything other than a fatal accident. Even the manufacturer's apologised and admitted they were at fault. So now we're waiting on a compensation claim. But the money won't bring my sister back."

Christian considered her words and answered quietly.

"I'm fortunate I guess. I've never lost a family member."

Jodie lay for a while composing herself so that she could continue and share what was really troubling her most of all. What she'd been keeping back and had tried to push away for so long.

"Did you know that Holly was the second person to die from that expedition?"

Jodie didn't expect an answer, but continued talking as Christian shook his head.

"First the Russian astronaut Alexander Leshenko died. And then Holly."

Christian shook his head again. This time because he was worried that he was about to have to listen to yet another conspiracy theory.

"It might sound peculiar but it's not impossible is it? Did he die in a car accident as well?"

"No he died of a chest infection. During a holiday in Odessa."

Christian got up from the bed looking for a cigarette.

"Well, there you are then."

He lit the cigarette and looked around for an ashtray without success.

Jodie got up from the bed and went out into the kitchen to fetch a bowl. Then she padded back. Naked. The sight aroused Christian again.

"I don't want you to think that I see conspiracies everywhere I look. But it's a bit like what you've been through. There are things which just don't add up," said Jodie, as she gave him the little plate.

"I don't see any conspiracies right now. All I see is a beautiful woman."

He reached out to grab her hand but she managed to avoid him and continued in the same serious vein.

"Well, the conversation I had with Holly the day she died, makes me see things in a different way. I mean not like I'd normally do."

"You make it sound as if there *is* actually some conspiracy at work."

Christian sat down by the window and took a puff on his cigarette as he watched while the light grew brighter and brighter in the sky.

"Conspiracy or not. It doesn't matter really. But I'm more and more convinced that Holly's death was no accident. Someone planned it. Someone had her assassinated."

Christian felt his stomach begin to churn. Suddenly it was all a bit too much.

"I've got this very unpleasant feeling that this is some sort of perverse competition. First I recount a murder, then it's your turn?! What next?"

"I had hoped you'd be a little more understanding," said Jodie, disappointed.

"Look, I can understand that you're upset about losing your sister, and you're right it seems pretty weird that not just one but two astronauts from the same mission die just as they get home, but, like I said before, it's probably just really bad luck. An unhappy coincidence. And there's therefore no reason to suddenly go looking for other explanations for something that was just a matter of bad luck. Otherwise everything just ends up as one big conspiracy theory."

Christian could feel that he was becoming irritated. Typical American, he thought. Couldn't they just relax a bit. Just for a second or two and not go round seeing things that weren't there. He wished, all of a sudden, that he was home.

Jodie wasn't to be put off, however. Not now when she was just getting into gear.

"The day I talked to my sister she said something that we both knew was a lie. She said, that when she saw me with my new boyfriend it made her think of Mr. B."

Jodie pronounced the words carefully. Emphasizing each word and leaving pauses between them.

Christian smiled and glared at whatever was under the bed.

"He's well hidden."

"Exactly. And Holly knew that. I mean, of all the people in all the world Holly really knew how much I missed having a boyfriend."

Christian turned serious again. What she said had affected him in a most unpleasant way.

"And as if that wasn't enough. Why name Mr. B?"

"I couldn't say. Who is Mr. B?"

"Well, I guess as a foreigner you wouldn't know. Here in the States, you should at least have heard of him. He was a whistle-blower. A CIA agent who took his story to the press - *me* - with evidence of CIA human rights breaches. Torture. And not just of terrorist suspects. Even though I only ever referred to him as Mr. B - and I was very careful about my sources by the way - they managed to find his true identity."

"And?"

"Well, it was classified information. He got thirty years. And that despite the fact that the only things he revealed were actually all completely illegal. Nobody else has been punished or even brought to trial."

"Okay. So when you say that Holly referred to Mr. B and that that made her think of your new boyfriend, well aware that you didn't have one then..." Christian had to search for his next words and he could hear how melodramatic he was starting to sound: "...Then she was actually speaking in some sort of a code?"

"But you obviously don't." Once more, Jodie sound disappointed. Maybe she had got her hopes up too high. Yes, it had probably been naive to think that a man like Christian would be able to understand her. What could he possibly know about their relationship anyway? Their childhood together and the confidences they'd shared?! Nothing! Jodie kept her thoughts to herself and reached out for Christian's cigarette packet.

Christian sensed Jodie's discomfort though and decided to convince her, once and for all, that she'd been mistaken. That it had all just been an unfortunate coincidence.

"Okay. Let's say Holly was speaking in code. Why would she do that? Was she involved in projects that had to be kept secret or something?"

Jodie just stood listening while she lit her cigarette. She inhaled deeply and talked as the smoked billowed out from her mouth.

"There were a lot of things she did that she couldn't talk about, but it wasn't exactly top secret. At least I can't imagine it was."

"And she hasn't felt as if she was under any special pressure at any time or anything like that?"

"I can hear you're not much of an expert on astronauts. Have you any idea what sort of training these people have to go through? How hard it is and how long it takes? How inhuman it actually is. The demands they make of astronauts' physical and mental stamina are just indescribable. So when you ask me whether Holly ever said she felt she was under any pressure, well, the answer's yes. That's also why I can't understand how a man like Leshenko could suddenly develop a deadly chest infection. Why hadn't they spotted it earlier?"

"Okay, okay. But what about words? What she said. I mean it could've been a slip of the tongue."

Jodie was deep in thought.

"The only thing I can think of that reminds me of the way she spoke that day, was a time when she said that, actually, it was all just about a load of ones and zeros."

Christian felt an ice-cold chill come over him. Like a shadow that made everything freeze to ice.

"What did you say? What was that you said there?" he almost whispered.

"What's wrong? You look like you'd just seen a ghost."

Christian exhaled slowly. Then he grabbed his shirt and began putting it on hurriedly.

"Does the word Nibiru mean anything to you?"

"No nothing. Why?"

"Okay. Listen. The material which I've got hold of came from a guy who used to *write* stuff in ones and zeros. But what really interested him was Nibiru."

"What is this stuff you've got hold of and what's Nibiru?"

"Nibiru is a planet in our solar system. A so-called planet x with an orbit that takes it into and out of the solar system. Right now it's supposed to be on its way back. This is all stuff that I've just heard, I've never had any direct access to any of it. But that's what this guy in L.A. is going to help me with."

"I'm starting to think that we're both working on conspiracy theories."

"But it's interesting that both people, independently of each other, took an interest in ones and zeros."

"So you think there's a connection?"

"Look. It's definitely made me think."

What, just a few seconds ago, had seemed completely impossible was starting to turn on it's head and Christian suddenly felt like a very small pawn in an enormous game, a game of astronomical dimensions, where he, more or less freely, was being drawn down deeper and deeper into a world of improbabilities. Nonetheless he was determined to see it through. He didn't really see that he had a choice anyhow.

As they had talked the sun had risen high in the sky and the noises from the street were growing louder and louder.

Christian went back to the bed and sat down. He was planning his next move. A train ticket to California couldn't cost that much. Or could it?

Jodie looked at her watch, before she lay down again and pulled him across to her. And, as if she was reading his mind, she interrupted him just as he was about to speak.

"I think we should take my car, and that we should leave straight away. I'll call my editor and tell him I'm going to have to be away for a couple of days. On research."

"We? You mean, you're coming with me?"

"Yes, I said we. If there's a chance that what you've got can bring me any closer to an explanation of the crime that I believe was behind my sister's death then I want to know about it. I am willing to take the risk."

"And it won't be thought strange that you just head off for a couple of days?"

"Look. I'm not just heading off just like that. If I say I'm on to something my editor normally backs me up and tells me to go for it. That's the way it's been up to now and I've no reason to believe things have suddenly changed. But, before we do anything else I'm going to have to catch up on some sleep. It was a very... active night."

Jodie smiled to him kissed him on the nose and fell asleep almost straight away. Christian couldn't sleep though. All he could do was speculate about loose ends, secret agencies probability and far-fetched conspiracy theories.

The black Cadillac CTS-V eased smoothly across the asphalt on its way into Manhattan. A great way to travel, if you're in the mood to notice. Wedlock wasn't. He was far too busy issuing orders into his cell phone:

"I need both units present at the briefing." He glanced at his watch and continued: "I'll be with you in thirty minutes, and I want everything ready when I get there." Wedlock ended the call, and looked out at the skyscrapers on the tiny island. The island of Manhattan.

The Cadillac rolled to a stop right in front of the glass-doors that formed a skyscraper's entrance. A building that, officially, housed a division of the *United States Department of Agriculture*, but which to the trained eye had too many security personnel and access procedures for it to be just an ordinary administrative centre. A building which, according to the sign outside, housed the FAS or *Foreign Agricultural Service*.

Wedlock left the car quickly and strode purposefully through the swing doors, flashed his ID and logged in using an iris scanner. He continued through an extensive foyer, took a flight of steps in a few quick bounds and was admitted to a large room by a couple of broad-shouldered security staff. A room that was chock-full of high-tech equipment from floor to ceiling with three gigantic screens covering one of the walls. A constant stream of IP addresses rolled down one of the screens, whilst another showed a map of Manhattan.

The third and final screen featured highlighted words such as '*UFO*', '*black helicopter*', '*2012*' and '*Nibiru*'. Words captured from e-mails sent from all around the world.

This was one of the many local branches of *Echelon 2.0*.

"Where are my crew?"

A woman pointed towards a connecting door.

"They're waiting for you, sir."

"How far have you got?"

A man at one of the consoles swivelled in his chair and answered:

"There's nothing on his laptop, sir. Technical Analysis just sent it back to us. Oh, and he's bought himself a phone card..."

"And we got the number, right?"

"Yes, from an e-mail to someone called Talon Karrde."

"Talon Karrde?"

The man shrugged his shoulders.

"A smuggler character from a *Star Wars* book. Apparently he was based on *Han Solo*."

Wedlock stopped him impatiently.

"Okay, okay, okay, okay. Anything else?"

"Well, amongst his own kind, Talon Karrde is considered a kind of a Robin Hood figure. He's had this reputation for being the best hacker in the world for years. He was the guy who brought down the FBI's network, you know when erm..."

"Okay, I want to know everything about this guy! Eve-ry-thing! The schools he went to, the size of his dick - everything. Anything else?" said Wedlock braking off.

"We're getting close to finding where Talon Karrde lives."

"Good, let me know when it happens."

"We're working on it, sir."

Wedlock made directly for a door at the other end of the room and went in.

Everyone straightened up spontaneously as Wedlock almost stamped into the room. His body and spirit were infused with so much energy that, naturally, it affected his behaviour. Wedlock had grown with his promotion, and he had no intention of resting on his laurels.

"What's the status from Copenhagen?"

The four agents made no reply, but just stood there, obviously embarrassed. Finally one of them broke the silence. A young woman with regular and appealing features.

"We did get counter orders, sir. But they came too late."

Wedlock cursed Bob Harris once again, but had neither time nor inclination to dwell on things. It was time to move on.

"Okay, okay, okay, okay. This man hasn't come to the US for a holiday. And we have every reason to believe that he's well on his way to damaging national security. So we gotta bring him in. Alive and discreetly, very discreetly. Is that understood?"

"The target has made calls to a Jodie Green, sir. A journalist on the New York Times."

"And the surveillance team?"

"No-one, sir. We were told to remain passive."

"*Fucking nightmare,*" said Wedlock to himself, and shook his head.

"Okay, two things. I want to know everything about Jodie Green. Eve-ry-thing! The schools she went to, the size of her tits - everything. And the sooner the better."

"And the other thing?"

"The other what?" answered Wedlock.

"You said there were two things. Up until now you've only mentioned one of them. Sir."

"Oh, yeah. Right. Actually it's two more things," said Wedlock and clicked his fingers by way of recognition in the direction of the female agent who'd just asked him.

"Why do you need a hacker, if what you're in possession of has already been hacked once? Huh? And is there someone who can get us some coffee? Please!"

The red two-door General Motors *Pontiac Solstice* was only about three years old and it still ran very, very smoothly. A convertible that had been put in production after the success of a 2002 concept car and which had four cylinders, 177 horsepower, five automatic gears, a 2.4 litre engine and a top speed of about 115 mph. Not the fastest car ever made perhaps, but it was very manoeuvrable.

Christian was impressed that he couldn't actually feel the wind at all, even though the roof was down. Only if he stuck his hand out above the windshield. Then he could really feel it.

Jodie drove the red sports car with a routine elegance. The car and its driver were as one. A perfect symbiotic relationship, thought Christian, and studied Jodie's profile. She looked good. Great, in fact.

They had made it about half-way through Ohio on Interstate 70 and Christian was feeling unusually relaxed, pleasantly full and well dressed. He was wearing the spare shirt he had brought with him, the black jacket, the black trousers and the black boots, plus a pair of sunglasses he had stolen from Jodie's cupboard. And he was feeling alive. Like a fifteen year-old who had run away from home he felt victorious and free. No matter how hard he tried he couldn't manage to make himself serious. The desire to just go for it and seize the day was far too strong for him. In the end he just gave up and let it happen. Gave in to his desire to just curse the entire fucking world and his fucking life. They could all go to hell for all he cared. In fact, it was just like the old days.

The next few hours passed in virtual silence, and even though Christian had just taken the wheel from Jodie he was beginning to think that they should probably start looking for a place to spend the night. He didn't really feel the need to just drive for the sake of driving. He wanted a good bed for the night and a good dinner. And he wanted her. Christian started to keep a look out. For the more humble cheap motels.

The joint that Jodie, and not Christian, settled on was more upmarket. In a little town in Indiana. In the town of Centerville at junction 145. A motel where a room for the night costed about 70 dollars. For a so-called *Two Queen Bed Room*, even though neither he nor Jodie had any thoughts of using the other bed for anything other than their luggage.

The next morning Christian took the wheel whilst Jodie dozed or smoked. More than she would normally, Christian suspected, as he considered her temperament. A side of her that really came out when they were in bed together.

It was seldom that Christian met a woman who took so much of the initiative as Jodie did. With an infectious sexual appetite and a desire for submission that seemed to be in-born it was really a pleasure to be around her and he really had to search his memory hard and long to find a person with similar qualities.

When two people hit it off that much, at both the physical and the mental level, then it was something special. Christian knew that and that was why he liked to dwell on it. Was he in love? Not yet. Could he fall in love? Never. He shook the thought off. The very thought. It made him feel strange and almost put him in a bad mood.

"Where did you and Helena meet?" asked Jodie suddenly.

A question that made Christian start.

"Helena? We worked on the same paper."

"Okay."

"It's natural that people find their husbands and wives the places they spend most of their time. Unless, of course, they meet on the Internet. All these different little worlds are sort of closed off in one way or another. Teachers meet teachers, actors meet actors, doctors meet nurses," laughed Christian.

"And Jodie meets Christian," answered Jodie suddenly serious.

Christian looked at her several times, whilst keeping a firm eye on the traffic.

"True. And it's a good match too. I'm an author and you're a journalist. We both write. Fiction. And try to make it so plausible that people actually believe it."

"Well, my job's not exactly fiction but..."

"What is it then? To find the truth? There's no such thing."

"Bullshit."

But Christian persisted.

"Every time you're presented with something you give it an angle. Every time you see something you interpret it and describe it as you yourself experience it. Someone else standing right next to you would have experienced something different. You'd see the same thing but you'd experience it in two completely different ways and you'd write two completely different stories."

"That's one of the reasons we use sources."

"Yes, but even so it'll be sources you've selected. Most of the time anyway. People who share your way of looking at things."

"You forget that sources sometimes contradict each other and that they're just as important, if not more important, to a story than when sources confirm each other."

Christian never answered Jodie's remark directly.

234

"Actually, that's why I became an author. So that I no longer needed to bother about being objective or looking to uncover the 'truth'."

"So it wasn't because of Helena?"

"Hele...? Why should it have anything to do with Helena? Is it something she's said?"

Christian's voice sounded a little too harsh. A little too accusatory.

"No, it was just a thought."

The conversation stopped for a while. Christian drove on whilst Jodie sat and looked at him. Something that caused Christian in turn to snatch quick glimpses at her every now and then. *For fuck's sake!* He couldn't work her out. What normally took him ten minutes had now taken two days and he still hadn't gotten anywhere. Who was she actually? On the one hand she came across as very self-assured. But at the same time there was a sort of fragility about her. And why had she suddenly started going on about Helena? *Shit!* It wasn't like him to go all defensive like that.

"You say you haven't got a boyfriend. It can't always have been like that. I mean, not with your looks..."

Jodie withdrew her gaze and answered without showing any sign that his flattery had affected her.

"I haven't had that many. Two, wait no, three. And the last one actually wanted to marry me. Even... All he ever seemed to do was talk about it, but... It took me a long time to get over my trip with Steven. A very long time. And the other boyfriends could, of course, sense that. I didn't have anything to offer."

"Steven?"

"Yeah. Steven. We took off. A bit like we're doing now. To California, where we went completely off the rails. We were just too young I think. I haven't actually seen him since. Not since the day when my sister suddenly turned up and took me home. It wouldn't surprise me if he was dead."

"It sounds like quite a time."

"It was. Though I could have done without..."

Jodie interrupted herself without completing her sentence.

Christian looked at her quizzically a couple of times.

"What? Done without what?"

"Nothing," said Jodie and shook her head.

They sat in silence again for a while until Jodie spoke again.

"I had an abortion."

"Okay? You must have really been far out. How many weeks were you gone?"

Christian had difficulty in appreciating the importance of things like that. And in that he was just the same as the vast majority of other men all over the world. Not that he didn't understand the unpleasantness of the physical procedure. No, it was more the psychological effects that passed him by. For Christian a foetus wasn't really alive - didn't become a child - before it was born. An abortion was pretty much the same as appendicitis. And all that stuff about respect for life. Well, it was just hypocritical. A zygote - a fertilized egg - was that life? What about the ants people crushed under their feet every day?

"Five months," answered Jodie.

Christian returned to the situation and nodded attentively.

"If my sister hadn't turned up, I..."

"So now you feel indebted to her?"

"I don't know. But I know that I miss her and know that I'd do anything to find out what really happened to her."

"I just hope you won't be too disappointed."

Jodie shrugged her shoulders and her gaze moved out to the countryside as she was lost in her own thoughts.

They continued on their way. On, across the vast country. Heading south west.

Made it, finally, to Interstate 44 and ended up in East Tulsa, Oklahoma where the motel they stayed at was slightly more down at heel than the first one.

They had also established a peculiar routine. As if they'd known each other for years.

The first time he noticed it was at a *pit stop*, where Jodie automatically, and of her own accord, bought a bottle of bourbon for them to take with them. And not just any bourbon, an *Old Grand-Dad*. The other time was now when he'd thought how nice it would be to have a joint, but had nothing to make it with. That very instant Jodie chucked a little bag over to him. In it was, as she called it, the best pot on the east coast, and a pack of rolling paper.

And then there was the sex. An ever recurring theme in human history and something which for modern relationships to work just had to click. If it didn't you got a divorce, left each other or got yourself a lover. But with Jodie things just clicked. And Christian knew that Jodie felt the same way as he did. As if they were an extension of each other. Without a thought for their 'performance' or going to exaggerated lengths to accommodate each other. Just with pure natural lust and the desire to give. It sounded almost religious he thought, but he had to admit that she took her place and filled it well. Unusually well, when he thought of all the other women he'd known.

Christian had pushed the door open and sat himself down on the carpet with a couple of glasses and an ashtray. With his back to the end of the bed and with a fairly uninteresting view of the parking lot in front of him. Still, it was something.

He took another drag from his joint and held the smoke in his lungs for a while, whilst Jodie came by and took up a position next to him. Almost naked and with a sleepy smile on her lips she lay down with her head in his lap.

Neither of them paid any attention to the news item playing almost silently on the TV in the background where a reporter was describing yet another UFO sighting. This time in Phoenix, Arizona.

On the third day they crossed Albuquerque, New Mexico and Flagstaff, Arizona.

And it was here they had their first fight. A fight that started with a stupid detail, but which grew and grew out of all proportion.

An innocent question about Jodie's role in their upcoming meeting with Talon Karrde.

"Maybe it's a good idea if you let me do the talking," said Christian. The remark that started them off.

"What had you imagined I'd do?"

"Nothing. I just wanted to make sure beforehand. I've had bad experiences with that sort of thing that's all," answered Christian.

"Did you think I'd scare him off. Was that what it was?"

"Who knows. He doesn't know there'll be two of us. And that you work for a newspaper, for example"

"I've done this sort of thing a lot of times, so I don't think you can teach me anything about how to be a journalist, all right," answered Jodie indignantly.

"I wasn't questioning your ability. I just wanted to avoid any surprises. As I said, I've had trouble in the past tackling this sort of thing with someone else."

"Well we're not tackling it together are we? You've got your agenda. I've got mine."

"Well, then we agree," answered Christian.

"I just think it's rude. Even though you say you're not questioning my ability, that's the way it feels anyway."

"That could just mean it hit home then. If there was nothing in it then you probably wouldn't have been offended."

"You're not listening to what I'm saying," answered Jodie. "What I'm talking about is...,"

"I hear you loud and clear," interrupted Christian.

"And please don't interrupt me when I'm speaking, thank you very much."

"Well what more is there for you to say? We've talked it through now surely."

"I just won't have you comparing me to other women. That's all."

"Who said anything about other women?" asked Christian surprised.

Jodie didn't answer but just stared out through the windscreen.

"If it's Helena you're talking about..."

"That's what I mean. You shouldn't be comparing me with other women."

Christian suddenly felt as if he owed Jodie an explanation but said nothing at first. The fact that, at one time, he had given Helena too much space, and that she had abused it, had been one big regret. Because, in reality, the responsibility had always been his. He had just been in love. In love and naive.

"Okay. I'm sorry. All right," he finally answered. "I must have got things mixed up. Sorry... Really."

Jodie looked at him seriously. Then she nodded curtly.

"Okay... and thank-you for saying it."

Finally, Christian and Jodie reached their destination. The city of angels - Los Angeles. They holed up in a cheap place near Echo Park which was known as an area in which many aspiring actors, directors and show biz wannabes lived.

The hotel, *Best Western Dragon Gate Inn*, was a small quiet place with a marble desk in the lobby and a relaxed atmosphere.

They settled on a *King Bed Room* and were both ready to just lie down and go to sleep. Long and deep until next morning where they had their breakfast in a little cafeteria to the left of the atrium area.

After the meal Christian went out for a cigarette, while Jodie went back to the room. Then he went back to reception and asked to use a computer. He then sent Talon a mail to let him know he'd arrived.

A minute later Christian received an answer in the form of a text message:

'Don't use e-mail anymore. The bloodhounds seem to be on our trail. I will contact you later.'

"Fuck!" shouted Christian and hurried up to the hotel room where Jodie was on her way out of the bathroom.

"We're going to have to leave. Now!"

"What's happened?" asked Jodie surprised.

"Every time I use mail I tell them where I am. They're evidently in a position to track my correspondence. Come on. Let's get out of here. The sooner the better." Christian grabbed their luggage, quickly shoved a few things into their bags and left the room together with Jodie about ten minutes later.

After they had left the hotel they decided to just drive around a bit and wait until they were contacted. Finally, they ended up driving out to Venice Beach.

The beach was full with all sorts of people. Skateboarders, roller skaters, fortune tellers and scammers of all kinds. Drug dealers, body-builders, musicians and street artists, but if it wasn't for the history of the place it could just as well have been a local beach back home in Denmark.

They had just got themselves an ice cream, when Christian's cell phone beeped again. Another message from Talon Karrde. This time with an address they could meet him at.

Echelon 2.0's high-tech control room buzzed with activity as the staff went about their business.

Including the young black man sitting in front of his keyboard and who now stood up enthusiastically.

"I got him!"

Wedlock was lying on a leather couch trying to catch up on some sleep, but jumped up in the very instant the man called out and rushed over to the keyboard.

"Where?"

"Topanga Mountains. Los Angeles."

"We're outta here."

A small motorcade of vehicles left for LaGuardia Airport at high speed. They passed straight through security and on to an unmarked black *Hawker Horizon* aircraft. Wedlock jumped aboard accompanied by a small retinue of agents.

After take off the plane turned - heading due south west.

"Have we got anything more on the woman?"

An agent sat down in front of Wedlock and read directly from the case folder:

"Jodie Green. 38. Caucasian... etc. etc. Employed as a reporter on the New York Times since 2001. Author of a number of controversial articles. Best known for her coverage of the Mr. B CIA case. Sister of the deceased Holly Burkana."

Wedlock was too tired to concentrate further and scratched his forehead.

"Okay, okay, okay, okay. That's fine. Wake me up twenty minutes before arrival, okay?"

He reclined the seat and pulled a blanket over himself and fell asleep. One of the advantages of being a former special ops soldier. You could sleep anywhere, any time.

Five hours later the plane landed again. This time on a small anonymous landing strip in a Los Angeles suburb. Three black Lincoln Navigators were waiting for them on arrival with their engines' running.

As soon as everyone was aboard they set off for Topanga Mountains.

The agents jumped out of the cars shortly before a small wooden house on Grandview Drive. A building that seemed, primarily, to function as a summer house.

They crept up to the house with Wedlock taking the lead. Once there he issued further orders. The team moved forward soundlessly using the classic hand signals for the so-called C.R.E's. - Close Range Engagements.

Wedlock and the other agents spread themselves and took up positions on various sides of the building, keeping a watchful eye on all entrances and exits, these being the windows door and roof. No activity.

Wedlock took the lead, crept up to the front door and picked the lock so deftly that not a sound was made.

The ground floor of the building was completely empty. Except for some well-maintained furniture and household items it seemed deserted and unlived in. Wedlock could sense something, however, and he moved forward to the basement door. Once there he made additional silent hand gestures. This time they were orders to the others to follow him, and together with two other agents, Wedlock now crept on down the stairs.

Down to a basement which was full of computer equipment including an array of small monitors on which a number of different geographical coordinates were mapped.

In front of one of the computers a young man was sitting hard at work and deep in thought. Sitting and watching his monitors as he entered line after line of code.

Wedlock and a couple of agents stood up behind him. He'd heard nothing.

"Using the force, Talon?!"

The young man jumped and turned around completely petrified.

"Shit!!"

Then they heard the characteristic sound of a gun being cocked.

"Don't move a muscle."

Wedlock and the two agents stiffened and Wedlock raised his hands slowly into the air.

Two other men stepped out of the basement shadows with their weapons pointing at Wedlock and the two other agents, who now lowered theirs.

"May I see some ID please?" asked one of the men. A question which made Wedlock start. It wasn't the sort of question you expected from a criminal under these circumstances.

"NSA - National Security Agency. Who's asking?" asked Wedlock and ignored the threatening barrel of the automatic weapon that was pointing straight at him. Slowly, and in full view, he moved his right hand inside his jacket and pulled out his ID.

The two men lowered their weapons and looked extremely confused.

"Will someone please explain to me what the fuck is going on here? Has someone fucked up big time or what? Morgan Edwards, CIA." Morgan

Edwards held up his own ID whilst Wedlock laughed angrily. "Okay. First blood to Mr. Talon Karrde."

It wasn't the clichéd zitty teenage nerd that greeted them, and Christian actually felt embarrassed at having, somewhere along the line, expected it. The man who opened the door didn't suffer from acme, and was actually about Christian's own age. With long swept-back dark hair which he wore in a ponytail. He had a thin narrow face, green eyes and a beard quite in keeping with the relaxed style of Talon Karrde. He was wearing some sort of white robe. And looked the part from top to toe.

"Who's she?" asked Talon and looked at Jodie who, until now, had stood passively behind Christian's shoulder. Talon was almost six foot five and was used to looking down at people, both literally and figuratively. Something that seemed to satisfy him immensely.

"This is Jo...," began Christian, only to be interrupted by Jodie who extended her hand.

"Jodie Green. New York Times. Pleased to meet you."

"You don't know that yet," answered Talon, but he did at least return her handshake.

"You haven't been playing games with me now have you?" asked Talon, and took a long hard look at Christian.

Christian didn't answer but left it to Jodie to justify her presence, since she'd now introduced herself.

"I'm also here, perhaps primarily, as a private individual. However, if we uncover something that's in the public interest then I look forward to reporting it."

Talon nodded drily and seemed to accept Jodie's role.

"It'll be from memory. No notes. No hidden dictaphones, okay?"

Jodie nodded and opened her jacket to show she had nothing to hide.

Talon smiled and changed the topic:

"Who is it that's tailing you?"

Talon's comment made Christian start. His experiences in Copenhagen and New York had left their mark. He felt insecure and vulnerable. So vulnerable that he spun round straight away.

"Not here. On the web. Every time we've exchanged mails someone's been listening in," said Talon seriously but with detachment.

Christian relaxed slightly but still wasn't quite comfortable with the situation.

"Listening in?"

"Someone's been intercepting our mails, yeah."

"I don't know but I have a pretty good idea."

Christian looked at Jodie. She shrugged her shoulders cautiously.

"Our guess is that it must be some branch of the secret service."

"Yes, and unfortunately there are more than one of them," said Talon winking in a friendly manner to Christian who continued seriously:

"They've followed me right across the Atlantic, that much I know. Obviously pretty resourceful. And apparently even ready to kill to get hold of the material. This material right here."

Talon shook his head and rolled his eyes. Then he stepped to one side and admitted them.

"They'll kill for anything these days. It's as if they're no longer capable of sorting things out any other way. Primitive. Really primitive. If you ask me."

The flat they were now entering was on Hilldale Avenue in West Hollywood. A quiet back street in a middle-class suburb right next to Beverly Hills. The apartment block wasn't anything to look at, and Christian was surprised to find that Talon actually had a pretty nice apartment. Okay so there were a couple of cockroaches that sometimes mixed it with the ants in the bathroom, but apart from that it was all very much to Christian's taste. There was a large square living room containing a worn, beige/off-white patterned couch in front of the room's sole window. This large window was in turn equipped with vertical plastic blinds. There wasn't much of a view, the window looked out on to the building next door no more than six to nine feet away.

Still, there were wooden floorboards and a large coffee table.

Christian's gaze travelled across the room from left to right and he noted everything, as he always did, without thinking. To the far left just opposite the front door was a door that led to a walk-in closet. It was so large that it could actually be used as a mini bedroom, as Talon pointed out. Perhaps that was why it was kept empty thought Christian. The next thing he noticed was the large TV. It was sat on top of an iron-bound box and was showing Steven Spielberg's 'Close Encounters of the third Kind', constantly interrupted by a stream of annoying commercials.

To the right of the main door along the wall opposite the window there was a small blue wooden bookcase with three shelves but without any books, which struck Christian as odd though he said nothing.

Then there were two old, high-backed wooden chairs. One on each side of a large table on which three laptop computers were running.

Once again, Christian had to admit that his preconception was mistaken. He'd expected a room full of electronic gadgetry and flashing lights - not this.

The fourth and final room started with a door which lead into a tiny mini-room. A mini-room which evidently functioned as a sort of small office with an inbuilt wardrobe the only fitting. Opposite the door to the mini office was another door. A door that lead into a large bathroom.

Yet another door to the right lead off into a bedroom, which was very similar to the living room. Just on a slightly smaller scale.

In the bedroom there was also a back door. A back door that lead out into a small yard. The only thing in the bedroom was one large double bed. *Kingsize.* Another door - it began to make Christian dizzy - he had never seen a flat this size with so many doors before - opened on to a kitchen and opposite that door, was a further door leading back on to the living room.

Then Christian noticed the noise. The noise of helicopters. The sound of flickering rotor blades.

"What's that I can hear?" he asked, nervous again.

Talon listened but couldn't hear anything out of the ordinary, shrugged his shoulders and shook his head.

"I don't know. I can't hear anything."

"Can't you hear it? Helicopters!" said Christian.

At this Talon smiled a broad smile.

"Aahh. You're a long way from home kiddo. It's just police choppers. They're scouting the area all the time."

Jodie nodded understandingly and patted Christian lovingly on the back.

It was probably because he was so close to achieving his goal, thought Christian. It was probably also why he was so nervous.

Christian nodded and pulled himself together.

"Well, shall we take a look at it?"

Talon remained standing where he was. Calm and cool.

"I'm afraid there's not that much to choose from, but I can offer you a beer - or a joint."

For the first time for a very, very long time Christian only needed one thing. And that was to be able to think completely straight. He therefore shook his head as he heard himself refuse the offer.

Jodie, on the other hand, accepted a beer. Talon soon came back from the kitchen with two cold *Millers*.

It felt like some kind of séance, thought Christian impatiently and looked to Jodie for support. She, however, seemed happy to lap it all up and appeared to be perfectly at ease. The only thing missing was a couple of joss sticks and some candles. Christian had a bad feeling.

Talon seemed, finally, to be ready. He sat himself at the computer closest to the wall and held his hand out to Christian.

"The subject, please."

Christian was temporarily baffled. *Subject?* What subject, he thought. Then he cottoned on and coyly handed Talon the flash drive. The drive that held secrets that were so compromising that their release would have more than dramatic consequences. Or what? Suddenly it was hard to believe that a little thing like that could be so important. But there had to be something on it surely.

Talon put the flash drive into his computer and looked questioningly at Christian.

"Oh yeah. Sorry. You want the folder with all the numbers," said Christian and tried to point at the 0100001100110010 folder.

"C2," answered Talon. "With a capital C."

"What?"

"That's what the numbers mean - the abbreviation for *Condor Deuce*," answered Talon and opened the folder.

"Okay," nodded Christian and continued:

"Perhaps I should mention that you only get three attempts. If you don't manage to crack it, or you try to copy it it'll be erased. By a piece of software I assume. That's what the little movie is all about anyway."

"Impressive," answered Talon and paused for dramatic effect. "But also kinda trivial."

Not the description Christian would have used, but for someone like Talon things were probably different, he reflected.

Then it was suddenly as if Talon Karrde had hit some sort of barrier. He just sat there, with his eyes closed and his hands in front of him, fingertip against fingertip whilst Christian and Jodie exchanged glances and Christian rolled his eyes.

Then Talon broke the silence.

"I will be seriously disappointed if the hash function in this cipher isn't collision-free and at least at the SHA-2 level," he suddenly blurted out. Without opening his eyes.

Even though whatever it was Talon was talking about sounded like complete nonsense as far as Christian was concerned he couldn't be bothered to ask any questions and just kept up a pretence of understanding.

"Okay. If you say so..."

Then Talon opened his eyes and ran a rapid command-prompt, a little black window in which he entered line after line of commands at ridiculous speed, before finally finishing with a flourish on 'Enter'.

Nothing. Absolutely nothing. It had looked good though. Very dramatic. Starting from some sort of Yoda posture and followed by such an elegant performance.

"Two attempts le...," started Christian, but Talon interrupted him with a rapid arm movement.

"Ssh," Said Talon harshly.

Christian and Jodie exchanged glances once again but said nothing.

"Brute force is the method people normally use to break in."

"Yeah? And?"

"That's what I'm doing now. The problem is just that I only have two more attempts. The third time I have to crack it," answered Talon.

Talon leaned himself back in his chair and closed his eyes despairingly whilst he let his head fall slowly back and exhaled from his nostrils. He nodded to himself a few times before he began to speak.

"I'm afraid he's probably used a one-time pad."

"Which is?" asked Christian.

Talon remained in the same position as he explained.

"A cryptological algorithm, where the code is the same length as the text."

"You what?"

"Forget it. The point is that it's impossible to break."

"I think you must be mistaken. He wouldn't have set it up like this if he'd already ensured that the code was unbreakable."

"Hmm," was all Talon said, straightening up in his chair.

Then he closed a little program called 'Cain & Abel'. One of the most popular code-breaking programs and, apparently identical to the one Mikkel had used, at least as far as Christian could see. A program that had evidently been running alongside Talon's manual attempts.

"That would have been too easy," said Talon to himself, apparently referring to his use of the said 'Cain & Abel'.

Christian thought for a while, trying to come up with a better approach.

"Did you know Condor Deuce? I mean were you familiar with the way he worked? Perhaps that could help us."

"Condor Deuce was good - an equal. We used to swap tips. Both on

252

hacker forums and via Trillian - a chat program - though it was actually me who…"

Talon interrupted himself as an idea seemed to strike him. He bent forward over the computer again and started to type. He finished off by pressing 'Enter' with a further flourish.

"…who introduced him to… …his first… …hacker… …tool."

The 'Bingo' folder opened.

"How the fuck did you do that?!" asked Christian surprised.

"I took a chance and used the algorithm I introduced him to back then. Call it a gift," answered Talon, not without evident pride.

All three of them were now glued to the screen, as the folder revealed its contents. A folder which - of course - contained yet another subdirectory. This one, however wasn't password-protected. A folder labelled 'Caret'.

As well as the folder there were a number of documents including various payrolls and a single document entitled: 'Above Black - Operation: Nibiru 2012'.

Talon simply opened the document with a double-click and without any further comment.

A document with an NSA letter-head and which was classified as above Top Secret.

"Officially there is no level of secrecy beyond Top Secret, so a document that's classified as 'Above Black' is… Well, it's pretty secret," said Talon drily.

Christian mumbled something semi-audibly:

"Eyes only. Copy one of one… briefing document… prepared for president Bush…?! …possessing Nibiru level clearance… Government Leaders Americas, Asia & Europe. What is this?" asked Christian.

Talon shook his head.

"I don't generally take an interest in these sorts of things. I'm only interested in money. You know, large sums moving between Swiss bank accounts. That sort of thing. Oh, and American ones of course."

Jodie interrupted in surprise:

"You steal money?" she asked with an indignant expression.

"I steal from the rich. And I mean the really rich, giving to the poor. Keeping a little for myself, of course."

Jodie seemed to have concluded that Talon was actually nothing more than a common criminal and returned her attention to the computer screen as she answered Christian's question:

"It seems to suggest that the names on that list are the people who met at The Government Leaders Forum. And that some sort of Executive Order will be issued in 2012."

"And what exactly is The Government Leaders Forum?"

"A place where business leaders and politicians from around the world meet once a year. It's arranged by Microsoft, by the way."

"They're actually the only ones I don't take anything from," said Talon and continued: "Do you know how much Bill Gates donates to charity out of his own pocket?"

"As if that's any justification," answered Jodie sharply.

"And do you have any idea of how many banks just choose to suffer in silence? If it got out that they'd been hacked and that a couple of accounts had been emptied, well it's hard to imagine worse publicity for a bank than that. And of course the hackers know that, so, times are good."

It was horrendous timing, but something suddenly struck Christian. Something he had to do.

"If I gave you the name of an organisation. One of the real blood-suckers of course, how long would it take you to transfer some money?"

"To you?"

"No... Let's call him an acquaintance."

"The transaction itself is instantaneous. It's what goes on beforehand that takes the time... On average... a couple of hours I guess."

"Perhaps we could get back to the point here?" said Jodie impatiently.

Christian lifted his hand demonstratively.

"Just a minute. This is almost as important as all the other stuff. And we've done the hard bit now."

Jodie shook her head and coughed impatiently.

"If I say the organisation is called 'Danish Aryan Resistance' and the man's name is Carsten Clausen."

"That'd help of course... Denmark? That's the capital of Sweden right?"

Christian shook his head.

"No, Denmark is a country and its capital is called Copenhagen. But could you do it? You could of course take a bit yourself while you were about it."

"Who is the guy?"

"Someone who needs to be taught a lesson. You'll find his name in the register of the Danish Secret Service. PET dot dk. Carsten Clausen."

Talon nodded, suddenly understanding and smiled.

"I get you. There's almost nothing worse than money you suddenly have to account for. Especially if it's a large amount and it comes from the wrong place. You must really be mad at him. Are you sure he deserves it?"

"Absolutely," nodded Christian.

"I'll do it when I have the time, okay?"

"Thanks," Christian answered. And not without a certain satisfaction.

"What about the other folder?" asked Jodie again, as she finished skimming the document in front of her.

Talon didn't say anything. Instead he collapsed the active window and was just about to open the subdirectory when Jodie suddenly stiffened.

"Hey. Wait a minute. Go back will you."

Talon expanded the document again and let Jodie read on.

"Michael Dale," she said seriously and pointed at the screen. "Dr. Michael Dale was Holly's colleague, before she became an astronaut."

"And?" said Christian.

"It all fits in," said Jodie simply.

"I don't get it," replied Christian.

"It all just fits together. I can't tell you any more than that. What's in the other folder?"

Talon waited before opening the subdirectory, as he reflected on Jodie's observation.

"Like in *Six Degrees of Separation*," he said.

"What?" asked Christian.

"An experiment developed by Stanley Milgram from Harvard, though it actually relied on earlier experiments from MIT. Anyway it seems like there are no more than six chains - six people if you will - between all the people in the world. Irrespective of cultures and boundaries. You can try it yourself some time. Everyone knows everyone. It all fits together. Really, we're all just one big family."

"We ought to tell the Klu Klux Klan and all the terrorists, then," answered Christian drily.

"Yeah, absolutely."

"What's in that folder?" Jodie asked insistently.

Talon double-clicked the subdirectory entitled '*Caret.*' It turned out to contain a large number of photographs. All of them very high resolution. No blurry images or faked details. All photographed with professional equipment by professional photographers. And all labelled with locations and dates. Photographs of UFOs, parts and components.

"UFOs?!" said Christian, disappointed.

"That not enough for you?!" For the first time that day Talon sounded genuinely surprised.

But Christian was far from satisfied. *Was that it? A couple of documents with a dollar stamp and some photos of flying saucers? That was what they were prepared to kill for?!*

Christian shook his head to himself, whilst Jodie nodded quietly. Then she withdrew slightly.

"Pictures of UFOs," said Christian. This time with an even more obvious edge of disappointment.

"Well that really does change a thing or two, wouldn't you say?" Talon replied, whilst he studied a couple of the outlandish vessels. "Take the religious aspect, for example."

Christian shrugged his shoulders but could feel that Talon seemed to share his lack of enthusiasm. At least in part.

"Yeah, you could always start by asking them if they believe in God... Caret? Why Caret?" Christian wanted to know.

"It's just a name. Caret is a secret project that's supposed to be about reverse engineering. The idea that you can work out how something works and acquire similar technology by looking at the way it's put together. Taking it apart basically."

"I thought you said this stuff wasn't really you."

"Well, you can't help picking things up here and there. Not if you move in the circles I do."

"What circles?"

"Have you ever heard of the Internet?"

Christian ignored him and returned to the matter in hand.

"Can you tell me anymore?"

"No, not really. It's just that it confirms what millions of people all round the world already believe. Even though, you may have missed one little detail."

"Which is?" asked Christian.

Before Talon could answer they were interrupted by a noise and turned to Jodie.

Jodie had moved away without the others really noticing and was now tapping away eagerly at one of the other computers.

"What are you doing?" asked Talon.

Jodie looked up quickly as she continued to type.

"I'm just mailing my editor. Don't mind me. I can listen and type at the same time no problem."

Talon remained standing. Serious.

"On the computer I use in my spare time?! Can I ask you what you've written?"

"Nothing secret. Don't worry. Just a bit of general information about what we've found."

"And what terms did you use?"

"Terms? I don't get it. What do you mean?"

"Which words did you use in your e-mail?!" Talon wasn't just serious now. He was angry.

"I'm sorry. I don't quite see what you're getting at?"

"Words like UFO, NSA, CIA... Caret or Nibiru, for example. Those kind of words. Did you use any of them?"

Jodie nodded quietly as she slowly realised that she'd made a mistake. A big mistake.

"Okay. The blood hounds now know where we are. Well done, Jodie Green."

Christian stood without saying anything looking from one of them to the other.

"What? How? I don't get it."

Talon shut the three laptops, threw Christian the flash drive and was already on his way out of the back door when Christian called after him.

"How?!"

"Echelon 2.0," answered Talon and shrugged his shoulders with a little smile.

That made sense, thought Christian. Especially in relation to what had been happening recently.

"Are you going to be okay?"

"A proper hacker always has something up his sleeve. I rent this place under an assumed name. Best of luck." Talon looked at Jodie and shook his head with a gleam in his eye.

"Women and technology," he said, and was gone.

"I'm guessing we're going straight to the paper?"

"I need to know why my sister was killed first. And I'm certain Michael Dale knows something. If not, then there are others on the list."

Christian nodded, almost to himself.

"The first rule of journalism."

Jodie looked confused.

"I don't get it."

"Have you not heard that? I thought all journalists knew that one. *'A story without sources is like water without a cup.'*"

Christian illustrated the analogy with his fingers.

"It just runs through your fingers."

Jodie laughed quietly.

"I think you dreamt that up yourself."

Christian shrugged his shoulders.

"Sounds good though, eh?"

Christian and Jodie were on their way up through California on Highway 1. On their way to Stanford university in Palo Alto.

"Who is this guy Michael Dale anyway?"

"He used to work with my sister. They were on the same research project, just before Holly was selected for astronaut training."

Then she thought of something.

"What was the detail that Talon thought we had maybe overlooked?"

"I never got an answer to that. And you know why," smiled Christian.

"How was I supposed to know they could track us?"

Christian shrugged his shoulders.

"There's nothing to be done about it now anyway. And it may not have been all that important... What is important is that we get a copy made - a hard copy. If we're going to get a story out of this then..."

"We'll do it straight away. I just wanted to get out of Los Angeles," answered Jodie, as they reached the Point Mugu Naws suburb near the town of Oxnard.

"I'm getting fucking paranoid. Every time a car goes past I expect it to swing round and set off after us." Christian leant his head right back against the headrest and looked at Jodie and the water behind her.

"Look they're not that good, all right. They've no way of knowing where we're going. None whatsoever," said Jodie and looked despairingly at him.

"What do you call that then?" asked Christian and nodded his head whilst keeping his eyes on the road.

About fifteen hundred feet ahead a road block had been established with a number of police cars blocking the road. Their lights flashing.

"Shit!" Jodie hissed and braked without thinking.

"Of course, it could be completely unrelated," said Christian drily.

"You wanna try?"

"Well, like you said... they can't be that good, can they? How would they know that we've taken this road?"

"It's the logical one," answered Jodie, pulling a u-turn.

"What are you doing?"

"I'm gonna go back to Solromar and up Mulholland. That'll take us straight to the 23rd and we can get there that way instead."

Christian shrugged his shoulders.

"Fine by me. You're the one who knows where we're headed."

"I'm afraid we're gonna have to be cautious."

"What about the copy?"

"That'll have to wait."

"Look, this is stupid. If they catch us and confiscate the material we'll have no evidence at all. Nothing."

"Do you have a better idea? Right now it's just as important to get this backed up by a reliable source."

Christian shook his head.

"If he really is part of this Nibiru-bigtime-Above-Black-Top-Secret-My-Ass-Operation. Why would he suddenly talk, then?"

"We'll figure that one out. Guilt, a desire for justice, anything. Right now we just have to get there. As fast as possible. Before they work out that we've got through. If they haven't already done so."

The little red Pontiac Solstice returned to Solromar and turned left up the twisty Mulholland main road.

Wedlock sat in his mobile headquarters in one of the black Lincoln Navigators and talked into his phone.

"No idea at all? What about the police? Okay, dream up an excuse and drop the road blocks. Say we got 'em. Bye."

Wedlock looked at the three other agents in the car without saying anything. Then he thought long and hard as he looked out of the tinted window. He had an idea.

He snapped his fingers at the nearest agent and pointed at a folder.

"Hand me my folder, will you."

Wedlock took the folder and opened it. He flicked through the case notes for what might be the fourteenth time and stopped at the description of Jodie Green. Holly Burkana's sister... *Holly Burkana's sister.*

Wedlock thumbed through to his notes on Holly Burkana.

Ph.D. ...research project 'Relativity and unifying Electromagnetism'... Dr. Michael Dale... Stanford...

Bingo! Just the words Wedlock had been looking for. He turned his attention briefly to the driver.

"Highway one. North-bound. Step on it!"

Leland Stanford Junior university, better known as Stanford, was located in Palo Alto about 40 miles south east of San Francisco, and was one of the world's leading universities. Founded at the end of the 1800s by railway-man, and later governor, Leland Stanford and his wife Jane. It opened officially on October 1st 1891 and was named after their son: Leland Stanford Junior.

Today it was home to about 2000 educators and thousands more students. All on a campus about half the size of the municipality of Copenhagen. A huge area with everything from housing and parks to a shopping centre and a post office. It held its own concerts and events and amongst other things, housed the largest collection of Rodin sculptures outside Paris, France.

Former pupils included large numbers of Nobel Prize winners, even more Pulitzer winners and an even greater number of astronauts. Making it a real breeding ground for people who'd made a difference.

Christian and Jodie walked the last part of the way from the parking lot on Serra Street to Stanford Quad, or just 'the Quad,' which was to the right of the Oval. From here they made their way to the lecture halls in the Department for Physics and Astrophysics behind Lomita Mall.

Whereas Stanford Oval was a place for hanging out, picnicking or playing volleyball, the Quad consisted only of offices and lecture halls. Almost only, it was also a great place for moonlit sex, preferably inter-generational.

Dr. Michael Dale was putting the last of his books back into his bag and getting ready to leave the auditorium when Christian and Jodie arrived.

"Dr. Dale?"

"Yes?" answered Dale somewhat taken aback.

"Jodie Green. I'm Holly Burkana's sister."

Dale rearranged his features to reveal an unexpectedly mild side to his nature. Particularly as he now recognised Holly's eyes in Jodie's gaze.

If he'd cared about anyone then it was Holly. Both as a colleague, and as a friend. Especially as a friend. Her death had deeply upset him.

"Holly? Yes, of course. I can see her in you." Dale looked briefly at Christian and just nodded seriously, whilst he, for a brief second, felt awkward. Then the moment passed and he returned his full attention to the matter in hand.

"Christian Bang. There's something we'd like to discuss with you."

Michael Dale closed his bag and straightened up.

"Space ships," continued Christian.

"And my sister's murder," added Jodie.

Michael Dale kept his cool and looked directly at both of them as he straightened his jacket and adjusted his trousers. Even though he was more than slightly overweight, his trousers were too big for him and seemed to be continuously on the point of falling down. Despite the belt. Or perhaps it was just a movement that had become a bit of a habit.

"Shall we go outside?"

They went out to the Memorial Church, known amongst the students as *Men Chu*, where they sat in the shade of one of the many palm trees. On a low stone wall slightly to the left of the church. With Jesus, who blessed everyone who happened to pass by from his position as part of the building's extensive façade painting.

"I'm afraid I don't quite follow you," Dale began.

"Drop it. We have documents that confirm your involvement in Nibiru," answered Christian harshly.

"Nibiru? Never heard of it."

"Operation Nibiru 2012. Above black, Caret. I think you know what we're talking about."

Michael Dale nodded slowly. It seemed as if he had made a decision of some sort. At any rate he began to speak.

"It all started with P.A. Sturrock. I was his pupil. Here, at Stanford. Of course, I'd heard all about his criticisms of the Condon report from the University of Colorado."

"Which are...?" asked Christian.

"The Condon committee was formed to provide a scientific analysis of the UFO phenomenon. It was led by the physicist Edward Condon. Hence the name. Many critics, including Sturrock were of the opinion that the fact that the report was commissioned by the American Air Force had influenced its conclusions. That it was biased, in other words. Non-scientific. Because of this, Sturrock founded his own committee. A committee that published its conclusions in 1997. At which point I, of course, was somewhere completely different."

"And what did they conclude?" asked Jodie.

Just then, Michael Dale's phone rang. He picked it up.

"Yes?"

It was Wedlock.

"Two people by the name of Jodie Green and Christian Bang are in all probability on their way over to you. If they reach you before I do you'll have to delay them."

"Can you hurry? I'm actually quite busy right now."

Wedlock seemed to understand.

"They're already there?"

"Yes... I have another meeting. When can you be here?"

"In twenty minutes. Max."

"Okay. See you then. Bye."

Twenty minutes. Twenty minutes lecturing was less than nothing for Michael Dale.

Dale finished the call and put the phone back in his pocket.

"I'm sorry. A student wanted to talk to me... Where were we?"

"Sturrock's conclusion and what it meant," answered Jodie.

"Yes, yes. That UFOs were a worthy subject of scientific investigation. There were just too many things that didn't fit for everything to just be mass hysteria or optical illusions. Unfortunately I was never able to help them clear up the matter as the information that was available to me was, for good reasons, kept absolutely top secret... *Above Black*."

Michael Dale sighed deeply and his considerably overweight body heaved. He breathed heavily through his nose and Christian noted that the sun's warmth was already troubling him.

"I was very attached to your sister. Both as a colleague and as a friend. And I'm very sorry about what happened. But... we had no choice. She was about to go public... Things just got out of hand..."

Jodie shook her head.

"It doesn't make any sense. What do you mean?"

"The International Space Station is perfect for our work. That's why we used the ISS for all our trials."

"You said that things got out of hand?"

"We were working on some tests based on a technology we've actually mastered since the end of the World War Two. Since Roswell. A technology that... How can I put this... Is based around an extreme power field. Many times stronger than the most powerful neodymium magnet."

Christian and Jodie looked quickly at each other. A detail that made Dale change tack.

"Have you heard of John Searl or John Hutchison?"

They both shook their heads.

"Nikola Tesla? Hans Christian Oersted? Albert Einstein? I'm assuming you've heard of them?" Dale continued without waiting for an answer. "It's that sort of direction we're working in. With electromagnetism. These forces are so great that they can affect not just the earth's but actual interplanetary magnetic fields. In other words the electromagnetic sheath around the sun."

Dale was already getting carried away by his enthusiasm for his work.

Jodie interrupted. "And that was enough for you to kill Holly? Is that it?! The interplanetary magnetic field?!"

"The window we operated in on the expedition was over Indonesia and... yes, we haven't yet managed to quantify the damage that this mistake has caused. However, the destruction that followed in the wake of the tsunami would tend to suggest that..."

"The tsunami?! But that killed thousands and thousands of people!" said Jodie aloud. A little too loud for Michael Dale's liking as he looked around nervously.

"As I said. We haven't yet fully assessed to what extent the disaster was a consequence of our activities. Magnetic fields are very sensitive and that's why our safety precautions are as extensive as they are."

"Well they can't have been that extensive. Not given what's happened."

"We don't yet know if it's the result of human error. That's what the calculations we're working on now will help to tell us. But there's no doubt that Holly pushed the wrong buttons, as it were. And it was that realisation that gave her this urge to reveal what she knew. A revelation which we, of course, could not in any way accept."

"So she had to die. That's why you killed her. One life more or less, huh?"

"It's very expensive to train people like Holly, so it definitely hasn't been without its costs. It wasn't an easy decision I can assure you."

"A decision none-the-less. You refer to my sister as if she was some sort of product. She was a human being for Christ's sake! Flesh and blood. No-one had the right to kill her."

"Everything comes down to money, Miss Green. I thought you knew that. At the end of the day everything comes down to money. The financial interests that are at stake here are phenomenal and far, far too large for us to allow a breach. Those are the conditions we all work under. Holly knew that. In fact, she was about to undermine national security. Not to mention international security."

Christian scratched his neck. There were a number of things that didn't add up.

"According to the documents we have access to, what you're doing is supposed to relate to space ships and reverse engineering. It would also appear that you plan to go public with all this in 2012. Is that when they're going to land? Officially?"

Dr. Michael Dale's expression was quizzical at first. That was until he understood what Christian was driving at. Finally it became too much for him and he began to laugh. Initially only gently, but then more and more.

Neither Christian or Jodie could see the joke though. and they had therefore no choice but to sit waiting for Dale to finish laughing.

"I'm sorry. Excuse me," said Dale wiping the tears from his eyes.

Christian felt certain that Dale was laughing at him.

"Was it something I said?" he wanted to know.

Dale became serious.

"These documents you've got hold of. They're the ones that were stolen from the archive. Is that correct?"

"Downloaded and copied yes."

"Why hasn't the story got out yet then?"

"We wanted to give you an opportunity to comment on it first," answered Jodie.

"I don't buy that. I think you came to look your sister's murderer in the eye. Or one of the people who gave the necessary orders anyway."

"Perhaps. Anyway, I've come here to hear what you know."

Dr. Michael Dale breathed deeply. He knew they'd never be able to reveal anything anyway. Wedlock would see to that. Fifteen minutes to go. He began to talk. To really talk.

Neither Wedlock nor any of the other agents had ever been to Stanford. It therefore took them some time to find their way and locate the nearest parking lot and neither their GPS nor any other high-tech equipment was of any use to them.

Even though it might be expected that secret agents would come rushing in at high speed and throw themselves out of their cars in a forward somersault, that was not standard procedure. Maintaining their cover for as long as humanly possible had always been a touchstone of their operations. That was the whole art of what they did. To avoid making a scene at any cost and instead to operate quietly and discretely. That was what gave the best and the most elegant solutions. Where the occasion demanded they could of course just use brute force. As was the case with the police road blocks, for example. And, of course, it made sense to exploit their position and status. But, as the ancient Roman poet Horatius was supposed to have said: *Vis consili expers mole ruit sua* - strength without wisdom will collapse under its own weight. An excellent motto worth living by, reflected Wedlock, as he surveyed the surroundings.

Wedlock and the other agents had reached their target and were now proceeding towards it slowly and cautiously and from the rear.

Closer and closer. Still anonymously. Still discrete.

Something in Michael Dale's expression betrayed them just too soon though, and Christian and Jodie turned and spotted them straight away. Their clothing, moreover, meant that they stood out sharply from the area's habitual users such as students and lecturers.

Christian recognised Wedlock instantly, took Jodie by the hand and disappeared into one of the characteristic arcades and on around the nearest buildings. From there Jodie took the lead and brought them safely back to the parking lot and the car.

They started the car instantly and drove out past the gas station as a breathless Christian, kept a close look out behind them.

They were in the clear.

They set off again, heading out of town. Just to be on the safe side and so as to avoid the regular police. And just so as they could get around more easily.

They drove quickly back up El Camino Real, left on Sand Hill Road and right on Portola.

"One of those guys was one of the people who followed me in Denmark."

"You know him?!" asked Jodie surprised.

"Not really. But I'll always be able to recognise him."

"And you've no idea who he is?"

"No... What now? They've seen our car. They know what we're driving."
Jodie nodded.

"Yeah. If we're going to make it back to New York we'll have to get ourselves another one."

Christian's adrenaline was still pumping but he tried a flippant remark anyway.

"Then it'd probably be best if it was a Cadillac. You can't go cruising around the States if you don't have a Cadillac."

His joke fell totally flat. Jodie was thinking about something completely different.

"There must be others on the list who are ready to speak out now. With the knowledge we have it'll be easier to get them to talk. Especially when I tell them that I'll do the story no matter what. That normally helps."

Christian became serious again.

"Can you do that?"

"No. But they don't know that. And that's to my advantage."

Christian sat for a while staring out of the window.

"This must be the weirdest thing that's ever happened to me. It's gonna make a fantastic novel."

Jodie looked at him quizzically.

"You're going to write a book?"

"What else do you think has kept me going for so long?"

They never heard the shot. All they knew was that suddenly the wind shield had shattered. Christian turned and looked behind him. Right behind them an unmarked black *Enstrom 480B Turbine* helicopter was hovering just above the road. A man dressed in black sat halfway out of the little cabin door with one foot on the landing skid, whilst he took aim at them with a rifle. A serious twelve pound *XM21* military rifle, with a telescopic sight. The type that snipers had used right from the Vietnam war to the conflicts in Iraq and Afghanistan.

The man dressed in black took his eye off the sight in order to adjust the rifle and reload.

They had to get off the road, but on the section of La Honda they were travelling on there was nowhere to go apart from straight ahead. Jodie began throwing the car from side to side, as the only way to avoid being hit. The man in the helicopter fired a second shot.

This time it found its intended target. The car swung wildly. Right across the Cabrillo main road and down towards the coast. It finished up in the rubble immediately behind the beach with a dull thud.

The rough journey from the side of the road to the beach had taken so much of the speed off the car that Christian was able to jump out straight away and run round to the other side, without any other injuries than the shock of the attack. He managed to get the driver's-side door open and hauled Jodie out.

Yes, the man in black's shot had hit just where he intended, bringing them very effectively to a halt. The shot had punctured the left rear wheel and the car's further course over the bumpy terrain had removed what remained of the tyre.

But, even though they were both unhurt and could now run away across the beach the situation was hopeless. Both because of the endless beach stretching out in front of them but also, and perhaps especially, because of the bullet which immediately ploughed into the beach just a few centimetres from their feet. They gave up their escape attempt, took each other by the hand and slowed down until they reached a dead halt and turned to face their pursuer face to face.

The black helicopter just hovered in the air in front of them, and then suddenly veered off and flew away. Just as noiselessly and quickly as it had come. Seconds later it was replaced by the, now familiar, huge four-wheel drive vehicles. The black Lincoln Navigators that were now rolling toward them at high speed.

Wedlock stepped out of the first car, whilst his men began automatically positioning themselves at a strategic distance and kept watch for any signs of danger.

Christian took a little step towards him.

"Are you Danish?" asked Christian, in Danish.

"Huh?" answered Wedlock. Then he understood Christian's question and shook his head.

"No. I'm from the good ol' US of A."

Christian seemed almost disappointed. Wedlock quickly changed the subject.

"Do you realise how many resources we've already used on you guys? Checking every single post office, Internet café and office supplies store between L.A. and Stanford. Just to make sure you haven't made any copies."

"I assume it was you guys doing the dirty work?" Was Jodie's only answer.

"And, as you can see, for very good reasons. I'm afraid sometimes there just isn't any other way."

"You couldn't just have locked her up? You seem pretty good at doing that on Guantanamo, for example. You were going to publish everything in 2012 anyway."

Wedlock smiled in a friendly way.

"Guantanamo's not my department. But no, the risk that something would be revealed was too great."

"We could have used our cell phones," interrupted Christian.

"To do what exactly?"

"Send data," was Christian's naive answer.

"We would have caught it. Believe me," answered Wedlock convincingly.

"What happens now, then?" asked Christian.

"You give me what belongs to me. That's all."

No threats, no weapons. No drama. Just a friendly request. He could have been asking for anything, thought Christian. A light for example, and Christian realised that it was several hours since he had last had a cigarette.

They both knew that anything else would be futile. They knew it was game was up. There was no other way out.

Christian put his hand in his pocket and fished up the little flash drive. He looked briefly at Jodie before handing it to Wedlock, who immediately nodded to one of his colleagues who then began searching them.

Wedlock took the flash drive with outstretched hand; palm up. Then he allowed his fingers to tighten around the little object and shook it quietly a couple of times. He opened his hand again and let the drive fall to the ground before crushing it under his heel.

The man who'd performed the search on them shook his head quietly and stepped away from them.

"So are you going to shoot us now?" asked Jodie.

"Yes, that's the way it should be. But things were different with young Mr. Mortensen. He would just do the same thing all over again if he could get away with it. But with you two... no," answered Wedlock and shook his head slowly. "I don't think that'll be necessary."

Even though Christian and Jodie were overwhelmed with relief they were also very confused. Was he really just going to let them go. Surely not.

"I hope you can find peace now," continued Wedlock and looked long and hard at Jodie. Then he turned and walked back to his car.

"What about us?!" shouted Christian.

"You can't tell the people," answered Wedlock. It was the last thing they heard him say. An answer they didn't understand, but which seemed to imply that they were to be allowed to live. Given that, there wasn't really much else that mattered, thought Christian.

The heavy Lincolns reversed back up to the road and set off in a cloud of dust and dirt whilst the waves rolled lazily up onto the beach and the Californian seagulls dived after food.

Christian sank down onto the sand, completely exhausted, whilst Jodie just stood there with the wind in her hair.

Christian stood slightly to one side whilst Jodie walked energetically back and forth across the blue carpet.

The editor sat behind his desk. One of his hands strayed to the keyboard every now and then, partly hidden by the flat screen monitor. He was listening to Jodie who was speaking enthusiastically.

"The same year as Kenneth Arnold, and the first observation of UFOs as we understand them there's an accident at Roswell. Why? Because it was in 1947, that the first test flights were held. Flights that were made possible by designs and technology developed by a small team of German researchers during the Second World War. Researchers who survived the war and fled to USA, taking their knowledge with them..."

"A project called '*Paperclip*'," said Christian, whilst Jodie nodded affirmatively.

Christian's interruption seemed to irritate the editor but he questioned him anyway.

"Paperclip?"

"The code name for a covert operation initiated by the American secret service immediately after the Second World War. The idea was to bring German researchers to the US."

Jodie continued:

"With knowledge and designs for motors based on electromagnetic principles. They could start the development of some of the most highly secret weapons ever developed. A weapon that's to this day kept secret from the public despite peak oil, pollution from combustion engines and fatal errors during continued testing. The recent tsunami in Indonesia is a good example. And if it hadn't been for so-called black technology from private companies, technology that Boeing has spent a lot of time and money developing, they'd have kept it secret for years to come. Private sector technologies are now reaching the same sort of levels of sophistication as the government's own vehicles, however. A development they're planning to make public at The Government Leaders Forum in 2012. Which will give Boeing time to phase out their current technologies."

Jodie paused. And waited excitedly for her boss' reaction whilst Christian rounded of:

"Not to forget Russian scientists' recent attempt to patent technologies based on John R.R. Pearl's invention. An invention which was simply stolen by the NSA, whereafter he has been widely discredited. He's still alive, by the way."

The editor remained seated without making any sort of response. He looked at Jodie without speaking. She for her part looked as if she was getting ready to run a hundred meter race.

Christian moved over to the window so as to be able to study the traffic weaving around beneath them. Then he became aware of the silence and returned his attention to the office and to the editor who began speaking just as he did so.

"The pictures you saw weren't alien space craft then? They were vessels that we'd developed? Is that correct?"

"Yes," said Jodie.

"Yes, there was a little detail we missed... at first," said Christian, interrupting.

The editor now considered Christian with surprise bordering on distaste. Like some peculiar insect he wished to study more closely before crushing it under a newspaper.

"Yes? And what detail was that may I ask?"

"The flag. The stars and stripes. On the pictures we saw, all the craft had a little American flag stuck on them. Discretely, but clearly. We we're just too focused on the spectacular."

The editor nodded repeatedly and turned his attention back to Jodie.

"Okay, lets summarize. The UFOs we've already seen and the ones we'll see in future, aren't of alien design. We made them. Correct?"

"Yes. And as long as people think that they're UFOs then no-one's the wiser," answered Jodie backing up Christian whilst her editor continued undisturbed:

"Based on a technology developed by the Germans during the Second World War which will be kept secret until 2012, at which time, and as a result of pressure from within the industry they'll reveal some at least of what's been going on. Is that correct?"

Jodie just nodded this time without answering.

"Okay. And what you're also telling me is that the evidence you had has gone. Confiscated by some secret service organisation. Is that also correct?"

Jodie nodded once. This time more weakly.

"Yes."

"Good. And the sources you've spoken to, they deny all knowledge, right?"

Jodie just looked at him without answering.

The editor started tapping away on his computer.

"And why on earth... if I may ask... should I... at any rate... let you... do an article based on this? Not to mention putting the paper's entire reputation at stake."

A statement that, of course, provoked a response from Jodie. She was surprised at her boss' rejection.

"The public have a right to know that they've been deceived. That people are being killed. That the UFO reports from all over the world are really just man-made secret weapons. And that my *own* sister was killed. Assassinated for that same reason. Because her conscience told to go to the press. Because test flights were costing thousands of human lives."

The editor interrupted impatiently.

"Look. People get killed for lots of reasons these days. Take the Middle East for example. And there's no reason to get your own personal feelings mixed up in this more than they already are…"

Jodie interrupted again.

"But that's what makes a life and death issue what it is. You *have* to take responsibility. Personal responsibility. And as a newspaper we have a responsibility too."

The editor shook his head.

"Okay. Number one, you've no evidence. Number two, you've no sources, and number three…"

The editor turned his screen in their direction.

"…This story's already on the net. And believe me, it's probably been there for a very long time," he said by way of conclusion.

Both Christian and Jodie could now see the website's large red heading clearly: thebiggestconspiracy.com.

Christian and Jodie exchanged glances. Then they reached the same conclusion. This was why Wedlock had let them go. The website that Jodie's boss had just shown them had been financed by the NSA. Not that that was something you could see anywhere on it. They just knew it was.

Christian and Jodie stood clasped in an embrace. A long one. Despite all the thousands of people rushing around them. Then Jodie stepped back slightly, put her hands in her back pockets and tried to smile. But she couldn't hide the fact that she was upset.

"Don't worry, you'll get them back again," said Christian, quietly.

"You don't owe me anything Christian. You know that. But, I'd really like to see you again."

"You mean you still don't believe me when I say I'll be back?"

"It's not because I don't believe you don't want to. I just can't see it actually happening."

"Just trust me," he nodded and turned halfway towards the escalator.

"Promise me I'll be the first to read it."

"It'll be in Danish."

"Jeg er ligeglad? - I don't care?" said Jodie, in her best Danish.

"Pretty good," said Christian laughing gently and smiled.

"Ciao."

Then he made his way onto the escalator without looking back.

It was both cold and windy when Christian landed at Copenhagen Airport.

He pushed his way through the terminal and out to the metro station where he could, finally, lean up against one of the billboards and enjoy a cigarette.

Several people looked askance at him, others giggled, most just ignored him. Finally it all got a bit too much for one particular over-zealous passenger. She pointed at the sign above Christian's head.

"You do know you're not allowed to smoke here."

"Yeah, thanks for letting me know. I'm almost finished."

He had to travel without a ticket on the metro. The bank would be the place to start, he thought. So he could get his card re-opened and access whatever was left of his grant money.

Back at the flat everything was as he had left it. And, actually, it felt like an age since he had been home.

He found a few inches of bourbon at the bottom of a bottle, got himself a glass and sat watching the clouds scudding across the night sky. Watched the way they seemed to spread themselves, making more and more room for the sky behind them. For space and the countless stars. Then Christian nodded to himself. Suddenly he knew where to start.

The hours flew by and Christian wrote like he had never written before. The quicker he finished the quicker he could head back. That was the decision he had made.

Christian ignored his complaining stomach. All he was going to ingest was coffee and cigarettes. All he was aware of was the text and the keyboard in front of him. Meaning that he missed the text message when it reached his phone:

'Jodie said you were short of cash.
So I divided up the 'Danish Aryan Resistance' money a little differently than agreed. Mine's in an account in VP Bank Liechtenstein. This is for you. Best of luck with the book. T.K.'

A text message that sort of made it a happy ending after all. That was what Christian thought anyway when he finally read it.